BOAT CAMP KILLER

Art of Murder Series
Book 2

Pam Fox

Bright Fox Books

Bright Fox Books

ISBN-13: 978-1-7328799-2-8

ONE

The sun warmed Kate's shoulders; she held her paddle lightly and drove it hard. Sometimes a breeze kicked up, but the ponds were small enough that it didn't have much fetch to build waves. On open water, she and her friend Ellen paddled side by side, sometimes talking, sometimes quiet, enjoying the flash of sunlight from their paddle blades and the gurgle of water under the bows of their kayaks. In creeks, they took turns leading. Turtles sunned themselves on logs, and herons stalked the shallows. An occasional kingfisher crossed overhead, shattering the air with its rackety call.

Along with the sunshine, peace soaked into Kate's bones. She'd traveled to the Adirondacks from an artists' colony in Maine, where her work had been disrupted by the death of a mentor, ruled accidental by the authorities. She'd suspected murder, and the quiet residency had become a harrowing struggle to discover the truth.

Being on the water soothed her. Ten days of kayaking was the perfect prescription to restore her spirits, and Ellen's company added to the pleasure. Kate had met her four years earlier, when they both worked as reporters for a small Massachusetts newspaper. They'd hit it off, hiking, biking, and paddling together. After two years Ellen had snagged a great job at a larger paper in Syracuse, but the two had stayed in touch.

When Kate's paper had downsized and laid her off, she decided to travel for a year in her truck camper before looking for her next job. The disastrous month in Maine, the first stop in her nomadic life, had made her more determined to focus on two things: spending time outdoors and developing herself as an artist. The goals were not only compatible but synergistic, since encounters with wildlife and wild landscapes excited her and fueled her work. She'd choose back roads to take her to parks and other protected land; life on the road would be simple and quiet.

As she'd driven west through New Hampshire and Vermont to meet Ellen, she'd discovered her true destination was every minute. Church spires glinted among trees brushed with gold, and hawks balanced on high thermals. Having grown up in Tucson, Kate had found New England's leafy canopy disconcerting when she'd gone to college ten years earlier in the Bay State. "What's all this green junk hanging around?" she'd joked. Another student from Tucson had dropped out in December. "It's too freakin' cold here," he said. "I want to go home, where there aren't any stinkin' trees."

Kate had learned to like trees.

Here in upstate New York's wilderness, there were plenty to like. *Adirondack,* Kate had read, meant *bark-eater*, a name the Mohawks used for porcupines—and for the neighboring Algonquins, as insult suggesting they were poor hunters.

No porcupine would go hungry around here.

On this first paddle, Kate had brought a notebook and pencils in a drybag, and she was looking forward to drawing when she and Ellen stopped for lunch.

She was so lucky. Her work, a good friend, and the outdoors: she was rich in all the important ways.

* * *

They'd been on the water a few hours when voices came up behind them, and a big green canoe surged past. The woman in the bow smiled and raised her paddle in greeting; the man in the stern nodded his hello.

Kate recognized the couple. "We met them at the outfitters' this morning," she said. "They're flying!" With two blades in the water and a greater length at the waterline, the canoe went much faster than the kayaks.

"Oh, right, the guides," Ellen said. "Molly and—I can't think of his name. It was an odd one."

"Shag," Kate said, surprised. She wasn't usually good at remembering names.

"They must know the area. We picked a good route."

"You picked a good route, you mean."

"Okay, I did," Ellen said. "A little from memory, but mostly from the map." She'd tucked the edges of the plasticized chart under bungee cords on the deck in front of her cockpit. "I had such a great time boating here as a kid. It's been a long time, though, so I don't remember if I've been on this pond before or not."

They were nearing the mouth of a creek, and Kate laughed out loud. Ellen, who'd moved ahead of Kate, angled her boat to look back. "What?"

"Oh, the way the canoe whizzed past us, it reminded me of this time I was out on my cross-country skis and a whole pile of people overtook me, so I got out of the way, side-stepped a little off the trail, you know? And a minute later this guy comes along and gives me a withering look and says, 'Well, *you're* off the pace, aren't you?'"

Ellen looked puzzled.

"I'd never heard the phrase 'off the pace' before," Kate explained, "because I don't do team sports. But the point of the story? I wasn't off the pace. He was. He was all sarcastic about me but he was the one who was struggling to keep up."

Ellen shrugged. "Okay."

"I guess you had to be there," Kate said, wondering why the incident had stuck with her. Maybe because it illustrated her lack of interest in competition. When the green canoe passed, her instinct wasn't to speed up. Even if she'd been with that group of skiers in her story, she wouldn't have cared if she was first, last, or in the middle.

She'd learned, though, that men often cared. A few men she'd known were always trying to beat the other guy. Even when the other guy was Kate.

They came around a bend and found Molly and Shag sitting in a sunny patch on the bank, eating lunch, the canoe half out of the water below them.

"There's room for two more," Molly called out.

"Hey, great, thanks," Ellen said. She glided to the shallows and did a graceful, paddle-braced exit. Kate's kayak, a lightweight Hornbeck boat with no upper deck, allowed her to roll forward onto her knees and step out. The two friends pulled their boats onto the sandy soil next to the canoe, then climbed the bank and settled on the grass near the guides.

Kate poked through her drybag for the sandwich she'd packed in a plastic box. The air was warm along the sheltered creek, and she pulled her paddling jacket off over her head. "We're like turtles sunning ourselves on a log."

Molly said, "Turtles don't wear sunglasses and hats."

"Not any turtles we've seen, anyway," Ellen said, and Molly laughed.

They were quiet for a while, eating. Then Shag said, "Muskrat alert. Below the big tree."

Kate spotted the animal, swimming upstream with some leaves in its mouth, then diving.

"Where?" Ellen asked.

"Gone. Do you know their lips seal behind their front teeth?" Molly said. "So when they're submerged they can harvest plants without swallowing water. Roger told me that." She looked at the kayakers. "Roger's our boss."

"Yeah, he knows that shit," Shag said. He rubbed his palm over his crew-cut.

A few minutes later, Kate said, "Food always tastes so much better outdoors." She'd wolfed down her peanut butter sandwich and was peeling a tangerine.

"For sure," Molly said. "Want some cashews?" She tossed a baggie to Kate.

"Thanks. They're my favorite," Kate said, taking some and passing the bag to Ellen.

"They get the bad taste of work out of your mouth," Shag said, popping a handful.

"Yeah, you had a rotten start to your day," Molly said.

* * *

That morning Ellen had driven her Toyota pick-up, which had four-wheel drive, down an unpaved road named Paul's Way to the outfitter's store, Kate riding shotgun. With its soft sides, Ellen's camper could be collapsed so it added only four inches to the cab's height, making her rig easier to drive than Kate's hard-shelled camper.

Ellen drove fast, gravel rattling in the wheel wells. She raised her voice to give Kate the latest news. "I broke up with Dan a week ago," she said.

"Oh, that's too bad. You were with him, what, eight months?"

"Right, and for the first five we were doing great. We were both busy—who isn't? But we made time for each other. Then he withdrew into his start-up companies. As if I was a box he'd checked off, a shipment he'd had delivered. I was in place and he could forget about me."

"That stinks."

"He's an outdoorsy guy," Ellen said. "Or he was. He grew up in rural Maine, hunting and fishing. I was looking forward to some backpacking trips last summer, but he kept putting them off. Took me a while to figure out he just didn't want to bother. He's consumed by his businesses."

She wiped her eyes with the back of her hand. "Let's forget about him. Let's think about all the kayaking we did in Massachusetts."

"Yes, we had some great paddles, didn't we?" Kate said. "The Sudbury River, so peaceful, right through that bird sanctuary. And the dam releases on the Deerfield, those were awesome."

"This area is even better. A lot of the ponds connect, so we can spend a whole day on the water with lots of variety—ponds, lakes, rivers, creeks. And portages, of course." She grinned at Kate.

"I'm game. Anywhere you want to go is good." Kate had always admired Ellen's ability to put the past firmly behind her; gloom about Dan was not going to spoil her vacation. In Kate's mind that ability was connected to Ellen's good looks, which went beyond her face. Tall and trim, she had what Kate called a "glow-in-the-dark nice" personality. "Hey, I haven't said it yet, have I?"

"Said what?"

"What I always say when I first see you—that you look like a movie star."

Ellen snorted. "And I always tell you you're nuts."

The building at the end of the road looked new, a two-story clapboard house that faced a lake across a gravel lot. Trailers parked in one corner of the lot were stacked with lime-green and orange plastic kayaks along with canoes in less conspicuous colors, tan and dark green. A jumble of wooden picnic tables took up another corner.

The porch was scattered with Adirondack chairs. An overhead sign read *BOAT CAMP*, and below that, in smaller letters, *Canoes — Kayaks — Supplies — Guide Services.*

Two men about Kate's age behind the counter looked up as she and Ellen entered. They were the only customers, not surprising in a vacation area on the day after Labor Day.

"Hi, I'm Tate. What can I help you with?" one of them said. He had a halo of curly blond hair and a sweet smile. A movie star to match Ellen's good looks, Kate thought.

"We're looking for maps, mostly," Ellen said. "Then we might have some questions about routes." She was looking around, didn't seem to notice how good-looking the guy was. Maybe she was off men for a while after having broken up with Dan.

"We've got folding maps on that rack," Tate said, pointing. "The big U.S. Geological ones are in drawers at the back. Let me know when you have questions."

"Browse away," the other man said. "Like deer." He was sturdy to Tate's slim, and his hair was clipped so short he looked like an Army recruit.

"Shag! In here, now." The voice came from an open door at the back of the store, and the second guy jumped, looked at Tate, and walked quickly to the back. Kate smiled to herself—a guy with a crew-cut was nicknamed Shag. Go figure.

Then it was her turn to jump, when the door slammed shut. Its sign read *OFFICE*.

Ellen was running her finger along a printed river and didn't seem to notice the noise. "This one's good," she said, folding up the map she'd been studying. "But I'd like one a bit farther north, too. Let's keep looking."

The rack was in a corner, so there wasn't enough room for both of them. Kate prowled around the store, perusing equipment and clothing. Shag was funny, telling them to browse like deer.

A short woman came in the back door, wearing the same color khaki shirt and pants as Tate and Shag. She gave Kate a quick smile and picked up a jacket that had fallen off its hanger. Her nametag said Molly, and she looked as if she'd been out in the sun a lot but tended toward freckles more than tan. She continued down the rack of clothes, straightening them.

The price tags knocked Kate over. She was glad she'd gotten her paddling gear while she had a good job. Her truck and camper, too—she'd bought them both used, but they were in good condition. With a double bed over the cab and a propane stove, fridge, and furnace, the camper had everything she needed.

A girl about ten skipped into the store, followed more slowly by her father, who asked Molly what they would need to get on the water besides a canoe. "The basics are a paddle and a PFD," she said. "And drybags are really useful."

"What's a PFD?" the girl asked.

"Like a life vest. It stands for 'personal flotation device,'" Molly said. "I know, acronyms. They're everywhere."

The girl still looked puzzled. "What's an acronym?"

The office door opened and Shag came out with another man, broad-shouldered, dark-haired, who joined Tate behind the counter.

Shag stayed near the back. "Come on, let's move the boats," he called, and Tate headed his way. They went outside, daylight hitting Tate's hair and brightening it like an aspen tree.

"Anybody want some coffee?" Broad Shoulders was pouring from a pot into a paper cup, and the way he stooped to put the pot down told Kate the coffee-maker was at knee height back there.

"Hey, thanks," she said. She never turned down java. "Ellen? Coffee?"

"Huh? Just a sec."

His nametag said Roger. He put the first cup down on the counter for Kate, poured a second, took a sip.

"Where are you folks from?" Roger leaned on the counter. Kate refocused on him and wondered if her face had given away her interest in Tate. Roger's brown eyes said he didn't miss much.

"I'm from Massachusetts," she said. "My friend's more local, from down the road in Syracuse. She used to spend summers here as a kid, so I'm letting her make the map-buying decisions."

"We're glad you're here," Roger said. "You'll love it. You can paddle for weeks and not see the same lake twice."

A couple of men in their fifties came in. The one in front, big and bearded, raised a hand in greeting. "Hullo, Roger. Going to help my friend pick out a paddle."

"Go for it, Hank," Roger said.

Kate's taste buds were sending out joyful reviews. "Hey, thanks for the coffee. This is excellent."

"Beans from Kenya. I grind them myself, right here."

"Amazing."

Ellen came to the counter with two maps and looked at Kate's cup. "You are one incorrigible coffee hound."

"That I am."

Molly had joined Roger behind the counter. "Want me to make another pot?" she asked him.

The ten-year-old girl, a beginner's canoeing book open in her hands, shuffled to the cash register, head down, already reading. Her father pulled out his wallet.

Molly leaned under the counter, came up with the coffeemaker basket and flipped the filter full of wet grounds into a wastebasket. Then she rang up the book sale.

"Ladies?" Roger looked at Ellen.

"No, I'm good," she said. "I don't know how she can drink so much." She cocked her head at Kate. "You can stand a spoon up in the stuff the way she makes it. Probably going to corrode her stomach lining before she's thirty."

Kate's and Roger's eyes met, with laughter in them. You could stand a spoon up in Roger's coffee, too.

"Wait a minute," Kate said. "I'm already thirty. Thirty-two, in fact. And counting."

"Oh, that's right. Well, forty, then." Ellen smiled. "How much do I owe you?" Molly rang up the maps while Roger stayed leaning on the counter. He had to be the boss because Molly was doing all the work.

Kate offered to pay half, but Ellen waved her off. "No, I want to keep the maps, so I'll pay for them. I'll be back here soon enough, I hope, but you won't have any use for them on your way to Tucson."

"Tucson? Wow," Molly said. "I've always wanted to see the desert. Are you flying out to Tucson soon?"

"I'm driving," Kate said, and laughed at the look on Molly's round face.

"Driving. Well, I can't say I envy you that."

"Oh, it'll be fun. That's why I'm doing it. Driving my camper, planning to take my sweet time. About a year, I think." Kate picked up some Clif bars and paid. She had tangerines and bananas, and she'd made peanut butter sandwiches, but food bars always came in handy on the water.

"Well, okay, now I'm jealous after all," Molly said. "Are you going too?" she asked Ellen.

"Oh, no, my editor would have a fit if I left for a year," Ellen said.

"Do you work for a publisher?" Molly's eyes got big.

"No, a newspaper. The one in Syracuse."

"The *Sentinel?*" Roger asked.

"Yes, that's the one."

"I read that all the time," Molly said. "The one on Sunday especially. It makes my weekend."

"Thank you," Ellen said. "I'm glad you like it." She tucked her credit card in a pocket with the receipt.

"Thanks for stopping by," Roger said, lifting his cup in salute.

Kate and Ellen went out into the sunlight. "I found a route we can take from where Paul's Way meets Floodwood," Ellen said. They'd camped the previous night at sites along Floodwood Road, free but without electricity or water.

"That's handy. Right outside our front doors." Kate looked at the map. "Eight miles, a couple of carries," she said. "Let's go!"

* * *

When she'd visited Boat Camp with Ellen that morning, Kate hadn't expected to be eating lunch with two of the guides on the bank of a creek. Or getting such inside information about what it was like to work there.

"Roger's so hung up on his Navy dream," Shag said. "He acts like he's an officer and we're recruits, for Pete's sake. I just wish he'd lighten up."

Molly looked past him to Kate and Ellen. "Our boss is kind of a tough guy."

"No he isn't," Shag said. "He's a goddam marshmallow."

"Okay, okay, take it easy." Molly rubbed Shag's shoulder.

"Yeah, I know, he really got to me this morning," Shag said. "I don't respond well to criticism. Especially when I don't deserve it."

"Roger overreacted." Molly said to the kayakers. "He jumped all over Shag for telling you guys to browse like deer. Roger said it was disrespectful." She looked down. "He gets on Shag's case all the time."

"Oh, heck," Kate said, "I thought 'like deer' was funny."

Shag jumped up. "Come on, let's go," he said to Molly.

"Thanks for the cashews," Kate called after them.

After the guides launched, Ellen lay back on the grass while Kate got out her sketchbook. She drew the boats, then Ellen, who had her hands behind her head, elbows out, eyes closed in the sun.

A great blue heron coasted in and landed silently in the shallows. Kate couldn't ask for a more cooperative model. The huge bird barely moved. Picked up a foot slowly, slowly. Put it down the same way, a few inches farther on.

Magnificent creature. Wingspan of six feet. The yellowish bill was grooved, the long neck straight out over the water like a boom. When these birds flew, their necks folded into a deep S, bill couched on the breast.

That bill was a formidable weapon, sometimes a spear and sometimes tongs. Kate had seen a great blue catch an eel once, tossing its beak up to swallow the head while the long body thrashed, the area of its manic scribble slowly shrinking, the heron's throat bulging and warping as the eel slid to its fate.

The bird in front of her struck, recoiled. Nothing struggled in its beak, no fish or frog.

The heron was almost as tall as Kate, its eyes yellow, fierce, as round as her own. She felt drawn toward them, into them, and she let her mind flow and float until she was half-heron herself.

She studied the water with avian eyes. The reflection of trees and sky looked black and white, the fish visible only in the black patches, their bodies iridescent, tantalizing. Such detail: every scale, gill slit, and fin—

The scene exploded. The heron had struck. It pointed its bill skyward and swallowed a silvery fish.

Released from her heron dream, Kate felt a breeze touch her neck as the two long crest feathers at the back of the tall bird's head lifted and fell. She and the heron were both creatures at large, abroad in air and water. They wore the atmosphere, the same clothes the earth wore. The planet was a network in which they were equals, creatures who lived in light and slept in darkness and supported themselves with the bounty around them.

Ellen stirred, turned, opened her eyes, smiled. Kate put away her notebook and pencils. Maybe she'd surprise her friend with the drawing of her, if it came out well enough. For herself, Kate would never forget that heron.

She and her friend paddled until late afternoon, carrying the boats on two short portages.

Sometimes, in the shadow of her boat, she saw fish as big as her paddle blade.

Kate loved water: she loved the sound of it, and the way it played endlessly with color. When the air was calm, the wavelets on the ponds reflected the sky in rounded-off triangles of light and dark: watching them was hypnotic, like watching the flames of a campfire.

Hypnotic and healing.

* * *

When Kate and Ellen got back to the Floodwood Road pull-out, Molly and Shag were lifting their canoe onto a pick-up truck with BOAT CAMP on the side. Shag saw the women land and came over as they got out of the kayaks.

"Hey, I'm sorry I exploded about Roger," he said. "I, I'd—" He looked uncomfortable. "I'd really appreciate it if you didn't say anything, to anybody. South Portage is a small town."

Kate and Ellen looked at each other, startled. "Oh, no," Ellen said. "Why would we? I mean, no, of course not."

"My lips are zipped," Kate said.

"Thanks," Shag said. "There aren't too many jobs around here. Well, not too many jobs where you get to test-drive canoes." Kate was glad to see a smile overcome the worry on his face.

"You've got the best job in the world," she said.

TWO

"I know a nice place in Saranac Lake," Ellen said. The two friends had decided to go out to dinner, a rare occasion for Kate.

"In a lake?" Kate blinked. "So you were thinking of fish. Sushi, maybe?"

Ellen snorted. "It's a town, silly. I used to go to this restaurant with my family. I checked on my phone and it's still there. C'mon, I'll drive."

Outside the Put-In Pub, Ellen bought a copy of the *Adirondack Daily Star* from a vending machine. "Got to support our fellow reporters," she said. Kate was happy to be included. When she'd had her year off maybe she'd find another job in journalism.

And maybe not. Newspapers weren't doing so well these days. She sometimes worried for Ellen, although the *Syracuse Sentinel* was a much bigger paper than the *Danvers Daily News*.

Maybe Kate should look into writing for magazines.

She pushed job possibilities out of her mind. The time to explore them was when she was ready to go back to work.

The round table had plenty of room to spread out the paper, and the two of them shared it after they'd ordered. Kate got the front section, a mix of national news and regional teasers with jumps to inside pages.

"Hey, here's an article about that guy Roger," Ellen said from behind the local pages. "He's organizing a Paddle of Silence on Veterans Day, trying to get as many people as he can to sign up."

"Paddle of Silence? Is that like a Ride of Silence?"

"You got it."

Bike clubs in cities all over the world sponsored Rides of Silence in mid-May every year to educate motorists and to commemorate riders killed in car-bike accidents. Lists of their names were read before the rides. Both Kate and Ellen were cyclists and had ridden in two of the annual memorials together in Boston.

"Roads should be safe for people, no matter how many wheels they have under them," Kate said.

She met Ellen's brown eyes. They were both thinking of her accident a couple of years ago, when a van turned without signaling and nearly hit her. She'd swerved and saved herself, but went into a ditch and broke her arm. At the rate of speed the van was going, she'd told Kate, she was sure she'd have been killed if it had struck her.

"This paddling event is to raise awareness of veterans issues," Ellen said. "I'm all for that. But November 11? It's pretty cold up here by then. In the forties."

"Yikes. Not much fun, especially if it's raining."

"Must be a Polar Bear Plunge kind of thing," Ellen said. "Like when those crazy Canadians jump into the ocean on January first."

"Ouch. I love to play in snow, but not ice-water. I'll save my swimming for the summer."

Ellen looked up and smiled, then her eyes went past Kate.

"Hello, you two." Despite his height and broad shoulders, Roger moved with a cat-like grace as he took the last few steps to their table. "You're the women I met at the store today. Welcome to the Adirondacks, the best place on the planet. Did you enjoy your paddle?"

"Roger," Ellen said, folding the paper. "I was just reading about you."

"That's flattering." His head went back as he laughed. "At least I hope so."

"It's all good," Ellen said.

Surely he'd read the piece already. Kate used to read her own stories in the *News* more than once, even though she knew every word already. And they weren't even about her.

"Mind if I join you for a bit?" Roger asked. "I love meeting folks from out of town, and I'll only stay a couple of minutes while I finish my preprandial beer." He lifted the glass mug in his hand.

Kate and Ellen looked at each other. What kind of a guy used a word like that?

"Sure, have a seat," Kate said, and Roger slipped into a chair.

"So how many takers do you usually get for this Paddle of Silence?" Ellen asked.

"Don't know yet," Roger said. "This one's the first. Wish I'd thought of it years ago."

"It must be pretty cold by November 11," Kate said.

"No, it's in October, a month before Veterans Day. It can still be in the fifties or even the sixties in mid-October." he frowned. "If I had my way, there'd be a Veterans Day every month. Damn. Does the paper say November?"

"Take a look." Ellen passed the paper to him.

"Right you are," he said. "Glad you mentioned it. I'll get a correction run. My brother and I are the only sponsors so far, and the set-up is a lot of work on my end, so we want people to have the right date."

"What do you do? Supply boats?" Ellen asked.

"Boats, paddles, PFDs, transportation to the launch site, snacks, water. Takes my whole crew of guides, plus a few special hires."

"Gosh, that is a pile of work," Kate said.

"At least your brother contributes," Ellen said.

"He lives out of town, so I do almost everything. He's volunteered to show up and take photos, and the best one will be featured on the front page of the *Star* the next day. The city editor really liked the idea."

"Why do you need to provide transportation?" Ellen asked. "You could have the event at your store, people could park in the lot or along that road, Paul's Way, and launch right into the lake that's at your doorstep."

He raised an eyebrow, looking impressed. "You're a good planner, Ellen. Maybe I should hire you."

Kate was surprised to see Ellen blush. But she said, "Sorry, I've got a job."

"Right, right. My loss." He glanced at Kate, then back at Ellen. "I'd thought of that—it would be a lot simpler, and I could serve hot cider afterwards at Boat Camp. Not a bad thing, to get people inside the store. But I'd rather take them to out-of-the-way places, maybe catch sight of a fox or a roosting owl, or let them paddle right up to a beaver dam." He shook his head. "It's amazing how people who live in this glorious place get caught up in their daily indoor routines and forget what's around them."

"Getting people outside is a wonderful goal," Kate said. "Most people spend most of their time thinking about other people. I don't mean relationships aren't important, of course they are, but there's a whole planet out there."

"Wonderful goal, Roger, but ambitious," Ellen said.

He shrugged. "I can do it."

Part of his attraction, Kate thought, was his confidence. Yet he wasn't overbearing. And he cared about issues she and Ellen cared about.

He talked for a few minutes about some of the lesser-known wildlife of the region, pine martens and fishers and little brown bats. "It's a daytime event," he said. "So we won't be seeing the bats, or beavers, or flying squirrels. If we're lucky we'll see otters, or a bobcat."

Kate was enchanted. This guy knew the local waters and woods the way most people know their back yards. Too bad she wasn't staying here long enough to join the Paddle of Silence.

He took a sip of beer and changed the subject. "So Ellen, you work for the *Syracuse Sentinel.* That's a good paper."

"Thanks. You read it out here?"

"It's the nearest big-city paper," he said. "When I was a kid and my dad was posted in Portsmouth, New Hampshire, we used to read the *Boston Globe,* the Sunday one. Great cartoons. Kept us kids quiet. For at least half an hour." He smiled. "Now my big-city paper is the *Sentinel."*

"I'm happy when I hear about my paper getting read," Ellen said. "Or any paper. Circulation is doing a nose-dive all over the country. People get their news from TV and social media these days."

"Not only newspapers. A lot of businesses are hurting," Roger said. "Not mine, of course. Boat Camp is doing great." His dark eyes on Ellen, he said, "I think journalists are heroes. Word heroes."

She looked startled. "That's not what most people think these days," she said.

"Say, didn't you write a series on homeless veterans a while back?" he asked.

"Yes, last spring. You not only read, you remember."

"It was pretty memorable stuff. Some of those guys were in sad shape."

"Yes. The scars you can see are bad enough. But the ones you can't see can be devastating."

"You did a great job on that series, Ellen," Kate said. "What was it called? Battling for Peace?"

"Fighting to Find Peace: the Invisible Legion," Roger said. "You think you could have been kinder to some of those guys?"

Ellen's expression stiffened. "What do you mean? Kinder how?"

"I'm talking about the ones who couldn't cope. Eating from dumpsters, sleeping in the woods."

"Yes," she said slowly. "That's what some vets were doing."

"You could have helped them more, is all."

"Some of them didn't want to be helped," Ellen said. "I'm not a social worker. I hope social workers read my articles. And politicians. I hope the publicity led to improvements in the lives of veterans."

"Let's say you're right and some of them didn't want to be helped," Roger said. He was looking away from the table and out the big front window to darkness, a darkness tinted red by the restaurant's neon sign. "Some of them didn't want to be exposed, either." He looked, for a moment, as if his mind had taken him somewhere far away from the Put-In Pub.

Ellen and Kate looked at each other. Roger must have read every word of Ellen's stories. One of them had ended with a vet threatening her with a knife if she didn't leave. She'd left, of course, immediately.

"I was trying to help them," Ellen said, "in the only way I know how."

Roger pulled his gaze back to the table, waved a hand and said, "Oh, what do I know? I didn't talk to the vets you found to talk to. And I'm no writer, that's for sure." His voice had gone from flat to friendly. "How long are you staying in town?"

* * *

He left when their dinners arrived—almond-crusted salmon for Kate and steak au poivre for Ellen, with broccoli and butternut squash sides. They dug in.

"A day on the water really makes me hungry," Ellen said.

"Me, too." The salmon flaked under Kate's fork; the bright green broccoli was slightly crunchy. "This is great." After a few minutes of dedicated eating she said, "Impressive guy, Roger. He really knows wildlife."

Ellen nodded.

"I didn't know fishers have retractable claws," Kate said. "That must be why they're sometimes called fisher-cats even though they're weasels. And they eat porcupines. I didn't think porcupines had any predators."

"We learned a lot. Except about Roger."

"That's true." Kate took another bite of salmon. "But isn't it nice to meet a guy who isn't so full of himself that his only subject matter is him?"

Ellen smiled, then looked serious. "His dinner-conversation manner, which was charming, doesn't fit very well with what Shag said about him being so difficult."

"Maybe he treats employees differently from other people. Which makes him not a good manager. Employees are people, too."

"That could be it. Or maybe Shag pushes his buttons somehow. Or Shag is sensitive."

"People are complicated," Kate said.

"I wouldn't mind seeing that particular set of complications again," Ellen said. "He's at least interesting. I like trying to figure people out."

* * *

Kate was surprised at how late they stayed, over post-prandial cups of coffee (decaf for Ellen). Talking in a restaurant was different somehow from talking anywhere else. Maybe it was the glass of wine they'd had, or the atmosphere—the place was dim but definitely not gloomy, with real flowers at the tables, and cloth napkins. Maybe it was different to talk surrounded by other diners, making her and Ellen part of a community, even if a temporary one.

Or maybe it was Roger who'd set the tone. Despite his moment of criticism of the Fighting to Find Peace series, he'd boosted their spirits by admiring what Ellen did, and what Kate used to do, for a living, and his knowledge of the area made them feel connected to it. Beyond their table, beyond the town, the vast Adirondacks were not still. Great-horned owls ghosted above moose asleep on platter-size feet; raccoons searched edges of ponds for frogs, and weasels slipped into mouse tunnels with deadly intent.

Ellen told her more about Dan, about how difficult he'd gotten about the break-up. "I thought he wouldn't care, but I was wrong. He had a major league fit. Told me I was an idiot to give him up, asked me who else I was seeing. Yelled at me that I was lying when I said there wasn't anyone else. Man, it was a nightmare."

"How awful."

"He's still sending emails, lots of them. So he does care. But I sure don't like the way he's showing it."

"Or the way he treated you when you were together," Kate said, "after the first glow faded."

"I'm almost thirty. Still hoping to start a family. But not with Dan." Her eyes filled, and she and Kate were quiet.

After a few minutes Kate described her summer at the artists' colony in Maine—how a new but dear friend had been murdered. How she'd found his killers, getting herself kidnapped in the process.

"God, Kate, you've been through so much."

"That's why I'm grateful to have this peaceful time with you. Nothing's more calming than being on the water. It's even better than biking, though that's great too."

"You're right, flatwater paddling is soothing," Ellen said. "I'm so glad you called and suggested meeting. I'm loving our time together, and getting away from Dan's craziness is a bonus."

"Maybe by the time you go back, he'll be over it."

"I hope so." Ellen looked doubtful. "He's actually scaring me a little. He's still emailing and leaving tons of voicemails. He just won't give up."

"Well, you can forget about him here," Kate said. "Don't read or listen to his messages, just delete them. He'll get over it."

"Yeah. And when I go home it'll only be for a couple of days. I've got three weeks of vacation, and for the last week I'm planning to join my parents in Aruba. They're already on the cruise ship—I'm doing the last leg with them."

"Aruba! You lucky duck."

"The tickets are a present from Mum and Dad, of course—I couldn't afford a trip like that on my own." She smiled at Kate. "So I've seen the last of Dan Lindquist."

"And you're free to hang out with me. I win."

"I'm happier than I've been in months. You're a great friend."

"So are you, Ellen," Kate said. "Here's to friendship." She held up her cup.

"Friendship." Ellen clicked her cup against Kate's, laughing. "Of course you'd toast with coffee."

They drained the cups. Ellen dug into her big purse for her wallet, and Kate pulled her credit card out of her pocket. They looked around for their server.

Kate caught her eye. Tall and red-haired, she came to the table looking flustered. "I'm sorry, this is so unusual—"

"Oh, you must be closing," Ellen said, pushing her chair back. "I'm sorry we stayed so late."

"No, no, not at all. Stay longer if you'd like—you're not the last. And, well—"

"Thanks," Kate said, "but I think we're ready to leave. Can you split the bill on these two cards?"

The woman laughed. "That's what I'm trying to say. You don't have to pay. It's so unusual, I didn't know how to tell you."

Kate and Ellen looked at each other. Ellen was faster. "Did Roger—the man who sat with us—did he pay?"

The server looked startled, then beamed. "Yes. How did you know?"

"A wild guess," Ellen said, with an odd look on her face. She was not entirely pleased.

"Tell us the total, so we'll know what to tip you," Kate said. She could probably figure it out herself, dinner plus wine plus coffee, but she didn't know what the tax rate was in New York. Easier to ask.

"Please don't do that," the server said. "Mr. Benedict's tip was more than generous. It was—outrageous."

"Oh." Kate looked at Ellen. "Okay. Well, thanks."

* * *

"What's the matter?" Kate asked. They were driving back to the campground, and Ellen hadn't said much.

"I don't know how I feel about Roger paying," Ellen said slowly. "It's odd for a guy to come on that strong. I mean, not when he sat with us—his conversation was pleasant. But paying for our dinners? That wasn't a cheap meal, but I really started thinking harder when the waitress said he gave her an outrageous tip."

"How much do you think 'outrageous' is?"

"While you were in the loo I asked her, nicely. Roger gave her a hundred bucks."

"Holy cats," Kate said.

"Holy something." Ellen flicked on the high beams and the roadside pines glowed green. "She said he told her he had something for her, pulled out his wallet and showed her a picture of a man he said was his father. Called him a hero and slid the C-note out from behind it."

"She must have been thrilled."

"Yeah," Ellen said. "Me? I'm not so thrilled. I've just met Roger and he seems like a great guy in a lot of ways. But a hundred bucks? It makes me nervous that a guy would throw money around like that." Her face was lit by the dashboard as she glanced at Kate. "I don't want to get involved with someone who's all about money. I don't want to waste time on another guy like Dan."

THREE

Rain drummed on the roof of the camper as Kate awakened.

Rats. Not paddling weather.

Ellen had said she had ten days in the Adirondacks. This was only the second, but a rainy spell could put a big dent in the fun. Time is slippery.

Kate made a pot of coffee and carried it to the next site, a routine they'd set up when she and Ellen had first camped together years ago in Massachusetts. The first time Kate had done it, she'd made a fool of herself trying to get up the steps and through the low door to Ellen's pop-up camper with a full pot in her hand. Since then, Ellen always took the pot before Kate climbed in.

"The mouse of time is nibbling at the cheese of your vacation," Kate said. She sat on the bench seat that ran along one side of the tiny camper while Ellen filled a kettle and put it on the propane burner. She liked to dilute what she called Kate's "viscous brew."

Ellen hooted. "The mouse of time. That's a good one, Kate. You'd better have another dose of that black stuff."

"Don't mind if I do." An open camera bag lay next to her on the bench. "How's your photography going?"

"Oh, you found my new Canon." Ellen looked fondly at the camera as Kate took it out of the bag. "I don't get to take pictures to go with my stories the way I did when we were at the *News,"* Ellen said. "The *Sentinel* is too big a paper for that. But I still love taking photos, and that Canon goes with me everywhere. Except on the water."

"I've been taking a lot of pictures with my cell phone recently," Kate said. "Reference photos, you know?"

"No. Tell me."

"I use the phone to collect images I can use later. I don't draw exactly what's on the screen, but I like looking at a bunch of photos before I start working. Sometimes I'll take pieces from different shots and combine them in my head. Or sometimes the pictures are for inspiration, to bring me back to the place where I started a drawing."

Ellen shook her head. "Heck, that sounds like a lot of work. Just take the shot and call yourself a photographer, like I do."

"I don't think you'd want to brag about photos you took with your phone. What I do is spontaneous, quick, a grab-bag of images."

"You're right. I want a camera, not just a phone. I need the control—exposure, depth of field, stuff like that." Ellen sat beside Kate and they looked at the Canon's small screen together while they waited for the water to boil. Ellen scrolled through stored shots, sharing her favorites. Most had been taken at Onondaga Lake Park or on the Erie Canal and its adjoining trail, both urban recreation areas.

"Hey, you've got to get out of Syracuse more," Kate said.

"You're right," Ellen said. "The *Sentinel* keeps me wicked busy."

Wildflowers, the shadows of ferns on rocks, a close-up of British soldier lichen: Kate could be looking at her own work done in pixels instead of pencil strokes.

Half a dozen photos showed Ellen with a tall man wearing a black T-shirt with INNOVATE OR DIE in white letters. She paused for the first of them and skipped past the rest. "That's Dan. I should delete those."

A few minutes later she stood and stretched. "Enough with the pictures," she said. "I've got muffins." As she reached into a cabinet under the tiny sink, a gust of wind buffeted the soft sides of the camper.

"Are you still happy with this little pop-up?" Kate asked.

"Absolutely. It's perfect for me. When I lower it to drive, I can forget it's there." Ellen gave Kate a pumpkin muffin on a paper towel. "The only down side is that I can't raise the camper if my kayak's on the roof rack—the boat's too heavy. How about you? Still like your hard-shell?"

"Yes, I'm still a turtle, my house on my back," Kate said. "I need the space—especially the dinette table for drawing. I can stop the truck and get right to work. And the storage is great, much more than you have, because I'm planning such a long trip. With art supplies."

"Remember our first trip in these rigs? You thought you could extend the legs on your camper, drive out from under it, and have your truck free for us to go exploring and get groceries—"

"Oh, please, don't remind me," Kate laughed. "I was thinking how much gas I could save if I left the camper at the campground. And I was right. We got great mileage that day."

"We had a good time, too. But then came the fun part."

"If I had a newer truck with a back-up camera, it would have been a lot easier to get the truck lined up straight to go back under the camper."

"But then I wouldn't have had the pleasure of watching you sweat bullets," Ellen said.

"How many times did I try? Man, it had to be a dozen. The clearance between the truck and the camper legs is about an inch on each side, and I had to line the truck up absolutely straight. I'd be halfway in, and you'd check it for me, and wave me off to try again."

"It was getting dark by the time you got the job done."

"Yes. You were using a flashlight," Kate said. "That was a bear of a night."

"So why are we both smiling?"

"I hate to admit it, but my technique hasn't improved much. I didn't have an extra parking space for the camper where I lived in Danvers, so I just stored it on the truck. Only had to take it off once, when the truck needed a brake job and the mechanic didn't want to put the whole shebang on the lift."

"Good thing you won't have to go through that process again anytime soon," Ellen said. "Hey, I have an idea about what to do on a day like this. Let's go Wild."

"Sure. Wild's one of my favorite things. How?"

"There's a place called the Wild Center a few miles from here," Ellen said. "It's an indoor-outdoor museum, and I think it's well done. I've been there a few times, but not recently."

"Cool. I thought we were going to spend the day cooped up in our campers, reading and listening to NPR." She'd probably spend a day like this on her drawings if Ellen weren't here, but her company was a treat and Kate wanted to see as much of her friend as possible.

"You can do that if you'd rather." Ellen glanced at Kate.

"Hell, no."

"I think you'll like the place. They have some live animals. An owl, I think?"

They dropped Ellen's camper and locked it down, then Ellen drove, the truck's wipers thwacking back and forth. On the way she said, "Just so you know—the people at the Wild Center spell W!ld with an exclamation point instead of an I."

"I'm going to like this place," Kate said. "That's how I'd spell it, too."

* * *

It was midweek and the place wasn't busy. Since the rain had become a downpour, Kate and Ellen prowled the inside exhibits. An animated map showed how the continents and seas had changed over the millennia. Another display showed a view of Earth from space with actual air traffic: swarms of tiny planes made Europe look like a seething anthill.

But the animals were the best. River otters played in a huge tank, and a caged porcupine gnawed on a carrot.

Kate looked at the screen on Ellen's camera. "How did you do that? They look like they're in the wild."

"Watch the angle to avoid reflections from glass, and use depth of field to make wires disappear. It's easy."

In the middle of the exhibit hall, a raven stood on a man's well-padded arm and eyed a group of admirers with reciprocal curiosity. Kate and Ellen joined the small crowd.

"Ravens are as smart as dolphins," the handler said. "They've shown the ability to recognize individual human faces and to remember them, even after a year, well enough to heckle and scold the researchers who were assigned the role of being annoying." When the murmurs of appreciation faded, he said, "So don't piss off a raven."

Ellen couldn't eliminate the handler from her photos, so she made the most of it: close-up portraits of the two faces, avian and human. She turned the camera around to show the best photo to its subjects.

The man had a large nose. "The raven's name is Edgar," he said. "We're cousins. Notice the family beak?"

The two friends were settling down for a movie in the half-filled auditorium when Ellen turned in her seat and made a muffled noise.

Kate looked back too. The double doors were closing.

"What?" Kate asked.

"I thought I—" Ellen turned forward, then looked over her shoulder again. "Thought I saw somebody I knew, but it wasn't. It couldn't be." She looked rattled, an uncommon condition for her.

"The way you cranked your head around like an owl, it must have been somebody special," Kate said.

"Oh yeah, real special," Ellen said. She gave Kate a grim look. "I thought I saw Dan. But it wasn't him. He's glued to his computer in Syracuse. Marketing. Figuring angles. Making money-money-money."

Her face faded as the house lights dimmed for the movie. Soon Kate was immersed in pre-history, when mastodons roamed the Adirondacks and tapirs swam its rivers.

* * *

"Coming here was a great idea," she said when the movie was over. "That was an excellent film. The animation was almost too convincing."

"It was good, yeah," Ellen said, but she seemed distracted. On their way through the hall she looked around a lot.

"You're sure that wasn't Dan you saw, right?" Kate said. "He wouldn't follow you here, would he? That would be crazy."

"I only got a glimpse, and the guy looked like him. But I couldn't see his face—he had on a jacket with the hood up—but his figure, you know?"

"Yes, you can recognize some people in silhouette." Kate thought of Farley, the friend she'd lost so recently in Maine. He'd been unmistakable, with his stooped posture and generous head of hair.

"Dan will get over our break-up," Ellen said. "He has a business to run. Businesses. And he loves them. It's all he thinks about."

Kate kept her mouth shut. He sounded obsessive, and Syracuse wasn't that far away. A three-hour drive.

"No, he wouldn't leave his work to follow me around, I'm sure of it." Ellen sounded as if she were trying to convince herself. "He cares much more about those stupid start-ups than he cares about me." Her voice was bitter.

"Then you're better off without him," Kate said.

FOUR

It was raining again the next morning. Kate turned on the radio and got a forecast for good weather the following day. She looked out at her kayak, overturned on the picnic table and cable-locked in place. Scratches on the hull were evidence of good times in the past, while the boat's graceful lines promised good times to come.

She made coffee, but decided not to go over to Ellen's because the curtains on her camper weren't open. Unusual this late. But let her sleep—she was on vacation, after all.

Kate read the rest of the paper she'd brought home from the Put-In Pub, including the article about the Paddle of Silence. The last paragraph mentioned that Roger's father had "served with distinction" in the U.S. Navy. Funny Roger hadn't mentioned that, since they'd talked about veterans.

She put her feet up on the settee and found her place in the book *H Is for Hawk,* written by a British woman who was training a goshawk to fly from her fist. It was so absorbing that a full hour went by before Kate got up and stretched, and looked at her friend's camper again.

A man stood at Ellen's door. He was wearing a dark rain jacket with the hood up. She felt a little shiver. Could this be the man Ellen thought she recognized yesterday? Dan, following her around to harass her or urge her to come back to him?

Don't be an idiot, Kate told herself. Anybody standing in the rain would put his hood up. And anybody walking around outside on a day like this would be wearing a rain jacket. The only conclusion was that some normal person wanted to talk to Ellen.

The door opened, and Ellen looked out. A gust of wind blew her hair all over the place, but she smiled at her visitor. They were chatting. And then Ellen stepped out into the rain.

The guy grabbed her. Kate stared.

Oh, they were kissing. What a relief.

Another gust flipped the guy's hood off. It was Roger.

Hmm. Well, she'd always thought Ellen was super attractive. Kate hadn't been surprised that Dan had started dating her soon after she'd moved to Syracuse, so she shouldn't be surprised that Ellen had a new boyfriend a few weeks after dropping Dan.

Kate closed her curtain, poured herself another cup of coffee and went back to her book. A few minutes later she got a call from Ellen.

"So hey, I slept late, and now Roger's decided he needs to take me out for breakfast at the Saranac Inn." Kate could hear the smile in her friend's voice. "I hope you don't mind."

"Heck, no," Kate said. "I like it when my friends have fun."

"You're a sweetie, sweetie," Ellen said. "He's a hard man—to say no to."

"I understand," Kate said, laughing at the not-too-subtle sexual reference. "And with this weather you're no doubt quite wet."

"Tell you what, I'm soaked," Ellen said. "See you later."

* * *

Later, indeed: Kate didn't see Ellen until almost dinnertime, and heard her enthusiastic review of a day spent with Roger while the two old friends chopped vegetables in Kate's camper for a kitchen-sink salad.

"He's smart, he's funny, he's socially conscious and he's well-read," Ellen said. She was chopping celery with a rapid-fire technique Kate admired. "If I could have designed a boyfriend, he'd be a lot like Roger."

"Yikes," Kate said. "I guess you like him, huh?"

Ellen snorted. "Just a little."

"You left out how knowledgeable he is about plants and animals," Kate said. She sliced a red bell pepper lengthwise. "That's a big one in my book." She stripped out the white pulp and seeds and tossed them in the trash. "Any reservations?"

"Only the moments, every now and then, when I thought it was all too good to be true," Ellen said. "He likes you, by the way. Suggested the three of us paddle together tomorrow. Is that okay?"

* * *

The next day Roger led them on what he called the Follensby Clear Loop, bringing plenty of sandwiches and two huge thermoses. Coffee first, lemonade later. The day started cool—Kate had heard her camper's furnace come on several times during the night—but by the time they launched, the sun was throwing spears of green light deep into the water. The early mist had left all but the darkest shadows.

Kate tucked the copy of the map Roger had given her into a waterproof pocket and followed his lead. She recognized the Route 30 underpass into Square Pond, and the state campground where she and Ellen had spent their first night. But mostly she concentrated on her form, keeping her hands light on the paddle, putting her shoulder and torso into each stroke. What a gift to be on the water with friends.

Yes, after only a short time in his company, Kate considered Roger a new friend.

They stopped for lunch beside a creek and he told them more about Adirondack wildlife. How loons had solid bones, unlike most birds' hollow ones, because the weight helped them be good divers. How they could contract their feathers to press air out, making them less buoyant, more like underwater torpedos.

"They can really snag those fish," Roger said. "They're fast, they can turn on a Manhattan dime, and they have these one-way teeth that keep fish from getting loose once they nab them."

"No way. Teeth?" Ellen said. "Aren't loon's teeth as scarce as hen's teeth?"

Roger laughed. "Okay, spiky bones in their mouths."

Kate liked this guy. She said, "I've seen loons periscoping around—you know, swimming with their heads down so they can see fish to catch?" Roger was nodding. "And then they dive, and come up with nothing. Most of the time, they don't catch a thing."

"Ah, the plot thickens." Roger handed her a sandwich. "They catch a lot—they're aces—and they eat the fish right away. Downstairs. Underwater." He laughed. "Fresher that way."

"This sandwich has crab in it," Ellen said. "Thank you, Roger. It's yummy, and I'm glad I don't have to eat it underwater."

"Crab and cucumber," Roger said. "And the spread isn't mayonnaise, it's a yogurt mix I put together."

Kate shook her head. This guy was amazing. Ellen had fallen into the—what was the expression? Fallen into the pie? Or was it the cake?

Or maybe it was the crab-and-cucumber salad.

Roger paddled a solo canoe. It was narrower than most, which was good for speed, and he had an impressive J-stroke, powerful enough to outpace the kayaks even though he was using a traditional single-bladed paddle. The women's double blades meant they could take more strokes in a given time than Roger could, but even so they couldn't keep up with him.

"Yeah, I grew up on these lakes," he said at another afternoon break. Kate was happy that he didn't talk much while they were on the water. She liked to enjoy the scenery and look for birds and other wildlife while paddling or hiking, and it was hard sometimes when companions chattered as if they were on a city sidewalk.

"I used to be out here all the time with my father," he said. "He was an amazing man." He looked down and went silent for a long beat. Kate remembered a similar moment before dinner at the Put-In Pub.

Ellen looked at him with concern. "Roger?" she said softly.

He looked up, and his face flickered with an expression too brief to read. Then he was fine, fully there, pointing out a nuthatch across the creek.

Kate wondered if there was some trauma lurking in the man's past, something he hadn't told them. Roger wasn't a veteran—or at least the newspaper article hadn't mentioned any service except his father's—but the way he occasionally spaced out in conversations reminded Kate of Ellen's descriptions of some of the veterans she'd interviewed.

There was more to Roger than met the eye. Kate hadn't forgotten Shag's take on his boss, that he was a tough, driven man who drove others.

* * *

They were at the pull-out when Roger said, "We're having a cookout tomorrow at Boat Camp. You two gals want to come by? It'll be all my guides, Molly and Jennifer and Tate and Shag and Irving, and me—oh, maybe you haven't met some of them. The last party of the season, with corn on the cob and swordfish. What do you say?"

Kate was glad he'd included her in the invitation.

"Oh, that's so nice of you," Ellen said. "Thanks. That work for you, Kate?"

"Sure."

"Okay, we'll be there."

Kate turned away and spent a couple of unnecessary minutes fiddling with the gear in her boat. She wanted to give the couple some privacy in case they got involved in a kiss like the one she'd seen outside Ellen's camper the previous day.

When she heard Roger's truck start up she turned around. Ellen was facing the road, where the big pick-up with the solo canoe in the bed was gaining the pavement, and she had her hand up in a wave. But her expression wasn't what Kate expected.

"Why are you looking so grim? I think you've snagged yourself a boyfriend. Now you'll have to use your loon teeth to hang onto him."

Ellen dropped her hand. "I'm a little scared. Dan has a yellow Corvette, and one just went by. How common are yellow Corvettes around here?" She clenched her fists. "I'll kill him if he comes up here and screws up this good thing I'm getting started. I swear to God I'll kill him."

Kate couldn't think what to say. She rubbed a hand across Ellen's tense shoulders.

FIVE

As Ellen parked her truck in the Boat Camp lot on Saturday for the cookout, the first person Kate noticed was Tate, the good-looking guide she'd seen in the store earlier in the week. He probably didn't sleep with a pillow, his hair was so curly and thick. The thought of him lying in bed made Kate feel tingly all over. She tried to focus on that instead of on her reaction to the size of the gathering. More than a dozen people were already mingling and talking, and more cars were coming down the road. When she'd been a reporter Kate had had to meet people all the time, but this was different. On her own, without a job to do, she wasn't crazy about big social gatherings.

But Tate sure was handsome.

Then she realized his name rhymed with hers, and she laughed.

Ellen looked at her, but Kate didn't explain. "This will be fun." She didn't need to be a wet blanket to Ellen, who loved parties.

"You bet it will."

"Nice of Roger to invite us." Kate wished he hadn't made it sound like just a small group of employees, though. She hadn't braced herself for a crowd.

Two other guides Kate didn't know were helping Tate unload big coolers from a couple of pick-ups and heft them onto picnic tables. Considering what Roger had brought on the paddling trip the day before, Kate figured the coolers held something more than ordinary fare.

Tate came to meet them. "Kind of late in the year for a cookout, but we lucked out with the weather," he said. "You guys know Molly. Meet Irving—he's a Boat Camper—and Dusty, a former fearless guide. Guys, this is Ellen, and this is Kate. Ellen's, like, with Roger."

Kate had never seen Ellen blush so hard. Was even her hair turning red?

Tate looked embarrassed. "Oh, hey, I hope that wasn't—I mean—"

Ellen laughed. "It's okay. I'll get over it."

Dusty was dark-skinned, and like Shag he had such a short haircut that it looked military. Maybe that was the new cool style these days? Kate wondered. Irving was a tall guy who stood behind Dusty and didn't shake hands. He looked at the women briefly and then at the ground. Must be shy. All of the guides wore khaki work clothes with their names on the shirts, which helped Kate relax a bit. She wished everyone, everywhere, wore nametags.

Tate introduced her and Ellen to other people, and Kate of course couldn't remember their names a minute later. A tall woman with waist-length hair whose voice was so soft Kate could barely hear her, a silver-haired couple dressed too nicely for a cookout, the man who ran a bicycle shop in South Portage and a couple of his employees, a beady-eyed guy who used to be mayor. Then two bashful girls too young to be here on their own, but Kate couldn't figure out who their parents were.

Her head was spinning. Was the whole town here?

A green Subaru pulled up.

"Here come the girls." Tate said, and Kate's heart did a little flutter-kick. Of course, a guy like him already had a girlfriend. "It's Molly and Jennifer," he said to Kate. "Oh, and Shag's with them."

Molly waved, Kate and Ellen waved back. Then the three guides lugged more coolers to the picnic tables.

"What can we do to help?" Kate asked. She liked to have a job at events like these.

"Relax and have a beer, that's what," Tate said.

Molly and Jennifer joined them. Jennifer was probably the oldest of the Boat Camp guides, about forty, but only some faint lines near her eyes said so; otherwise she looked as fit and trim as the others. "Hey," she said, smiling at the newcomers. "You won't see much of me—I'm on store duty."

"What's the expression?" Tate asked. "'Somebody's got to mind the store'? Give me a wave out the door and I'll spell you, Jennifer."

"Thanks, Tate."

They all drifted toward the picnic tables. Irving was lighting a big gas grill: shy people like to stay busy. Shag was changing the propane tank on a second grill.

Molly looked around. "So the gang's all here, except Roger." She opened a cooler and looked inside. "Food," she said, and put plastic containers on the nearest table. Then she dropped the lid and opened the next cooler. "Ah. That's better."

She pulled out a bottle of Sam Adams and waved it around, offering it. "Anybody?"

Ellen reached for it. "Thanks."

"Oh, wait, I should say there's also Blue Moon, and Deschutes, and, um, Michelob, and Guinness—"

"Honestly, give me anything," Kate said. "Beer is beer. I must have really stupid taste buds, and they can't tell one brand from another."

"You'll never be able to convince me you can't tell the difference between a Guinness and a Sam Adams," Tate said.

"Her taste buds are so devoted to coffee that they've tuned out all other beverages," Ellen said.

"Oh, no, look what I found." Molly was peering into another cooler. "Budweiser. Ugh."

"Bud is beer," Kate said. "I'll drink one, if you want to get rid of them."

"No, it's not that," Molly said. "Roger really spoils us with all this great food. And he's kind of a beer snob. A bunch of Budweiser means his mother is coming."

"That's a bad thing?" Ellen asked. Molly and Tate laughed.

* * *

Roger drove up about ten minutes later in a big Boat Camp pick-up and helped a tall woman down from the passenger seat. Her hair, as dark as his, swept in bangs above hawkish eyes. She might have cut an imposing figure except for the slowness of her movements as she came toward the group. It wasn't far, now: so many people had arrived that half the parking lot was full and the guides had carried out more picnic tables.

Another man had gotten out of the pick-up. He looked like a younger version of Roger, with the same powerful build. A brother or cousin? He wore his hair longer, pulled back in a short ponytail; a camera hung around his neck.

"Howdy, everyone." Mrs. Benedict's voice carried over the chatter of the crowd. She gave a little wave, found a smile. "How's everyone doing?"

She got a collective murmur in response. Her son was a successful businessman in a small town. Everyone must know her.

Roger came behind her with a lawn chair he unfolded; he waited while his mother settled into it. "Care to introduce me, honey?" she asked him, looking at Ellen.

Kate winced. Calling a grown son "honey" in front of others was embarrassing.

Roger introduced them quietly and went off to the grills. He must be used to his mother's ways.

Mrs. Benedict asked Ellen a lot of questions. Where was she from? How long was she staying in the area? Did she have a boyfriend? Ellen looked startled and answered only some of the questions. She told the older woman how much she loved the Adirondacks, and how she'd come here often as a youngster, with her family. She named places they'd stayed back then. Long answers to the less intrusive questions avoided the ones she didn't want to answer.

Roger's mother's voice was loud, as if she had some hearing loss. Hoping to escape interrogation, Kate turned away and literally bumped into the man with the camera, who introduced himself as Roger's brother Will. He was drinking a Bud and waved the can toward the group.

"Roger's getting to be a popular guy," he said. "I've been to a lot of these cookouts over the past few years and this is the biggest by far. Looks like he invited everybody in town this time." He shook his head. "I used to think he was shy. Can't say I really understand my brother."

The camera on the strap around his neck was a small Leica. "Are you a professional photographer?" Kate asked.

He was, with a studio two hours away in Burlington, Vermont. "A really pretty part of the world," he said, then looked around at the lake. "Not that this isn't."

"So what don't you understand about your brother?"

Will shrugged. "Five years ago he was a wild man who lived in the woods. Now look at him. Mr. Pillar of the Community." He took a long swallow of Bud. "He's a fu—he's a magician."

His tone had an edge to it, something in it besides approval. Was he jealous?

Seeming to catch her thought, or perhaps reconsidering his tone of voice, Will added that he'd taught Roger a lot about running a business. "He's done well," he said, his voice warmer—maybe because he was taking credit.

Irving and Dusty were cooking burgers, which were pretty ordinary until you added your choice of fixings from a long row of dishes. Kate skipped the meat and went for mango relish, lots of red lettuce and a slice of sweet onion.

Roger came by as she took her first bite. "Definitely not your average burger," she told him. She didn't like to make waves about being vegetarian, and he didn't need to know what was inside the bun.

"We don't do ordinary around here," he said. "Dusty, Irving, don't forget the swordfish steaks—they're in the blue cooler."

"Oh, man, swordfish." Kate said, who liked fish but ate it rarely because it was expensive. She'd had salmon a few nights ago at the Put-In Pub, and Roger had stepped in to pay for it. Now he was offering another free seafood meal. "What a treat."

"No, we don't do ordinary." Molly, who'd been putting serving spoons in food containers, joined the group around Roger. "This is an amazing part of the world. You can paddle flat water or killer rapids, you can hike and bike and ski. And there are all kinds of classes—how to make Mohawk baskets or Mother Moon necklaces—and artists all over the place give lessons in every medium you can think of—" She was breathless with enthusiasm.

"Don't forget the festivals," Tate said. "The Moose festival is my favorite. Although, no, maybe the canoe-and-brew is."

"We've got a cardboard box boat race in July that's hilarious," Roger said. "I hope you come back for it, Kate."

"Face it, we've got everything." Molly said. "Eat your heart out, Cleveland."

"Don't forget that sports car show," Shag said. "That's wild. Enough Firebirds and Corvettes to choke a—" He looked around for inspiration. "A freeway."

Everybody laughed, and Shag celebrated with a long pull on his beer. He ducked his head to hide a smile and rubbed his crew-cut with the flat of his palm.

"When's the sports car show?" Kate asked.

"This weekend," Roger said. "Watch out when you're driving. Some of these muscle-car guys think the road's a race track."

"I think Corvettes are the worst," Molly said. "Those drivers take crazy chances. They'll pass you on a curve going 90."

Ellen was still in a face-off with Mrs. Benedict, so Kate couldn't tell her right away. But it was great news that there were Corvettes all over the area for a show. Ellen could stop worrying that Dan had turned into a weirdo who was stalking her.

"Do you like sports cars?" Tate was beside her, and Kate felt like she was on an elevator going down too fast. She had a flash that he might invite her to the show, and she didn't want to discourage him but she wasn't remotely interested in fancy cars.

"Oh, gosh, no, I asked about the show because Ellen's, um, Ellen—" She felt her face heating up. "I mean, I really love being outdoors, in a boat or on a bike. Engines? Not so much."

"Boat, bike. Gotcha. Boots?" He actually had dimples. Could a guy get any more attractive?

"Oh, yes, definitely boots," she said. "You caught me in sneakers today, but boots are better."

* * *

Kate had two beers, which she decided was half a beer more than she could handle: the party took on a glow she knew was alcohol-induced. Tate made sure her second beer was a Guinness, and she had to admit it was a different experience than the Bud. Thicker, stronger. Like beer soup.

She looked for patterns among the people she knew. Roger's mother was at the edge of the group, like a sniper, firing questions at nearby people. Sitting, she couldn't mingle, making group conversations impossible for her. Roger made sure she got a Bud and a plate of food, and he chatted with her at times, but he never stayed for long.

Tate talked mostly to Irving and Dusty—their nearly-shaved heads made his hair look even more like a halo. With a pang she realized Tate might be gay. Molly and Shag hung out together, and when the store wasn't busy Jennifer joined them. Not that the groups were locked in place—they split and got messed up as everyone but Mrs. Benedict circulated. But they often they came together again.

Tate-Irving-Dusty, then, and Molly-Shag-Jennifer. Roger, master of ceremonies, floated. Could a magnet float? Wherever he went, a cluster of people—Kate didn't know most of them—formed around him. His social skills were getting a workout, navigating so many groups. Hard to imagine him as the wild man living in the woods the way Will had described.

As newcomers, she and Ellen floated, too. At one point she found herself next to Irving. She'd wanted to chat with him; she sympathized with shy people, considering herself one of their tribe.

"How do you like working at Boat Camp?" she asked. Might as well collect some info—otherwise known as gossip—about the man who was fast becoming Ellen's new boyfriend.

"It's not that bad," Irving said, shrugging. He glanced over his shoulder and located Roger, who was well out of earshot. "The boss is kind of temperamental, but you get used to it."

"Temperamental how?"

"Oh—grouchy, now and then. And sometimes he doesn't show up for days, doesn't tell us ahead of time or say where he went." He had a cherubic face, but when he smiled his teeth were ragged. "Those are the good days."

"That doesn't sound like fun."

"Pays the bills," Irving said. He drained his beer and fished another out of the ice in the cooler beside them. Flipped the cap off with a church-key, wiped his hand on his shirt and took a good pull from the bottle. Then looked at her.

This was why Kate didn't go to parties often. For her, conversation was work.

"Is Roger's mother sitting down because she's ill?" she asked.

"Yeah, she's got asthma? Has good days and bad days. This must be a baddy."

What else to talk about? "So tell me about Roger's father," she said. "That newspaper article about the Paddle of Silence said Roger's the son of Paul Benedict, an 'important community figure' or some phrase like that. But it didn't give any specifics."

"Nobody knows where he is," Irving said in a low voice.

"Oh, I'm sorry, I didn't mean—" Oh, great. Roger's father must have run out on his wife. No wonder she seemed difficult.

"No, it's okay, no reason for you not to know. The whole rest of the town knows." Irving turned his back to Roger, and Kate shifted with him. "Paul Benedict is, or was, in the Navy, one of those special forces guys?"

Oh, that was different. Maybe not good, but at least he hadn't abandoned a sick wife. Kate nodded.

"He was on what was supposed to be his last mission? And he didn't make it back. Roger and his mother don't even know where he was or what he was doing. It's been a while now, four or five years? But I don't think she's over it, and the breathing problem doesn't help."

"Oh, I'm so sorry," Kate said.

"Roger and his father were super-close," Irving said. "You know, it's not a subject I'd bring up with him? I don't know if he'll ever get over it, either."

"Oh, wow, thanks for the warning. I'll tell Ellen, too."

"Yeah, that would be a good idea. It's kind of a mine field, talking about his parents, you know?" His eyes were bloodshot; he'd maybe had too much to drink. And the way he made statements into questions was driving Kate crazy. "Oh, jeez, I didn't mean that to be a joke, a mine field? Not too funny."

"No, I understand," Kate said. "Thanks again." She wanted to warn Ellen, but she was talking to Roger. Still— "Excuse me."

Kate made her way through the crowd. Ellen and Roger looked at her, two faces with the same cat-that-swallowed-the-canary look. Weren't sexy vibes great? This might not be true love, but it was at least a welcome segue for Ellen out of her disappointment with Dan.

Having eaten her improvised veggie sandwich, Kate asked Ellen if she wanted to split one of the swordfish steaks. A look at them on the grill had told Kate they were more than she could eat.

Ellen said yes, and as Kate hoped Roger went off to cook one for them.

"Hey, I wanted you to know that Roger lost his father. A special forces guy who ended up MIA. Irving said it's a sensitive topic," Kate said.

"You're sweet to tell me," Ellen said. "But I already know. He's a complicated man who's been through a lot." She looked away, her face clouding. "We've done a lot of talking in the past few days."

"Along with other things?" Kate asked. Like smooching in the rain.

Ellen turned back and beamed. "Yes, other things. However did you guess?"

Kate told Ellen about the car show, too, and then they drank their beers and looked over the crowd. Roger knew how to throw a party.

* * *

Kate did her best. She talked to people for a few minutes each. When she bumped into Will again it was a relief. At least she remembered his name. Ellen joined them; she and Will talked about photography for a while, amateur to pro.

"Taking pictures is such a great thing to do for your family," Ellen said. "I've got pictures of everybody, doing practically everything—I love candid shots the most, though I get called on for weddings and graduations and ducks-in-a-row situations like that."

"I'm with you there," Will said. "Candids really show who people are, what they're into. On their bikes, or at a potter's wheel, or painting a house. But a lot of people come to me for studio shots, so they're sitting in chairs with a toddler on their knee. Or they want portraits."

"I've got baby pictures of every kid born in my family in the last ten years," Ellen said. "I hope the later ones are better in terms of lighting and composition, but heck, they're all good for blackmail." She smiled at Will. "I bet you have a few you could hold over Roger's head when you want something."

Will shook his head. "No, actually, Roger isn't into photography at all. In fact, I think he destroyed all the pictures my mother had of Dad. There were a lot, all over the house, and one day a couple of years ago, they vanished. Back when Roger was living there."

"Strange," Ellen said.

"He never admitted that he took them, but I can't imagine who else would. Like a lot of older folks out here, Mum doesn't lock her house, so I suppose somebody could have gone in and taken them. But why would anybody else do that?"

"What about pictures of Roger? Did they disappear too?" Kate asked.

"There weren't any. He's one of those people who says he hates having his picture taken. Must be part Indian. You know, cameras steal your soul?"

Ellen shrugged. "So take the shot anyway."

"If you do that, all you get is a picture of the back of Roger's head," Will said. "The guy can move faster than a speeding shutter."

"Oh, too bad," Kate said. "These days, everybody's taking selfies and posting them. A dozen a day on Facebook."

"Nobody can say my brother follows the crowd," Will said.

"When he hears 'Say cheese,' he says 'Baloney'?" Ellen asked.

Will laughed. "You got it. I'm out of luck in the blackmail department."

That was going to be the last laugh for a while, because Mrs. Benedict stood up, edged around the chair and held onto the back of it while she scanned the crowd.

"Excuse me," Will said, putting down his beer. He'd been facing his mother while the three of them talked; he must have been keeping an eye on her.

Roger, who was talking to an older couple, put down his Guinness and went to her, too. He helped her into the Boat Camp truck while Will folded the lawn chair and tossed it into the bed. The pick-up rumbled down Paul's Way.

The party was quieter after that, and in a few minutes Kate gave Ellen a look, to see if she was ready to leave.

"Can we help clean up here?" Ellen asked nobody in particular.

"Heck, no, we're good." Molly turned to them. "We put this kind of shindig together all summer for groups who sign up for our paddling trips. We're experts by now, and Roger keeps us trained."

"Yeah, doesn't he though," Shag said, behind her. "South Portage's own special forces canoe outfitter. Why do you think it's called Boot Camp? Drop, seaman, give me fifty."

"Hey, cut it out, Shag," Tate said, looking around to see who'd overheard. "That's enough."

"Yes, sir." Shag's tone was sarcastic.

Molly put her hands behind Kate's and Ellen's elbows, steering them gently toward their truck. "Mrs. Benedict's health has gone downhill," she said. "Her husband was lost at sea a few years ago and she's never really recovered. She says she has asthma, but heartbreak is what I call it."

"I'm sorry for her," Kate said. "Losing her husband has got to be hard."

"Hard for her," Ellen said, "and for Roger and Will."

"And I'm sorry about Shag's outburst," Molly said. "He probably had a little too much to drink. You're not seeing us at our best." Kate was surprised to see tears in the guide's eyes as she gave them each a quick hug and turned away.

"Wow, Molly's really upset," Ellen said as she started up her truck. They were heading to the state campground, Fish Creek, where they'd moved from Floodwood Road to charge up their batteries and enjoy shore power for a few days. "She was almost crying, wasn't she?"

"Yes," Kate said. "Interesting how she said 'us.' I wasn't sure if she was including herself with the other guides at Boat Camp or with the Benedicts."

"Maybe she meant the whole village of South Portage," Ellen said. "Roger's kind of a big wheel around here, and his father, too. The guide service uses part-timers in the summer season, which means Roger probably knows everybody in town who can lift a paddle. That was a big crowd for a shoulder-season party."

"It was. Will called his brother a 'pillar of the community,'" Kate said. "Funny, though, Will sounded like he might be jealous. He's been running his photo studio for a lot longer than Roger's run the guide service. Maybe Boat Camp's success is bugging Will."

"Will doesn't have Roger's charisma," Ellen said. "Hey, I need to stop for gas, but after that want to throw the boats in Square Pond for an afternoon paddle?"

"Sounds good."

Ellen pulled into Stewart's, and while she filled the tank Kate went inside to buy a newspaper. As she came out, a yellow Corvette pulled up to the pump. Ellen did a double-take at the tall man in a camo jacket who unfolded himself from the driver's seat.

Even before she got within earshot, Kate knew the conversation wasn't pleasant. Ellen was leaning forward, her chin out, still holding the pump nozzle, like an attack dog straining at a leash.

Dan's posture was surprisingly relaxed. He might have been waiting for a bus. As Kate reached them, he looked her up and down with an amused expression.

". . .even *doing* here," Ellen was saying. "You're not impressing me by being persistent. Or you are impressing me, but not in a good way." Her eyes narrowed. "Are you following us? Were you stalking me at the Wild Center a couple of days ago?"

"Hey, that might've been me." His voice was quiet and smooth, like a salesman's. "You two are awfully close. Long dinner at the Put-In, wasn't it? I saw your new buddy come out of your camper early one morning, Ellen. Have you gone gay on me?"

"Oh, for God's sake." Ellen jammed the nozzle into place on the pump. "You're an idiot."

"I think you need to leave my friend alone," Kate said.

"Leave her to you, diesel dyke, is that what you mean?" He turned to Ellen. "You think it's over between us, honey, but it's not. You've always had your hissy-fits, but then you calm down." He smiled. "When you get over this broad you'll want me back, with everything I can offer you." He made a small, perhaps unconscious, gesture with his hand toward the car. The driver's door was open, a long yellow wing.

He couldn't possibly think Ellen gave a damn about a flashy car, could he? Maybe in his mind it stood for his money. Surprise, turkey. Ellen didn't care about that, either. She supported herself. And enjoyed doing so.

Ellen's voice was quieter now, but it wasn't any less angry. "Listen to me, Dan. Go home. Stay out of my life. I don't want to see you again. Ever."

"That's what you think now, honey. I can wait."

Ellen opened the door to her truck. "And don't call me honey!"

SIX

Even though temperatures had dropped into the high thirties on Saturday night, Sunday was another splendid day, with dark water and bright sun. The two women paddled south to the quiet end of Lower Saranac Lake, weaving among islands. They all had short names, Fern and Burnt and Bluff, as if they were too small to rate more than one syllable. The fall colors had brightened overnight, though they still needed a week or two to reach their peak. Kate had her cell phone handy as they approached Bluff, hoping for some interesting rocks, but the island's face was a uniform elephant-gray.

"That cliff is over sixty feet high," Ellen said. "Every summer people jump off the top. Adrenalin junkies. Some of them get hurt." She turned and pointed east with her paddle blade. "Whiteface Mountain is about twenty miles that way. I like descents that involve snow, and take a lot longer than free-falls," she said. "Whiteface is great, but it won't have snow for a couple more months."

She didn't hear from Roger all day, and Kate could feel her friend wondering why.

"Maybe we're not getting good coverage out here," she said, when she saw Ellen checking her phone again.

"No, it's not the coverage. I've got four out of five bars," Ellen said. "I'll have to back my brain up to Labor Day and stop thinking about him." After another few paddle strokes she said, "Although I'd rather think about

Roger than Dan—he made me so mad yesterday. He's turned into a nut case."

Dan had scared Kate more than he'd made her angry. "I'll race you to the end of the island," Kate said, to help get Ellen's mind off men.

And her own.

* * *

The day went well for a few hours after that. They took short walks on two islands, paddled some more, then climbed to the top of Bluff. Back in the kayaks, they explored the river that ran south toward Upper Saranac Lake and found a boggy patch crowded with pitcher plants. Kate took dozens of reference photos of the tubular beauties, and Ellen couldn't resist taking her own shots even though she had to do it with "a mere phone" instead of her camera.

Most of the plants were full of water from the recent rain. "This one has a fly floating inside," Ellen said. Leaning over the gunwale with her phone held over one of the bristle-lined botanical traps, her kayak heeling hard, she looked happy, the way Kate had known her in their outdoor adventures in Massachusetts.

When they pulled out for lunch beside Loon Bay, though, Ellen told Kate some of the sobering things she'd learned about Roger.

"He's kind of hung up on his father," she said. "Apparently he was an amazing man, physically and mentally. He took Roger out on the water when he was a toddler; he meant it literally when he said grew up on these lakes."

Ellen took a bite of a sandwich with a slice of cheese hanging out the side. It was chrome yellow. Nobody should eat anything the color of a school bus, Kate thought. Her own crunchy peanut butter on whole wheat was a boring tan but at least it was real food.

Both their lunches were blah compared to Roger's provisions. She wasn't going to say so, though. Ellen had more to miss about him than the food he'd supplied for their paddling trip and the cookout.

"Roger wanted to be a secret fighter, like his dad. They did all kinds of hard-core workouts together: weights, wicked-hard rock climbing, paddling in the worst weather, skiing all the black diamond trails they could find. There are a lot around here—Olympians train at Lake Placid. His father even took him skydiving."

"So why didn't Roger do that? Follow his father into the Navy?"

"He has only one kidney," Ellen said. "Born that way. He and his father never knew until the Navy processing center did a routine X-ray. Any missing organ disqualifies a guy, so he wasn't eligible to join."

"Oh, man. What a shock that must have been."

"It was horrible."

"If you want to hear God laugh. . . ," Kate said, starting a saying they both knew.

"Right. Tell Her your plans," Ellen sighed.

"They must have been really close, Roger and his father."

"Well, yes and no," Ellen said. "He had to call his dad Sir, and his room got inspected, like boot camp. And some of those trips they took were grueling. Paddle two days straight with no food. Sometimes Roger schlepped the canoe over a long portage, and then went back for duffel bags full of rocks."

"What?"

"Yeah. Instead of supplies he got to carry rocks. Sounds crazy, but if you're trying to make your son tough as nails I guess it makes sense."

Kate found her tube of sunblock and put a dollop on each forearm. "Second coat," she said as she tossed the tube to Ellen. "It doesn't last all day." She rubbed the lotion into her arms and face. "What did Roger do, when the Navy wouldn't take him?"

"He ran away. Got on a bus straight from the processing center, after the Navy told him. Couldn't face his father. Rode around on buses, says he can't remember where he went or what he did."

"Yikes."

"Yeah. Now he says he knows it was a bad decision. Nobody knew where he was for a week or two. Then he phoned home with the bad news."

"His parents must have been frantic."

"Yeah." Ellen's voice went low. "He doesn't talk about his mother much. She was so nosy at the cookout, asking me all those questions, wasn't she? He says her health fell apart after his father was lost at sea."

"Yes, that's hard." Kate said. "She didn't look too good yesterday."

"No."

They sat for a few minutes. It was good to talk to an old friend. And it was good not to talk, too.

A flock of chickadees came through, making those small, barely audible noises Kate loved. She thought about the sharpness of the senses of birds and animals. Bees can see into the ultraviolet range of light. And hawks' vision is so good they can target mice from a mile up. Owls hear voles moving under snow, where they must think they're safe.

It was an amazing planet, and she felt lucky to be alive on it.

On the trip back they saw teal and mergansers rafting in open water, feeding to ready themselves for the long haul south. Almost to Fish Creek, the kayaks glided around a bend and startled a doe and a fawn that had been drinking at the water's edge.

As they pulled the boats ashore, Kate said, "Did you see those deer? I couldn't put an age on the younger one, but it was half the size of its mother. And it was still spotted. Isn't it kind of late in the year for that?"

"Yeah, seems like it would be," Ellen said. "I'll ask Roger the next time I see him." A pause. "If I see him."

"I hope he doesn't pull a disappearing act on you." As soon as the words were out of her mouth, she wished she hadn't said them, but her friend didn't seem bothered. Maybe Kate was too sensitive, her own father having gone missing when she was a child.

Ellen's cell phone rang. She glanced at it and her face brightened.

Kate was glad. She emptied the boats, broke down the paddles, and put all the gear in the extended cab of the Toyota while Ellen wandered along the shoreline, phone to ear, with the aimless walk of someone who's not paying attention to what's in front of her.

Kate slid her Hornbeck onto the rack on top of Ellen's camper and strapped it down. It was a light boat made of carbon-fiber, only sixteen pounds, a gift three years ago from her then-partner. It didn't have an upper deck, so it looked more like canoe than a kayak, but it had the foot pegs, low seat, and narrow beam of a kayak. She'd spent the bucks for a super-lightweight carbon-fiber paddle when she was working, never thinking she'd be out of a job so soon.

Ellen's boat was too heavy for one person to handle, so Kate leaned against the truck and ate a tangerine, thinking how involved Ellen had gotten with Roger in only a few days.

Roger could be very pleasant. You'd never guess he'd faced a disappointment so huge it drove him away from home, or that he'd had a father with the personality of a drill sergeant. Or whatever the Navy equivalent of a drill sergeant was.

Then she thought of Roger barking out Shag's name the first time she and Ellen visited Boat Camp, and of Shag's resentment of Roger. And the way all the guides wore khaki pants and shirts with nametags, even at the cookout. Like uniforms. And the name of the business, a pun on "boot camp."

Yes, Roger had a great social personality, but underneath it was someone who'd been brought up tough. It sounded as if he'd been enrolled in a military school since he was born.

When Ellen got off the phone they loaded her boat. She practically hummed with relief.

"So he's okay?"

"Yeah, he asked me out tonight. Apologized for being out of touch today."

"Well, he's got a business to run," Kate said. "And a mother to help out."

"What, you were listening?" Ellen joked.

They got back to the campground and unloaded Kate's kayak first. Roger had offered to pick Ellen up so she wouldn't have to break camp and then set up again, late. Thoughtful of him.

"We're going out to dinner, then maybe back here or to his place," Ellen said. "He lives over the store, down at the end of Paul's Way."

"Romantic setting, out there in the woods," Kate said. "Hey, the moon's only a few days past full. Maybe you could go for a midnight paddle."

"It would be hard to paddle in the dress I'm going to wear," Ellen said. "And I hope I'm doing something else at midnight. Something—warmer."

"Oh, silly me," Kate said. "Of course you brought a dress along on a camping trip." They both laughed.

They got Ellen's boat down and locked to the picnic table, then raised her pop-top. Kate snapped open the latches around the edge of the roof, while Ellen got herself inside. Awkward to do that with the roof in its low position, but Ellen was used to it. Once in, she pushed the roof up and put its supports into place.

When that was done, standing room established and the camper plugged in, Kate said goodnight through the door. "Have a good time."

"Count on it," Ellen said with a wicked grin.

Kate took a couple of steps, then turned back. "We don't actually know Roger very well. He seems like a great guy, but keep your cell phone handy, okay? Call me if you need a ride."

"I don't think I'll be calling, but thanks for the offer."

Kate went back to her camper and made a simple dinner of rice and beans, adding cumin and ginger to stave off blandness. She looked in the fridge, found some green onions, and chopped them up for a garnish.

Headlights washed across her window as she sat down to eat, and she heard a truck door slam. Must be Roger. She pulled her curtains closed after the truck moved off.

Legs up on the settee and a pillow behind her head, she settled in for a good read.

Hours later, she woke up with her head at an awkward angle. The pillow had slipped: she had a sore neck and what felt like a dent in the side of her head. Not only that, the book was on the floor under the table. It had shut itself, so Kate had lost her place. Drat, she hated that.

Then she laughed at herself. This was definitely in the category of high-class problems, a phrase of her father's that still tickled her. Losing her place in a book wasn't exactly a life-altering disaster. It was the kind of problem that should make you happy because you don't have bigger problems.

Like the ones the Benedict family had.

She hadn't liked Roger's mother, but the woman carried the daily burden of not knowing the fate of a loved one gone missing. A burden Kate knew only too well.

She shared even more with Roger. They both had fathers who'd disappeared.

Ellen hadn't brought up that parallel. Kate knew her friend had left it up to her, and she would have talked about her father if she'd felt the need. But it was over twenty years since he'd vanished. There was nothing to say.

Roger was attractive, physically and otherwise—he was smart and funny and socially skilled and successful at running a business. But Ellen had gotten herself involved with someone who hadn't had an easy life.

Well, who did?

Kate climbed up to the over-cab bunk and fell asleep for the second time. She dreamed she was paddling, enjoying water and sky, and then the current got stronger, the gray-green water surged under her boat and she was rushing headlong toward rocks.

She didn't sleep for long. Chirping woke her, and she fumbled for the phone.

"Kate, can you pick me up at the end of Paul's Way? Right now?"

SEVEN

Ellen's voice was tense.

"Be right there." Kate was full of questions, but her friend sounded so stressed that this wasn't the time to ask them.

Still, they circled in her mind as she threw on clothes. Had Ellen had a fight with Roger? Or did his truck have a flat? Or worse, were they in a traffic accident? Kate dropped the coffeemaker into the sink so it wouldn't slide off the counter and went outside to unplug the camper. Her breath smoked in the cold.

Half past five: the waning gibbous moon drew silver scribbles on the surface of Square Pond. Not a likely time for Ellen and Roger to be on the road.

Kate drove the few miles north on Route 30 as fast as she dared. Under the trees, the road was dark. As she made the left turn onto Floodwood, a trio of deer stared at her headlights and then scrambled off the pavement, hooves slipping.

She slowed as she got near the campground where she and Ellen had stayed a few days earlier. Only one small camper there, unlit, like a boat floating in the night's dark waters.

A figure stepped from behind a tree. Kate's headlights picked out pale legs and face, and wild hair. Ellen, hugging her big purse. She hurried to the truck and climbed in.

"Let's get out of here." She shivered in her black dress and cardigan.

Kate turned the heater up and made a three-point turn. "What's going on?" she asked as she straightened the wheel and picked up speed. "Did you and Roger have a fight?"

"Did we ever. And then he proposed! Sort of. Oh, my God." Ellen's laughter was harsh, and she kept glancing in the side-view mirror as if worried Roger was following them. "Oh, Kate, it was so weird. Last night was great. And then this morning—"

"Wait. Tell me from the beginning." Kate dropped her speed a notch: Ellen's urgency was contagious.

"Okay. Last night." Ellen took a deep breath and pushed her hair back. "We chatted on the way to the restaurant, the Serendipity. You know how easy he is to be with. Or was, until—" She looked at the rear-view again. "Dinner was so darn normal. We talked about jazz, and about how good the cross-country skiing will be up here in a couple of months. I said I'd be into that, and he smiled and said he knew some great trails."

Kate kept her eye mostly on the road, watching for deer, but was glad her friend's voice was calmer.

"He told me more about his family. He's afraid his mother is kind of losing it. His father's been missing for five years, and she still celebrates his birthday—bakes a cake, invites her kids."

"How many does she have?"

"Two sons, Roger and Will, that photographer we talked to at the cookout, who lives a couple of hours away in Vermont. And a sister, Sarah, who moved to Minnesota and never calls or visits, not on her father's birthday or any other day."

"Ouch."

"Yeah. Roger said his mother is super disappointed. She always wanted a daughter, especially since the household was kind of macho."

"Yikes. Families sure can be difficult," Kate said, thinking of her own alcoholic mother and vanished father.

"Yeah." Ellen was quiet for a moment. As far as Kate knew, Ellen's family was relatively okay—everybody spoke to everybody, nobody missing—but of course there were tensions. Every family, every person has them.

"So we had a nice dinner, and then we went back to his place. He has an apartment over the store, which is pretty isolated, but he said he likes that."

"From what you've said about how he was brought up, I imagine him having a Spartan place. Does he sleep on a bed of nails?" Kate asked.

"No, the place is comfy. Real furniture." Ellen's laugh was subdued, but it was a laugh. "I remember the first guy I dated. He had a sleeping bag for a bedspread—you know, one of those rectangular ones that you can zip out flat? Had a flannel lining with cowboys on it."

"I remember those bags," Kate said, "from camping as a kid. The zipper was metal, right? I was always afraid I'd whack myself in the teeth or the eyes with the zipper while I was half-asleep."

"Yeah. And his bedside table was a wooden crate."

"You're talking your first boyfriend now, not Roger, right?"

"Right."

"Maybe the crate came from that store Crate and Barrel," Kate said. "That's upscale."

"No, it was the real thing," Ellen said. "Anyway, I was afraid Roger's place would be like that, because he's such an outdoorsy guy. But you can tell from his conversation he's not an overgrown Boy Scout. The first thing he did when we got there was put on some Thelonious Monk. He loves classic jazz." She sighed.

"Me, too," Kate said. "Then what?"

"We talked, and then we made love. It was—really sweet. Two-way, you know? Not like Dan, who was always focused only on what he needed, which I didn't realize for a whole damn lost half a year." She shook her head. "Roger was gentle, and afterwards we talked a little, which is really nice when you're all mellow like that, and then we fell asleep."

"Sounds like the perfect date," Kate said.

"That's what I thought, and I was expecting more of the same the next morning. But when I woke up, it was still dark and he was already up and dressed. He was in khakis, the ones he wears at the store, with his name on one side of the shirt and Boat Camp on the other. He'd made coffee. So I got dressed too. I said, 'Roger, it's five o'clock in the morning. What's up?'"

"He laughed and said, 'We are,' and handed me a cup. 'Black?' he asked and I said 'Yes' and he said 'Good.' And I asked again why he'd gotten up so early. That's when he got weird."

"He said weird stuff? Or did weird stuff?"

"It was what he said, but it was so odd that I didn't trust him anymore. First he said how much he liked me and how he wanted to make a permanent future with me. I said something like Whoa, Roger, it's a little early for that. I had a great time, I really want to see you some more, but I'm not ready to make a commitment. And he started saying the really strange things, the things that didn't make any sense."

"Like what?" Kate looked both ways at the intersection with Route 30. The road was dim with pre-dawn light. Not a car in sight.

"Like 'You don't know how much of a commitment you've already made, Ellen.' And 'We're joined for life.' So I said 'What do you mean?' and he said 'You're going to find out. And you're not going to like it.'"

"Yikes, that is weird."

"It sounded like a threat. And the look on his face, Kate. He was agitated. Feverish. Maybe he had an actual fever, but I decided if he was sick his employees could help him out when they came in. I grabbed my bag and ran down the stairs and left. I was in such a hurry I left my make-up kit in his bathroom, but I'm not going back. I can buy that stuff when I get home."

"He said you'd already made a big commitment? After one date?"

"Well, one date, one night in bed together. But still."

"You're right, that's It totally off the wall," Kate said. She pulled into her site at the campground. The truck cab had warmed but Ellen still had her arms folded tight around herself. "You want to spend the night here, Ellen? The dinette table drops down and converts to a bed."

"Thanks, Kate, but I'll go back to my camper. It's small, it heats up fast. I'm going to smoke a little weed to calm down. It always works. Want to join me?"

"I haven't had a toke in years," Kate said. "The stuff makes me paranoid."

"Doesn't mean they aren't out to get you." Ellen's laugh sounded almost normal. "Thanks for rescuing me, Kate."

"Any time." Kate heard what she'd said and amended it. "But I hope you don't ever need me to do it again."

"That was my last date with Roger Benedict," Ellen said. "And I sure hope you don't have to rescue me from anybody else."

* * *

Kate glanced at her phone when she woke up and was surprised that it was nine-thirty: she usually woke around seven. But of course most mornings she didn't get up at five-thirty to rescue friends from proposals of marriage. Or threats of same.

Sliding down from the bunk, yawning, she pushed the button on the coffee-maker. Ah, the convenience of staying at a campground with shore power. If she weren't with Ellen she'd be dry-camping to save money, running the noisy generator for the coffee-maker. Or using the stove, waiting for water to boil and watching it sink through the grounds in the one-cup filter.

While the little machine made its snorkeling noises, she opened the curtains and had a look at the oncoming day. Sunny. Perfect.

What a strange story Ellen had told. Roger thought she'd made a life-long commitment to him? He was nuts. Kate hoped he didn't follow Ellen around and make a nuisance of himself like Dan. What else had Roger said? "You're going to find out, and you're not going to like it." What the hell did that mean?

She yawned again, then picked up the full pot and went outside. She'd knock lightly on Ellen's door, not loud enough to wake her if she was still sleeping.

As she climbed out of her camper, a police car pulled in and two officers got out. The one in front nodded at Kate on his way to Ellen's door. He was a heavy guy, and his knock was loud. "Police," he called out. "Open up."

After a moment a voice answered, so muffled it was unintelligible. Ellen was probably still in bed, asleep until a few seconds ago.

Kate's arm was getting tired. She put the coffee pot down on the bumper of her truck and joined the officers. The one in front had just raised his hand to knock again when Ellen opened the door in a pale blue bathrobe. She looked startled when she saw who it was.

"Good morning, Ms. Waters." His tone was friendlier than Kate had expected. "We'd like to talk to you. Do you have a few minutes?"

"Yes," she said. "Please come in."

"The thing is, we'd really prefer it if you'd come on down to the station with us."

"Really? What's this about?"

"Well, now." The cop adjusted his dark-blue ball cap, a gesture meant to be folksy and reassuring. "A few minutes at the station would probably clear things up."

Ellen wasn't her usual quick self. She looked past the men to Kate.

"Why don't you give her a few minutes to get dressed?" Kate suggested. "I'm a friend of hers, and I think you woke her up. I'm sure she'd be happy to answer your questions when she's had some coffee."

The two faces that turned to her did not look pleased. "We've got coffee at the station," the smaller cop said. He was so young he had acne.

"Free coffee and a free ride to beautiful downtown South Portage," the burly cop said. "We'd really appreciate it."

They had quite the comedy routine, but what was going on?

"Give me a minute," Ellen said, and shut the door.

The two men looked at each other but kept their faces neutral. Neither spoke, and Kate didn't bother to ask any questions. Since they hadn't told Ellen what was up, they weren't going to enlighten her bystander friend.

Ellen reappeared, transformed. Even though she wore ordinary jeans and a soft ivory sweater, she was back in movie-star mode. Kate, who was used to her friend's good looks, wondered how she did it. Make-up? No, she'd left her kit at Roger's. Earrings? Just studs. But something important was different.

The other mystery was how she did her magic so quickly. Maybe it was only the way she held herself. A projection of her mindset when she presented herself to the world.

The big cop opened the back door of the cruiser for her. Ellen rolled her eyes at Kate before he shut the door and tinted glass blocked her from view. The engine started.

Kate didn't like it. She went around the front of her truck to the electrical post and unplugged the fat cord connecting her camper to shore power. Stuffed the cord into its compartment on the side of the camper and climbed behind the wheel.

It wouldn't hurt to go to the station. Even if she couldn't find anything out, she'd be there to give Ellen a ride back to Fish Creek when the police were finished interviewing her.

Busy thinking about Ellen, Kate had pulled onto Route 30 before she remembered she didn't know where the police station was. The cruiser was out of sight. She pulled into the parking lot of a general store and got her GPS out from under the seat. Waited for it to find satellites and calculate. Ten miles. She touched GO on the screen.

As she drove the scenic road, she worried that Ellen had taken some marijuana with her last night. But neither Ellen nor Roger was dumb enough to smoke dope in public. And even if they had, possession of marijuana was a minor offense, a misdemeanor, wasn't it? She and Ellen would go to lunch together and laugh about the morning's drama.

She parked her truck close to the police station entrance so Ellen couldn't miss it when she came out, and climbed into the bunk over the cab. She didn't want to sleep, but she didn't want to do anything else, either. Her concentration was totally shot.

Kate's phone chirped. She woke in a panic: sleep had taken her after all. She didn't recognize the number.

"I'd like to speak to Kate Corliss." A woman's voice.

"Who's calling, please?"

"South Portage police."

"Oh, good. This is Kate. Is Ellen Waters ready to go?"

A pause. "No. One of our detectives would like to see you."

That was strange. "All right. When?"

"As soon as possible."

"I can be there in half an hour," Kate said. She could be there in half a minute, but she needed to brush her teeth, comb her hair, and change the T-shirt she'd worn to bed the night before.

The police wanted to talk to her, too?

At least she'd get some answers.

EIGHT

Detective Jordan was dressed in jeans and a blue shirt wet under the arms. His maroon tie was loose. Kate was in no mood to be charitable: the man needed to lose at least 30 pounds. The number of chins under his fat face multiplied whenever he looked down at the legal pad on the table.

A security camera stared at Kate from the ceiling.

He asked for her address and she gave her old place in Danvers, Massachusetts, because it was easier than explaining that her boyfriend had thrown her out of there last Christmas. She'd changed her mailing address to a friend's house near Boston—Marjorie had agreed to forward anything important to Kate wherever she went. But until her Bay State license expired Kate was going to claim Danvers as home.

He didn't waste time. "I'd like you to describe where you were and what you did yesterday, Sunday."

"Ellen and I went paddling," Kate said. "We spent the day on Lower Saranac Lake." She told him when they'd left, what they'd done. His face was stern. "I have plenty of photos on my phone, if you need proof. So does Ellen."

"Only the two of you?" He took out a handkerchief and blotted his forehead.

"Yes."

"No contact with Mr. Benedict? You and Ms. Waters have been seeing a lot of him recently, isn't that true?"

Why was he asking about Roger? "He stopped by our table at the Put-In Pub on Tuesday night. We'd seen him—met him—briefly, at his store earlier that day, but the first time we talked to him much was at the Put-In, while we were waiting for our dinners to be served. We liked him; we all got along." She wanted to make it clear that the three of them were on good terms; if Ellen was in some kind of trouble maybe Roger could put in a good word for her. A local businessman on her side couldn't hurt. "Then the three of us paddled on Friday. A very pleasant trip."

"How about the weekend?"

"Saturday we went to a cookout at his store. He'd invited us on Friday. Quite a crowd there. Sunday he called Ellen late in the afternoon, and that night he picked her up at the Fish Creek campground."

"What time?"

She shrugged. "Don't know exactly. Around dinnertime. It wasn't dark yet."

"So Roger, ah, Mr. Benedict was clearly interested in Ms. Waters."

"Well, yes." Duh. You don't date somebody you don't like.

"Instead of you?"

He had been taking notes, but now he watched her closely.

"I think it's obvious Roger was interested in a relationship with Ellen and not with me." When the detective kept looking at her, she said it again. "To me he was a new friend." She emphasized the word *friend.* "To Ellen he was more than that."

"Perhaps you were jealous of Ms. Waters? She's the more attractive woman. She beat you out for his attention."

Kate almost laughed. "Look, I've known Ellen for years. There have been times when both of us have been in relationships, times when only one has been, times when neither of us was. We're very good friends, and when Roger showed interest in her I was delighted."

"Have you ever been in a situation with her before when a man chose her over you?"

"Oh, for Pete's sake. What's Roger got to do with anything? What are you fishing for? I'm not going to answer any more questions until you tell me what's going on. And let me see Ellen."

Jordan leaned a little closer. "Your friend isn't going to be released. She's being held without bail."

"What?" Kate was stunned. "Why?"

"She's a suspect in the murder of Roger Benedict."

"What?"

He was silent, watching her.

She was beyond thought. Her mind didn't have any words in it, only faces. Ellen's. Roger's. Both of them in the quiet light of the Put-in Pub. At the cookout, washed in sunlight. Ellen in her kayak, wind blowing her hair all over the place. Roger on the water, strong arms driving the paddle, his canoe's bow wave flaring white.

Tate's face came to her. What a shock he was in for, soon. Tate and all the guides. What would happen to friendly Molly and angry Shag? Shy Irving, responsible Jennifer?

So many faces, most of them people she'd known only a week. But they'd become important to her.

Mrs. Benedict. She would be hysterical. To lose a husband, and now a son.

Kate felt sick.

A couple of years ago she'd overinflated a bicycle tire, and the tube had exploded with such a bang that she couldn't hear anything for ten minutes. Her sense of balance had been affected too—she'd staggered, then had to sit on the ground until things stopped spinning.

That's how she felt now. The news was a huge, invisible explosion. And this time she knew it would be more than ten minutes before she felt better.

She had no idea how much time had gone by in the interview room. The faces of her friends, old and new, faded; she was looking at Detective Jordan again.

"When can I see Ellen?" Kate asked. Her voice was hoarse.

"Soon," he said. Then he changed tack. "So. You're—traveling?" He made it sound like something to be ashamed of.

"Yes. A job ended, and I've decided to take some time off."

"How much time?"

"Possibly as long as a year." Still shocked by Roger's death, she was answering from some automatic part of her mind.

"Living—where?"

"In my camper."

They looked at each other. He was frowning. She kept her face blank and refused to look away. She had nothing to apologize for. Full-time RVers were often older couples, but the fact that she was young and single wasn't criminal.

"I'll have an officer get Ms. Waters," Jordan said abruptly. "Wait here." In the doorway he turned. "Thank you for coming in, Ms. Corliss. I'm going to ask you to stay in the area until further notice." He shut the door.

Oh, great. She was a suspect, too?

A cop opened the door, motioned a shaken-looking Ellen through it, and said, "Fifteen minutes." He was the burly one who'd knocked on her door that morning.

Kate stood, and Ellen gave her a fierce hug. "Oh, Kate, I feel so terrible about Roger I can hardly move." Slumped in a chair, red-eyed, she didn't look like movie star any more. "And I'm scared. The police really think I killed him."

"The detective knocked me over, telling me that. But I can't imagine why they'd think so. Do you have any idea?"

Ellen shook her head. Her chin quivered.

Kate pushed some strands of hair, wet with tears, out of her friend's face. "I don't see how they can possibly charge you. You were with him at Boat Camp, okay. But somebody else went there after you left."

"That's what I told them."

"What's your motive supposed to be? Why would you knock off a great guy who takes you out to dinner and goes to bed with you? And how can they hold you with no evidence?"

"I'm not being held for murder," Ellen said. "Technically. At least, not yet. That's what Detective Jordan said: not yet."

"What do you mean?"

"You know that baggie of marijuana I had? It weighed a little over two ounces," Ellen said. "That's apparently some kind of cut-off. Below two ounces and you pay a fine. Above two ounces and they can hold you."

"Oh, rats."

"Yeah. Wish I'd smoked a little more. Or a lot more." She made a sound that might have been a laugh, but it didn't change her stricken face.

"I can't believe you have anything to worry about in the long run, Ellen. No motive and no means. Come on, you'd just met Roger."

Ellen's eyes were filling. "Jordan asked if he could look at what was on my cell phone, and I gave him the password. I don't have anything to hide, so why not?"

"That can't have turned out to be a problem," Kate said, but from the look on her friend's face she knew she was wrong.

"He saw the emails from my mother, and the e-tickets she sent me from the airlines and cruise ship. Aruba's off the shore of Venezuela, which doesn't often cooperate in extraditing people to the U.S. So he says I'm a flight risk and he has to keep me in that stinking cell." She wiped her eyes with the heels of her hands, but it didn't help. "He says he's going to hold me until he gets the results from lab tests."

"What kind of tests?"

"Fingerprints, I think. Although I heard him say something to another guy about toxicology."

"Well, your fingerprints will be all over the place. But that doesn't mean anything—you aren't denying you were there. What are you doing about a lawyer?"

"I called a legal beagle in Syracuse I know from a story I did on bankruptcy trends. Criminal law isn't his field, and his firm doesn't do it either, but he said he'd ask around and find me somebody good."

"Soon, I hope. Are your parents leaving their cruise? I mean, if you're charged with murder—"

"I'm not going to tell them unless I have to," Ellen said. "I'll see what the lawyer says."

"Right, you don't want to wreck their vacation if you're out of here tomorrow."

"They work so hard all the time," Ellen said. "I was thrilled when they told me they were going on the trip. They haven't taken a vacation in years."

"Well, I hope your contact hurries up with the referral. The lab results shouldn't be a problem." She gave Ellen a smile she hoped was reassuring. "Maybe you'll never have to spill the beans to your parents."

The door opened and the cop said, "Time's up."

The women stood and shared a hug. "I can't call you. They kept my phone," Ellen said.

Almost to the door, Kate turned. "Ellen, wait. What about Dan? Do you suppose he followed you to Roger's place? He knew we'd gone to the Put-In Pub, right? And the Wild Center?"

Ellen's face brightened. "Kate, yes! And he's so possessive—well, you saw him at the gas station."

"Jealousy's a big-time motive."

"But Roger didn't come between Dan and me. Dan was already history."

Kate laughed, relieved she'd thought of Dan. Ellen wouldn't be a suspect for long. "He didn't sound like he got it. He doesn't think he's history; he thinks he's the current event."

"Time's up," the cop said again, putting a hand on Kate's shoulder.

"I'll tell Jordan about Dan," Ellen called after her.

* * *

Wound up, Kate didn't know what to do with herself. Driving occupied her in a helpful way, and the automatic part of her brain put the truck on Route 3. But instead of turning left onto Route 30 toward Fish Creek, she used the intersection to make a U-turn and went back to South Portage. She needed distraction.

The village streets were busier than she'd expected. But it didn't matter—she wasn't going anywhere in particular. Her only goal was escape from the ugly facts of the day: Roger dead. Murdered. Ellen being held. Dan, who was probably guilty, free to zoom around in his stupid car.

Maybe not for long.

When her GPS showed the street she was on dead-ended at a pond, she took a random left. A small shop caught her eye: "Donuts," the sign said, and "Laundromat." Two life-sized pinto horses stabilized with guy wires stood on the roof, apparently to call attention to Native American crafts offered inside, according to a cardboard sign in the window.

Whoever ran this store believed in diversification. Add anything else and it might be easier to list what they didn't sell.

Kate had had only a sip of her coffee that morning, so maybe part of her fatigue was due to a caffeine shortfall. A cup of java wouldn't fix Ellen's plight, but it might help Kate's body get back to normal and cope with the stress.

Afraid she might start crying in public, she got a cardboard cup to go and a copy of the *Saranac Lake Daily Star*. She sat in the cab drinking and reading. Roger's death was front-page news, but the article had no details, only stating that he'd died of unknown causes and an investigation was underway. The paper had had to go to press before any solid facts were available.

The second paragraph jumped to the local page, but that yielded nothing but boilerplate biography. In the column next to it, ironically, was the correction for the date of the Paddle of Silence. Another correction would be required. The new date: never.

A pick-up truck went by, then a couple of cars, then a black Corvette. She been in a car like that once, back in college. All she remembered was how uncomfortable it was. The angle of the seats was absurdly low; she was practically lying on her back, like an astronaut. How do you drive the thing from that position? The owner, some friend of a friend whose name she couldn't remember, had been very proud of his car.

What difference did it make if your car cost fifty thousand or five thousand? If you lived in ten rooms or one? If you wore this year's fashions or got your clothes at Goodwill?

Kate found herself crying. She held it back long enough to get her coffee set down in the cup holder, then let herself sob, turning away from the street and putting her arm up to cover her face. The cab of a parked truck is not the most private of places.

Even while she was crying, she told herself it would turn out all right. Ellen was innocent. Kate couldn't imagine anyone, not even Dan, killing Roger—actually, she couldn't imagine anyone killing anyone except on a movie screen or on the pages of a book. It happened, of course, but not to anybody she knew. And certainly Ellen had had no part in ending Roger's life. The whole mess would be cleared up in a day or two.

Someone rapped on the window. She jumped and turned.

It was a cop, a brown-eyed young man who looked concerned. His voice came through the glass. "Is anything wrong? Do you need help?"

"I'm fine, thanks." She found a smile for him. "It's only, you know, life."

"You sure?"

"Yes, thanks."

He nodded and walked on, splitting his attention between the parked vehicles and the people on the sidewalk, nodding at a few of them. Kate focused on his kindness as an antidote to Detective Jordan's insidious suggestions that she was jealous of Ellen's attentions from Roger and might be enraged enough to kill.

She drank the rest of the coffee. Cooler than she liked, it still might help get her biochemistry back on track.

Maybe it was working already. Her mind lit again on those strange things Roger had said, which had turned out to be some of the last words he'd ever utter. "Joined for life" and "committed." Was he on some kind of high? Kate had smoked some marijuana in college, but she didn't know much about other illegal drugs. Surely some of them could distort the user's thought process. And what about prescription drugs? Maybe he was manic-depressive, and he'd made the extravagant claims because he was entering a manic phase.

Could the police question his doctors?

Probably not. Medical records were private. A dead end, like the street she'd been on.

She started up the truck and headed for the campground, her mind echoing the phrase "dead end." Very funny, she thought without humor.

When she pulled into her site and plugged in her camper, she was surprised to see her coffeepot tucked safely beside the gray pedestal of the electrical hook-up. She'd set it down on the bumper when the police showed up and then forgot about it. Somebody must have picked it up so she wouldn't drive over it on her way back in. Nice neighbor.

A piece of paper inside it turned out to be a note. "Hey, lose something?" it asked. "You better be a little more careful, girl. Or maybe a lot more careful." Below that was a frowny-face and the initial D.

D for Dan? He must have figured out where Ellen was camped, although how he could follow her in a car as conspicuous as the Corvette was a mystery. But why leave Kate a nasty note instead of Ellen? She walked around Ellen's camper and checked the electrical post. No other note.

Dan's manner when he confronted Ellen at the gas station had been oddly calm. He must enjoy provoking people. What a creep. Kate felt a twinge of anger, and then laughed at herself. Anger was exactly what he'd want her to feel.

She focused on being happy she'd gotten her coffee pot back. But maybe she should wash it, since Ellen had mentioned overhearing something about toxicology tests.

* * *

She called her good friend Marjorie in Massachusetts, whom she'd known since college. She'd stayed at Marjorie's house for a few months the previous winter, after her long-term relationship had ended abruptly. Gosh, that was nine months ago. Marjorie had majored in psychology and she was great to talk to about people problems.

Like a friend being suspected of murder.

Sure enough, she'd hardly said hello when Marjorie said, "Hey, what's up? You sound funny."

Kate told her what was up—Ellen's date with Roger, a little about him, the events of the morning.

"Oh, my God, Kate. That's so awful. Does she have a lawyer?"

Good old Marjorie. She always looked for solutions. "Not yet."

Marjorie had once said that men and women respond differently to conversations about a problem. Men want to solve it; they talk about what to do next. Women want to support the person with the problem; they talk about feelings. Marjorie, maybe thanks to her psychology degree, did both.

Kate described her interview with the unfriendly detective.

"He's playing Bad Cop," Marjorie said. "Don't let him rattle you. He's thrashing around in the bushes, seeing what he can scare up."

"Me. He scared me up." It felt good to laugh.

"This should be over in a day or two, Kate. Talk to Ellen's lawyer as soon as you can. There can't be any evidence, and if there's no evidence they can't—"

A child's wail replaced Marjorie's voice. She had two children, one of them an infant, which meant she was always near her home phone. But sometimes conversations were interrupted.

"I'll keep you posted," Kate said. She'd tell her friend about Dan the next time she called. Maybe he'd be in jail by then.

* * *

Making sure her cell phone was charged up, Kate went for a sunset paddle on Square Pond; enough campsites around it were occupied that she felt safe. She tried to look at the shapes light made on water, and to listen: the small plash of her paddle blades entering the water, the gratifying splashes under the bow, wind ruffling leaves. Someone was cooking outdoors: the wind brought her the odor of barbecued meat.

But it was hard to stay in the moment when her mind was so busy. Dan had obviously followed Ellen. Was he following Kate, too? That gave her the creeps, but she hadn't seen any yellow Corvettes.

Before it got fully dark, Kate locked her boat to the picnic table. She made hummus for dinner and ate it with carrots and celery.

What a long, sad day.

NINE

Kate left the coffee maker chugging away while she walked to the general store across Route 30 the next morning and brought the *Saranac Lake Star* back to her camper. Roger's story had retreated from the front page to the local section, but it occupied a lot of column-inches there with testimonials from friends and a picture of Roger that was so old it might have been from his college yearbook. He was the erratic son of a well-known family, his early death its second tragedy. This would be a high-visibility case.

She was sure Dan had killed Roger out of jealousy, but she didn't have a scrap of proof. She hoped the police would listen to Ellen and question the obnoxious entrepreneur, but she wasn't hopeful, considering the way things had gone yesterday. The police had decided Ellen was guilty way too fast. Was it possible they wanted someone who wasn't local to be the one responsible for such a major crime?

Heck, in that case they'd like Dan as a suspect just as much as Ellen.

Kate had to find out more about Roger. It was time to talk to the people who'd known him best. She'd already been thinking about the guides, knowing they would be suffering from shock and grief, and they'd also be worried about their jobs. She'd especially been thinking about Molly, who had been so friendly on that first paddle, inviting them to stop on the bank, sharing cashews. Molly, and Tate. She rinsed the coffee pot, unplugged the camper, and headed for Boat Camp.

The store was open—she'd had her doubts, but a Honda and a blue pick-up were parked out front, and Shag and Tate were slumped in the big chairs on the porch, looking dispirited. Shag was wearing jeans and T-shirt instead of the usual khaki.

"Hey," Kate said. Would they even talk to her, friend of the woman who supposedly killed Roger? Did they even know Ellen was in jail?

Tate said "Hey" back, and Shag raised a hand in greeting.

"You want anything inside?" Tate looked like he hadn't slept.

"No, I came over to say how sorry I am about Roger."

"Yeah." Shag rubbed his head with the palm of his hand the way he did. "Thanks."

"We're having a little trouble—we're having a lot of trouble getting used to the whole thing," Tate said. Then he shook himself a little, as if he were waking himself up. "Sit down if you want. There's coffee behind the counter."

"Thanks," Kate said, but she kept standing. "I want you guys to know that my friend Ellen didn't have anything to do with what happened to Roger. I don't know what kind of evidence the police are going on, but she really liked him. And even if she didn't, she wouldn't have—" She stopped. "This isn't coming out right."

The two men glanced at each other. Kate wished she could read their minds. "He charmed her socks off. And I've known her for years, and she's not somebody who would harm anyone, knowingly. She's—"

"Okay, okay." Tate held up a hand to stop her. "We're not the jury. I didn't even know Ellen was a suspect. Sit down before you fall down."

Kate realized she'd been holding onto a post, squeezing the rough wood fiercely. "Thanks," she said, and got herself into a chair.

"What, the police are questioning Ellen?" Shag asked.

"Not only that," Kate said. "They're holding her without bail."

Tate went inside and came back with a paper cup of coffee he handed to Kate. "You look like you could use this."

"Oh, man," she said. "Thanks. I think I can find someplace to put it." The day was bright but the porch was shaded and cool. A good hit of coffee somehow gave her goose-bumps. Roger had been alive the last time she'd had this Kenyan brew. He'd talked to her and Ellen. He'd been fine.

Why had he said those crazy things?

"I'm sorry to hear about Ellen," Shag was saying. "The cops questioned me, too, for a couple of hours yesterday. I was the one who found Roger."

"Where?" Kate asked.

"Upstairs. I came in early Monday, because I wanted to have it out with him. I was ready to quit, and I wanted him to know why. He's usually in the store by six, so at 6:30 I went up the stairs. Door was open. Found him on the floor. I called 911, but I could tell it was too late."

"The cops let you go instead of putting you in jail," Tate said. "So you're probably okay."

"Maybe. They told me not to leave the area, so I think I'm still on their shortlist of suspects. No wonder—I was always complaining about Roger. He didn't treat me very well."

"Why was that, anyway?" Kate remembered how Roger had yelled at Shag the first day she and Ellen had come to the store.

"He ordered all of us around," Tate said to her. "Shag took it personal. So did Dusty, and Dusty quit."

"I didn't like the way he ran this place like it really was boot camp," Shag said. "Making us wear khaki outfits like recruits, challenging us to do fifty push-ups in two minutes, the times he'd send us out in crazy weather, not to guide but to test our boat-handling skills when it was blowing like stink. It was a bitch." His voice had heated up. "Aw, shit. I didn't want him dead, I wanted him to back off." He got up. "I'm gonna go do inventory."

After Shag went inside, Tate shook his head. "Inventory doesn't really need doing. He gets himself bent out of shape, has to do something physical to calm down."

"Who's running the business now?"

"Nobody. We're showing up on our regular schedule until somebody tells us not to. I guess it depends on Roger's will. Whoever takes over, we hope they'll pay us for keeping the place open."

A car with a couple and a teenaged boy came down Paul's Way and parked, and the three went into the store.

"Good. Customers to keep Shag busy," Tate said.

"Do you close for the winter?"

"No. We sell skis and snowshoes, open year round," Tate said. "I sure hope it isn't Mrs. Benedict who takes over. She doesn't know which end of a paddle to put in the water."

"She seemed a little difficult. But if she doesn't know anything about the business, wouldn't she hire somebody?"

"That's what a reasonable person would do."

They sat for a while. A chipmunk came out from under the porch, sat on the bottom step and looked at them. Tate pulled a peanut out of his pocket and tossed it, and they watched the chipmunk hold it in his front paws and gnaw, still facing them, alert.

Tate sighed. "Roger hated these little guys. Called them vermin."

"Do they damage things? Eat electrical wiring, like pack rats in Arizona?"

"No, chipmunks aren't a problem. But porcupines? Dumb as dung, and they eat the grips off canoe paddles because of the salt from people's sweat." He looked at Kate. "Now how dumb do you have to be to eat wood?"

Kate laughed. "Pretty darn dumb." Then she thought of beavers needing to chew wood to keep their teeth from growing so long they interfered with eating. Did porcupines face some similar dental requirement? The only person she could think of to ask was dead.

"One of them was gnawing on a corner of the building a few months ago. Roger shot it a bunch of times. Buckshot. Shredded it. You could hardly tell it used to be an animal."

"Wow. So Roger could lose it, sometimes?"

"I think he didn't respond well to threats. The problems he had with Shag? My opinion is that Shag is as tough as Roger. He could do as many push-ups, and as fast. Could maybe out-paddle him, out-carry him, outlast him. And that bothered Roger. A lot."

"Sounds like all he thought about was the pecking order." Competition. Kate thought of the skier who'd accused her of being off-the-pace in the story she'd told Ellen.

"Yeah. And Shag's the fittest."

But not the most attractive. She kept the thought to herself.

"Roger wasn't like that with girls, though," Tate said. "He would never test Molly to see if she could do fifty push-ups, or Jennifer. Women mostly liked him, because he treated them differently."

"Yes. He sure did." Kate had been struggling to reconcile the macho, shotgun-wielding man Tate and Shag described with the friendly, intelligent paddling companion she and Ellen had spent time with. Two Rogers? Tate's comments helped.

"Oooh, man, what a mess. I'm sorry your friend's in jail." Tate stretched, arching his back away from the chair's wooden slats. "Hey, I'd better help Shag out. We should be getting those skis out of the storeroom." He pulled himself onto his feet.

"Need any help with that?"

He turned back, surprised. "We've got it covered, thanks. Don't get too many offers like that from our customers."

Kate felt let down. She wanted to be more than a customer. She started to get up, which wasn't easy: these Adirondack style chairs were deep, with slanted seats.

Then Tate was back, offering her a hand.

She took it and smiled up at him. She pulled against his firm grip and in a second was standing next to him.

Right next to him. His face was so close—

He brushed his lips against hers and gave her a playful smile. "Y'all come back now."

Kate grinned as he went inside. Hooray, she was more than a customer.

TEN

Kate stayed up late reading, and the next morning her phone chirped her awake. She fumbled with it, squinting at the screen, her eyes gummy from lack of sleep. Unknown number.

But a familiar voice. Ellen. "Sweetie, how are you holding up?"

"Oh, Kate. I'm so relieved. I've got a lawyer. And she wants to talk to you. Here she is."

"Hello, Kate." The voice was soft. "Would you come in to the South Portage police station to talk with me?"

Kate didn't answer right away because of a huge, jaw-cracking yawn. Not the best first impression for Ellen's attorney.

"Kate?"

"I'm here, and yes. I'll leave right away."

* * *

The woman didn't look at all like an attorney ready to take on a possible murder case—petite and pretty, with shoulder-length black hair that shone under the windowless room's fluorescents. She stood at a table, frowning at a document in her hand, but she put it down and smiled when Kate came in.

It was a different room than the one in which she'd talked to Detective Jordan. Smaller. Kate didn't see any security cameras.

"Ah, you must be Kate Corliss. Thank you for coming so quickly." The woman held out her hand. "Amber Banerjee. Please call me Amber." The lawyer's handshake was kitten-soft.

"I'm so glad you're here for Ellen," Kate said. "Can you get her out of jail?"

Amber held up a manicured hand. "We'll get to that in minute. "First, I'd like you to tell me everything you remember about last Sunday night and early Monday morning." She put a black box the size of a deck of playing cards on the table and pushed a button. "I'd like to record this, if you don't mind."

"No problem," Kate said. "But surely Ellen told you everything that happened."

Amber only smiled.

"Okay, so she and I spent the day in our kayaks and got back to the Fish Creek campground late Sunday afternoon," Kate said. "It was still light when Roger picked Ellen up. Maybe six o'clock? I'm assuming it was Roger—I heard the truck, didn't look out. But it sounded like his, an older diesel. And then I fell asleep reading, woke up and went to bed. Slept until Ellen called."

"When was that?"

"Around five-thirty. But Ellen could—"

"Please tell me every detail you can remember. Everything that happened. Everything Ellen said after you picked her up."

Kate did, even though she couldn't see the point. Ellen's call, the dark drive, the deer on the road, Ellen stepping from behind a tree, how upset she was, what she said about the previous night and Roger's strange comments in the morning.

"Thank you," Amber said, and pushed a button on the recorder. Its red light went out. "I wanted to make sure your account and Ellen's account matched. They do."

"So can you spring her?" Kate asked. "She's already spent two nights locked up."

"I'm afraid your friend will be incarcerated for some time."

"Why?" Kate was baffled. "Roger was alive when she left his place. Someone showed up after five o'clock or so, after Ellen left. I'm sure she's told you about her ex-boyfriend Dan. It could have been him, but if it wasn't him it was somebody else. It wasn't Ellen."

"I'm sorry. I'll do what I can, but we're dealing with more than the law here—we're dealing with small-town politics. Roger was a prominent member of the community, and there's pressure to move quickly."

"But a mistake would be a second crime. There can't be any evidence against Ellen."

"Her prints will show up everywhere. Probably hairs of hers in the bed."

"That's no proof she killed him," Kate said. "That's proof she was there, but she's never denied that."

"You are correct," Amber said. "Unfortunately, the police—and more importantly the district attorney's office—are convinced she did it. A DA whose mind is made up is an immovable object. I'm sorry, Kate. Ellen's going to be arraigned tomorrow."

The room was terribly bright. Had she heard Amber correctly? "I don't understand."

Amber leaned forward, her voice serious. "I don't believe Ellen committed this murder," she said. "But there's one piece of evidence that's going to cause difficulty for the defense."

"Which is?"

"Roger left a message. He apparently managed to scrawl a few words on the wall in the bedroom before he died." She hesitated. "The prosecutor hasn't told me what the message was yet, but I'll be able to see photographs of it after the forensics team has completed its work. It must be incriminating, or the prosecutor wouldn't have charged her."

Kate felt as if she'd walked into a scene on a movie set. This couldn't be real.

"Handwriting analysis, fingerprints on the pen—they'll be done quickly because of the seriousness of the crime," Amber said. "Given the circumstances, it's likely that the handwriting results will be inconclusive—Roger's state of mind would not be an ordinary one, and his coordination would deteriorate under the influence of the drug—"

"Drug?" Even one word was an effort.

"The preliminary report from the ME—the medical examiner—indicates the cause of death was some kind of poison. We should get full autopsy results by the end of the week. And the coffee in his cup will be tested." She sighed. "More tests. More joy for the forensic labs."

Everything in the room went two-dimensional. Lines and colors. Amber's face was a painting.

The face in the painting softened. "You can see Ellen for a few minutes. She's asked me to keep you informed, and I'll let you know as soon as I have any further information."

* * *

Ellen looked worse than she had the day before, pale and tired. "I'm numb," she said. "Amber told me there was some message on the wall, something Roger wrote. I don't know what to think."

"The killer must have written it," Kate said. They were in the larger room, the one with cameras on the ceiling.

"That's what I told Amber," Ellen said. "She said the handwriting's getting analyzed. They've already done fingerprints. Amber said that's why they let Shag go. His prints weren't on the cups or the light switches, and mine were."

"Of course they were," Kate said. "That doesn't prove you're a murderer."

"I wish I could remember more about the car that passed me on Paul's Way, when I was walking out to meet you. Amber is such a believer in the subconscious, she keeps asking me."

"I didn't see any vehicles. Didn't think there was anybody awake except us."

"Yeah, it was a big thing, boxy. Red, maybe, but I wasn't paying that much attention. I was cold, and I was afraid Roger would follow me, so I was running, and then I'd have to walk for a while to catch my breath. There wasn't enough moonlight to see the car well. All I'm sure of was that it had good road clearance."

"You told Amber that?"

"Yeah." Ellen's elbows were on her knees, hands cupping her face. "She wants me to remember more, but I don't think I can."

* * *

Kate stowed her paddle and let her boat drift as she watched the breeze play with the water's surface. Motion was the one thing she couldn't draw. She had to show it indirectly, the tall grass at the water's edge bending in the wind or a moustache of white water at the bow of a kayak.

She took some photos of the bridge over the narrows between Square Pond and Fish Creek Pond. She started some rough sketches of a loon, but it kept diving and resurfacing, minutes later, somewhere unexpected. She remembered what Roger had said about loons eating the fish they caught underwater. No wonder this one stayed down so long. He must be stuffing himself at the submerged buffet.

It was cloudy, but with no rain in the forecast.

Then she fell out of the good mood that working gave her. Her watch told her she'd been out on the lake for an hour and a half. That was all the vacation from worry she was going to get, because everything came rushing back: Roger was dead, Ellen was in jail, Dan was lurking, maybe even watching Kate this minute.

She couldn't float around enjoying herself—or trying to—with all that on her mind. She had to find out more about Roger. She had to find out what happened Sunday night.

Time for another visit to Boat Camp. Talking with the guides, the people who'd known him well, was her best shot at learning something that could help her free Ellen.

ELEVEN

"Hey, Molly. Hey, Tate."

They were setting up some kind of rack near the front of the store.

"Hiya, Kate," Molly said. "What do you need? More mint Clif bars?"

Wow, she was on the ball, remembering exactly what Kate had bought on her first visit to the store over a week ago. Molly's eyes were red and puffy—she'd been crying, and not long ago, but she'd pulled herself together.

"Yes, that would be great," Kate said. She hadn't planned on buying anything, but on second thought it would be a good thing to support this place. Her business couldn't help Roger, but maybe it could help Tate and Molly, Shag and Jennifer and Irving.

As Molly went behind the counter, Tate winked at Kate. A warm feeling spread inside her, and she sent him a smile that said so.

"I'll take the whole box, Molly. "I can always use Clif bars."

"Sticking around for a while, then?"

"Oh, God, yes. I want to help Ellen get out of this mess." She passed her credit card across the counter. "I mean, she's definitely not guilty, like I was telling Tate and Shag yesterday."

Head down, Molly was fighting tears. Kate said what she should have said first. "I'm awfully sorry about Roger. I liked him a lot even though I'd just met him, and it's a terrible shame he's gone. You and the other guides, you have all my sympathy."

Molly's head stayed down. "Thank you."

"I'm going upstairs to get some more skis," Tate said. "Want to help?"

Kate and Molly said "Sure" at the same time and then looked at each other.

"Why not?" Molly said, handing Kate her receipt. "C'mon."

Kate couldn't believe her good luck. Ellen had said Roger lived over the store, and she never thought she'd get a chance to have a look around. You could tell a lot from people's living quarters. Sweet.

The three of them trooped up the wooden stairs. At the top was a small room full of cross-country skis of different lengths, at least a hundred pairs. Down the hall was a shut door with a deadbolt lock. She wasn't going to see anything of Roger's place after all.

"Let's only take two pairs at a time," Tate said. "We don't want to scratch them up."

Molly nodded. "Better exercise that way. More trips up and down the stairs."

"Exercise. That's why Roger had us put them up here," Tate said.

"He's kidding." Molly looked at Kate. "We filled up our downstairs storage with kayaks this year."

It was indeed a good workout. Up the stairs, then down them with a set of skis in each hand. The pairs were clipped together, bases facing each other, with plastic bands that looked like an electrician's zip ties. That made them easy to carry—Kate slid her fingers into the space the opposing cambers made. Tate grabbed a binding in each of his big hands, and Molly hugged her two pairs. Down they went.

And up, down, up. "Didn't Roger live here, above the store?" Kate asked Tate, at the top.

"Yeah, a couple of years ago he renovated this building and expanded it big-time. Doubled the showroom area, added the second floor with the apartment. Before that he lived with his mother. Man, she was not happy when he moved out."

"Much better for him to be here, I bet."

"Yeah, he seemed a lot happier for a while." Tate grabbed another pair of skis. "Hey, think we've moved half of these planks?"

Molly had gotten busy ringing up a paddle for a fit-looking man in his forties. Kate and Tate kept ferrying skis, and Molly made one trip with them but then responded to another customer, a woman who asked questions about the correct fit for a PFD. A few trips later, Molly was sitting on the floor, clipping the ties off the ski pairs with a wire cutter.

"Hang on, Molly, let's wait for Shag to get back with the screws for the rack before we liberate all those skis," Tate said. "We already have enough screws loose around here." He winked at Kate again.

"Okay," Molly said. She stood, and cut ties scattered around her. "I'll get a broom," she said. "God, I hate all this plastic."

"Girl, the *skis* are plastic," Tate said.

"God, I hate all this extra plastic," Molly said. They all laughed.

Molly was sweeping up, and Tate excused himself to use the bathroom at the rear of the store. Spotting a paper coffee cup someone had left near the register, Kate decided to throw it in the trash. As she reached for it she saw a row of small boxes below the counter, with a couple of keys in each. The boxes were labelled FRONT, BACK and UP.

Before she could think about it, she'd slipped a key from each box into her pocket.

Tate came back and fielded a phone call from Shag. He'd had to go to three different hardware stores to get the right size screws, and it was too late to drive back to Boat Camp. He'd bring them in the morning.

"I guess that means we'll have to call it a day," Tate said after he ended the call. "I hope he isn't getting drunk. It sounded like he was calling from a bar—lots of voices in the background."

"He's been doing better with the drinking thing," Molly said. "But he had to stop somewhere to call." After a moment she added, "I wish he'd get a cell phone."

"Me too," Tate said. "Hey, you guys want to get some dinner?"

"I'm bushed," Molly said. "You two enjoy. Thanks for your help, Kate."

* * *

Kate followed Tate's green Honda to a locally-owned restaurant, a place casual enough that she might frequent it if she lived in the area and was working. But planning to RV full-time and live off her savings for a year, she rarely ate out—only when she was with a friend, which wasn't that often in her new lifestyle. Dinner at the Put-In Pub with Ellen would have been a splurge if Roger hadn't paid.

She wouldn't be going out with Ellen again any time soon.

"Sorry about the name," Tate said when she got out of her truck at the Jolly Roger.

Kate had a glass of red wine and a huge Greek salad. Tate ordered a beer and a burger, no onion.

Did he dislike onions or was he keeping his breath untainted for later in the evening? She was hoping he had plans for her that went beyond dinner. Ashamed to have such thoughts when Ellen was in major trouble, she couldn't stop them.

She and Tate were both hungry from the work of moving skis. It was a few minutes before either of them said much.

"I talked to Irving and Dusty and Jennifer today. We're all still pretty shook up," Tate said. "How's your friend doing?"

"Ellen's a wreck. This is a total nightmare. Her parents sent her some e-tickets so she could join them on a cruise in Aruba, so the police decided she's a flight risk and she's stuck in jail. If she could paddle and hike, she'd feel so much better. And then she'd have the energy to figure out who poisoned Roger."

"Oh, God, he was poisoned? That wasn't in the paper."

"That's what Ellen's lawyer said." Amber hadn't told Kate to keep it quiet. "It'll be in the paper tomorrow."

"If she's stuck here for a trial, will she lose her job?"

"I thought of that, but I didn't bring it up," Kate said. "You're right, though. Trials can take months to schedule. And they can last for weeks."

"Yeah." Tate looked worried. Maybe he was thinking about his own job being up in the air, too.

"Can you think of anybody in town who had a grudge against Roger? Anybody who fought with him, about anything?"

"I've been trying to think of who his enemies were. I don't know Ellen, but it doesn't make sense to me that somebody would come from out of town, know a guy for a week and want to knock him off." Tate pushed his plate away. "He wasn't liked by everyone, but he was pretty well respected. Business guys liked him, and tree-huggers. He was a bridge between those two groups. Not too many like that." He shook his head. "I was so worried Shag would get arrested. Ellen never crossed my mind. I wonder why they decided to grab her so fast."

Kate's instincts told her she'd already said too much, so she kept the fact of Roger's scrawled message to herself. Given the stakes, it made sense to be cautious, even with someone she liked as much as she liked Tate. "I'm hoping her lawyer can get her out of jail. And then clear her. She's no killer."

The waiter came by and asked if they wanted dessert, coffee? Tate looked at Kate and she shook her head. "Coffee maybe, but not here," she said. A hint she hoped he'd take her up on.

After the waiter left, Tate said, "I'm having a surprisingly good time, considering what's happened."

"Yes. I'm having a surprisingly good time, considering what's still happening." He must be talking about Roger; she was talking about Ellen.

He had a look on his face that said lots of things, most of them about the next few hours. He leaned across the table and said in a low voice, "So. Can we think of somewhere to go? For, ah, dessert?"

Kate smiled. Tate had said he shared a house with three other guys, so the ball was in her court. "Follow my taillights."

* * *

In the morning she made her usual coffee without thinking. He took a sip and made a horrible face. "Good God, woman. Are you trying to poison me?" Then his expression changed, and he put his face in his hands. "I'm sorry."

"No, hey, Tate." She touched his shoulder. "No need to be sorry. It was out of your mouth before you could think." She turned on the gas burner under the kettle. "I can dilute it with hot water and make it into that pitiful stuff you call coffee. That's what Ellen does."

"This stuff is so thick you must have to wave the cup around to keep it from setting like concrete. What do you do when it cools, chip it out of the cup?"

"Keep that up and you won't get any coffee."

"That's the way I am in the morning—words pop out of my mouth. Now's the time to ask me anything. My guard is down." His face had that slightly amused look Kate realized was habitual.

"Okay," she said. She slid onto the settee across from him. ""Who hated Roger?"

"You asked me that one already," Tate said. "I'm still thinking. I've been thinking all night."

"Oh, no. You didn't sleep?"

"Well, you kept me awake for quite a while," he gave her a grin that faded quickly. "That was the fun part. But no, I didn't sleep much. I keep going over people in my head, trying to come up with somebody Roger might have pissed off."

"And?"

"I came up with Kenny Smallwood. He was the mayor here for a while, and Roger and he disagreed a bunch of times. Smallwood was all about development—resort hotels, condominiums, golf courses, industry. Any business was good business."

"When was he mayor?"

"His term ended, let's see, it had to be three years ago at least. He was only mayor that once, partly because of Roger. Smallwood was in big with people in the business community, but he wanted too much development too fast. Even for them."

"Three years isn't so long," Kate said. "Not if you're nursing a grudge." She let a swallow of coffee sink in, its complex taste lighting up her brain, its warmth spreading through her all the way down.

"Yeah, he could have waited a while to throw off suspicion." Tate rubbed his blond stubble. "People hold grudges for decades sometimes. And Smallwood's got that competitive thing some guys have, you know? Always wanting to be in control."

"What if something happened, something recent, that could have riled him up again, reminded him of the old fight with Roger? Can you think of anything? Assuming he's still in town, of course."

"Oh, yeah, he's in town. He even showed up at Roger's cookout on Saturday. He ran for city council, last election." Tate brightened. "Hey, that could be it. He lost, and pretty badly. He could blame Roger for that, too. Smallwood was a big wheel before Roger took him on. They had a public disagreement over a proposed shopping mall."

A gust of wind rocked the camper, and they looked out at the lake. A cloud had gone over the sun and the water was steel-gray and ragged with waves.

"How about Dusty?" Kate asked. "You said he quit because he didn't get along with Roger."

"Dusty? You've got to be kidding. He's the most laid-back dude in New York State. No way it's him."

"How well do you know him? Maybe underneath that cheerful personality there's another Dusty." Kate raised an eyebrow.

"He's the kind of guy who knows how to take care of his karma. He's good enough to himself that he doesn't have to be mean to other people." Tate shrugged. "He wouldn't tie himself up in knots like Shag does. He'd walk away. Which is exactly what he did when Roger bugged him."

"Okay, Smallwood's a possibility, Dusty's not. Dan's a possibility." The previous night she'd told Tate about Ellen's ex-boyfriend and described the incident at the gas station. "He's tops on my list, and I hope the police yank him out of his garish yellow gas-hog today." She took a breath. "Now think about women."

"I'm always thinking about women," Tate said. "What would you like to know about them? I'm something of an expert."

Kate groaned. "Man, I sure handed you a line you could run with."

"Couldn't resist."

"I did a little thinking last night too, and it seems to me poison somehow suggests a woman. Maybe the police are thinking that way, too. They just picked the wrong woman." The last of her coffee was tepid. She stood up and stretched, then poured herself seconds. Tate put his hand over his cup. "Guys, you know, they want to hurt somebody, they pick up a knife or a gun," she said.

"Or a rock or a club. We're a bunch of cave-men at heart."

"Go ahead, make fun of me. I have to admit it sounds sexist, this theory of mine. But I think there's something to it. A poisoner doesn't have to be strong, or tough, or brave. Poisoning is sneaky, and it's planned. Not a fight that gets out of control."

"So women are sneaky, and men are thugs? I object, counselor. Some weak, wimpy men would think twice about getting into a fistfight. Some men—some people—smolder."

"I admitted it was sexist, didn't I?" Coffee definitely tasted better hot. "Do you think Roger used any drugs? He said such crazy stuff to Ellen, that last morning. Could he have been high?"

"Heck, no. He wouldn't touch street drugs. Called them pollutants."

"What about prescription drugs?"

Tate shook his head. "They were pollutants, too."

They looked at each other for a moment, then Tate put his hand over hers. "This is the weirdest thing I've ever been through. I'll get used to Roger being gone. It may take a while to really sink in, but it's a done deal. It must be worse for you because you're close to Ellen, and she's in the middle of her deal. We don't know how it's going to turn out."

"Yes," she said. "And think how weird it must be for Ellen."

Tate took his hand away. His face changed from serious to his baseline playful. "Any more questions, counselor?"

"Back to women," Kate said. "Did Roger date much? He was an eligible bachelor—good-looking, smart, successful, the works. And he sure came on to Ellen big-time. He must have a string of ex-girlfriends as long as his, um—arm."

Tate laughed. "You know, we were all blown away when you and Ellen showed up at the cookout. Roger hadn't been dating. He lived with his mother for while, and that doesn't go over well with most women. Even if his mother weren't such a barrel of laughs. It had to be awkward."

Barrel of laughs? Mrs. Benedict? Kate was getting used to Tate's dry humor. "Awkward as hell," she agreed.

"But still, he did date some, back then. And for a while after he moved to Boat Camp. Then he just stopped."

"Roger's father was a big deal, right? What was he like? Were they close?"

"Beyond close. His father was obsessed with fitness, physical and mental. What you call a man's man. Now I'm the sexist, right? I knew Roger in high school, but not well, because he couldn't hang out. His father had him training all the time."

"What kind of training?" She'd heard some of this from Ellen, but Tate probably knew more.

"You name it. Marathons, the running kind, and the skiing and paddling kind. That huge cross-country ski race every year up in Ontario. They did all those races together. Competing with his own father. Jeez. And those endurance biking events, randonneurs? Anything that would test him. Them. Would have killed the rest of us." He shook his head. "Killed. I can't say anything right this morning."

"No, no, you're doing fine." Kate tried not to feel like she was doing a newspaper interview. She wanted this information more than she'd ever wanted any story. It might save Ellen. "Did Roger go away to college, get away from his father that way? A lot of kids do."

"He didn't want to get away. He idolized his father. Too much. He always called him Paul, not Dad, to us. Called him Sir to his face. We all thought it was weird. And in high school some of the guys thought he was maybe gay, but I never thought so."

"College?" Kate prompted him.

"Yeah, he went, but not far away. Syracuse. Came home on weekends, sometimes his dad went over there mid-week." Tate sighed. "He was ROTC, of course."

"Yes, Ellen said the Navy wouldn't take him."

"He was being processed in, and they found something. He couldn't join up. Couldn't mimic his father's career in special ops or serve on a sub, which he and Paul thought was the second-most macho thing a guy could do. He never told me what they found, but he couldn't join." He smacked his forehead. "Oh, no, I'm not going to say 'washed up,' am I?"

"You just did." Kate couldn't laugh. She'd known much of Roger's story from Ellen, and it was still an intense case study in despair. She knew why Roger had been rejected—the congenitally missing kidney—but decided not to interrupt Tate's flow.

"He said he was stunned. He came back here and spent a lot of time alone. His father had no use for him. Called him a loser. That was the worst thing, even worse than not getting into the Navy."

"That's cruel," Kate said. "Abusive, in fact."

Tate shrugged. "All of the above. Then Paul was lost on a mission, and Mrs. Benedict staked Roger so he could start Boat Camp."

Kate looked out at the lake again. It was blue this time, but still rough. "What a hell of a life. He must have been traumatized. Everything he'd worked so hard for, everything he wanted, gone. Not only the career he'd been working toward, but his father's respect."

Tate was quiet for a moment. Then he said, "I guess it can't hurt to tell you, since Roger's dead. Probably Paul is too."

She waited.

"He told me once—he'd had a couple of beers, which didn't happen often—he told me he thought it was his fault that Paul didn't come back."

"Wow. What a burden, to blame himself," Kate said. "Why?"

"Because why would Paul want to come home to such a loser son?"

Kate shook her head. "I'm really having trouble connecting all this to the Roger I met. Don't get me wrong, I believe you, but he seemed so—"

"Normal?"

"Yes. And charming. Thoughtful, even empathic. Intelligent and well-read. Like that. Not a guy traumatized, rejected, probably depressed out of his mind."

"Well, a few years have gone by."

"Stuff like that marks you forever." Maybe one day she'd know Tate well enough, trust him enough, to tell him about her own father disappearing. She had a flash memory of him ahead of her on a trail above Tucson, looking back at her, telling her to be careful, to watch out for snakes.

She shook her head, came back to the present. "Job one, right now? We have to figure out who wanted Roger dead." She reached across the table, bumping her cup, and put her hands on his. "We simply must get Ellen out of that horrible place and back into sunlight and fresh air." Sadness for both Ellen and Roger welled up in her.

Tate's gray eyes met hers and held. "Roger getting killed was a disaster. Ellen's arrest is disaster number two, but it's the one we can do something about."

Then he looked down and snorted with laughter.

"What?" Kate looked at him. What was funny?

"Your cup says 'La Brea Tar Pit,'" Tate said. "That's a good one. Accurate, I'd say, for the stuff you drink. Where'd you get that?"

Kate hesitated. Her former partner had given it to her for her birthday when they were first dating. She should have thrown it out the way he'd thrown her out last Christmas, but she liked the belled shape, which kept coffee hot longer. "Oh, an old boyfriend gave it to me. A long time ago."

"What?" Tate's voice rose in make-believe outrage. "I'm not your first?"

TWELVE

"Ellen's been arraigned for first-degree murder," Amber told Kate on the phone. "If I were the prosecutor, I wouldn't have charged her so soon. But this guy likes to move quickly, to look decisive. It's a small town, and Roger's family is prominent. His father was legendary for his toughness, not an easy accomplishment in the High Peaks area."

Grim news, but not unexpected. "What happens next?"

"She'll have a preliminary hearing tomorrow, and I'll enter a plea of Not Guilty. Then some paperwork with the court system, after which a trial date will be set." She sighed. "It's a long road, Kate. Anyway, I'll be sure to keep you in the loop. But I'll call when there's something to tell you, not on a daily basis."

"I understand."

"It's a confusing case. Except for the message on the wall, the evidence against Ellen is circumstantial. She's an unlikely suspect, in my opinion. Nothing adds up. Roger was poisoned but the tests have come back to show the coffee left in his cup was poison-free."

"That's confusing, all right," Kate said. "What about the message? Do you know what it said?"

"Not yet." A pause. "I'm glad you're here to give Ellen emotional support."

"Has she talked to her parents yet? Told them what's going on?"

"She's told them she won't be able to join them on the cruise, but she still doesn't want to let them know how far this has gone. I think she's being unrealistic, but she doesn't want to spoil their vacation. She's hoping she'll be exonerated before they get back to Syracuse."

* * *

In the middle of Fish Creek Pond, Kate stowed her paddle and called Marjorie, who'd asked for updates.

"Here are my headlines. Roger was poisoned, Ellen's been indicted, and her lawyer doesn't sound optimistic."

"Kate, that's awful," Marjorie said. "So much for my theory the last time you called that all this would blow over in a day or two."

"I like the lawyer, and she sounds like she knows what she's doing. I'm hoping she'll figure this out," Kate said. Sunlight dappled her boat. The hull was so thin she could see the waterline right through it, a cross-section of fluttering wavelets. "Ellen's ex-boyfriend looks like the perfect suspect to me." She told Marjorie about Dan harassing Ellen at the gas station. "But for some reason the police are sticking with Ellen."

"Sticking it *to* Ellen is what it sounds like," Marjorie said. "Hey, the news is bad, but you don't sound as stressed as you were last time."

"The news isn't as new as it used to be," Kate said. "And it helps to be doing something. I got online at the library and did a web search on poison, but that left me more confused. Too many kinds to know what to look for in Roger's case. Snake venom, pesticide, lead, some compound in shellfish, even Botox."

"It had to be fast-acting," Marjorie said. "I think you can forget about lead."

"Maybe a rattlesnake bit him."

"In his house? On the second floor, and without Ellen noticing? Anyway, the lab tests would have been able to tell if the poison was something Roger could have encountered accidentally. It's got to be something more unusual."

"You're right," Kate said. "And Roger wasn't the type to get facial wrinkles treated with Botox." She was gratified by Marjorie's chuckle.

"I'm glad you're still able to crack a joke."

"Here's my last headline. Another reason I'm not as bent out of shape as I was the last time we talked? I'm sleeping with the coolest guy on planet Earth."

"My goodness, you lead an exciting life," Marjorie said.

"I don't mean to. But it's not going to get any quieter while Ellen's in jail. I want to find out more about Roger. If I get to know him better posthumously, maybe I can figure out who his worst enemy was."

"You're going to do some major snooping? Be careful. There's a bad guy out there."

"Or a bad girl."

"Either way, stay alert. I want to continue to get bulletins from my most adventurous friend."

* * *

She'd have to see Roger's apartment alone. That was a scary proposition, but she didn't want to admit to Tate she'd stolen keys from the store.

Asking him to let her in with his keys had crossed her mind, but she'd decided against the idea. He was a new and thrilling presence in her life, and she didn't think she could concentrate with him around. Besides, you don't ask someone you've known for a few days to join you in criminal trespassing, even if it's done with the best of intentions.

He'd apologized that he was busy that Thursday night, having a standing commitment to meet up with some buddies once a month for "beer, bullshit and pool." She'd moved to the Floodwood campground so she could walk the mile down Paul's Way to Boat Camp. That way, nobody would see headlights going to the store long after it had closed. And starting her truck might wake someone at one of the other campsites who could get curious about where she was driving so late. So walking made sense.

Trying to have a normal day, she worked on a drawing from her photos of the Fish Creek bridge in the morning and hiked up Baker Mountain in the afternoon. But she got a jolt of adrenalin every time she thought of her plan, and she was so preoccupied that after the hike she could barely recall the trail she'd followed or the view from the top.

She steeled herself by considering the stakes. A man dead, and the wrong person accused. She might be the only person who had a shot at figuring this out.

Setting the alarm for 1:00 a.m., she climbed into the cab-over bed and lay there wishing for sleep. At this rate she wouldn't need an alarm.

Then it went off, and she jerked awake. She'd slept for at least an hour.

She put on her jeans, a black turtleneck and her deep purple jacket. Feeling a little ridiculous, she put on a black balaclava and gloves. Hey, it was cold out there. But mostly she didn't want to be visible. She'd checked on her phone—the moon would rise at 1:20, so it would be too low to be a factor on her walk down Paul's Way. Depending on how long she stayed at the store, moonlight could be a factor on the way back.

But nobody would be looking. Right?

She topped her outfit with a headlamp, and went quietly down the step.

Night air splashed against her eyes like ice-water. She pressed the camper door until the latch clicked, locked it, then waited by the step for a couple of minutes to let her eyes adjust. The campground was half-empty, and silent. She wouldn't need her headlamp for the walk; she must be seeing by starlight.

She crossed Floodwood and was startled at how much noise her feet made going from pavement to gravel. She moved around on Paul's Way until she found a tire track where the gravel wasn't as loose.

Kate moved fast. She wanted to get this over with, and her fear had ebbed somewhat now that she was doing something instead of thinking about it. She wasn't afraid, really, only a bit anxious, like an actor with stage fright. Some anxiety is productive, right? And what is anxiety but excitement wearing the ugliest outfit in its closet?

A light through the trees told her she was close. It lit the store's front porch, so she went to the back of the building. As she eased around the corner a light came on. Kate froze. She was an idiot. Maybe this was only a motion-triggered light, but it reminded her that the place could have an alarm system.

Wait. When she and Tate had left the store after she helped move skis, he didn't set any alarm, just locked up. So she was okay getting into the building. Roger's apartment was a separate issue.

Back door key, then. Inside, she flicked the headlamp onto its red setting and hit the stairs. Unlocked the apartment door, and looked at the walls for an alarm box. None. Good.

In fact, the walls were all bare. No calendars, no photos, no art.

She pulled off the headlamp and stuffed the balaclava into a pocket. Kept her gloves on. Flashed the light around. The overall impression was not the coziness she'd expected from Ellen's description, but spareness. Yes, the furniture was tasteful, especially the curved leather couch facing windows that would give a great view of the lake in the daytime. But there was absolutely no clutter—no pillows on the sofa, no clocks or vases or books or plants, the kind of stuff most people have.

What was she looking for? A threatening note signed by ex-mayor Kenny Smallwood? That would be nice. Kate smiled at her own silliness. She glanced at the kitchen (the counters gleaming, bare) and the bedroom (not a slipper in sight) and chose what looked like an office at the back for a closer look.

A closet held half a dozen cardboard banker's boxes on shelves, each one labeled TAXES with a year underneath. No help there.

She turned to the desk, pulled out the file drawer. Manila tabs in neat writing: Expenses, Income, Inventory, Payroll, Personnel, Sales. She flipped open Personnel. About twenty application forms; she recognized some of the names. Tate Winchester. Irving Horst. Jennifer Hunter. Margaret Chaddick must be Molly. Oh, yes—"Molly" was written in pencil, hard to see in the red light. She switched her headlamp over to white. "Shag" at the top of Dennis Cotreau's application. In the margin, the word "attitude."

On the desk she laid out the rest of the applications, overlapping so that the tops showed names, addresses and phone numbers, and took a picture with her cell. Maybe somebody who didn't get hired had been angry about it.

A slide-out shelf under the desktop, designed for a laptop computer, was empty. The police must have taken it. Kate could only imagine what insight they might get into Roger's last days from his email. A moot point if the cops didn't read his messages.

But of course they weren't interested. That was the problem.

A map on the wall caught her eye. Unframed, attached at the corners with push-pins, it showed lakes and islands deep in the St. Regis Canoe Area. At the top, Hermit Island was circled in pencil. Kate looked closely. The map was smudged in places, but not randomly. It looked like someone had run a finger along two different routes from the nearby Floodwood Road put-in north to Hermit Island.

Outside the window, the motion-detector light went on.

Heart racing, Kate switched off her headlamp.

Probably a deer. Or a porcupine, or a fox.

She looked out the window. A man stood at the edge of the woods.

THIRTEEN

He was wearing tall rubber boots and a jacket with the hood up, his face shadowed.

Kate looked away, looked back. Was she imagining things?

No. Definitely a person, standing at the edge of the clearing behind the building, unmoving.

Was it Dan? The Floodwood campground ran along the edge of Middle Pond, the sites in a single row between the water and the road. She would have seen Dan's car.

Maybe this was a burglar. He could have read about Roger's death in the paper, figured the store would be unattended. A local would know the victim had lived over the store. She'd heard of thieves using news items to target the homes of people who'd died or were hospitalized, or had gone to relatives' funerals.

But this guy wasn't acting like a burglar. He wasn't trying to get in.

And he was looking up. At the office window where her light had showed until seconds earlier. He knew she was there.

Outside, the light went out.

It had a timer, of course. And he hadn't been moving.

She was panting. She made herself take deep breaths. Slow and deep.

Okay. If he was in the back, she'd go out the front. The light out front had to be ordinary, not motion-triggered, because it had been on, steadily, as she'd come along the road. It wouldn't alert him that she was leaving. She slipped out the front of the apartment and down the stairs.

At the front door, she looked through the glass first, then slid out onto the porch, locked the door. Halfway to the steps, a board squeaked. She kept on going, feeling exposed under the light. Instead of going back down the road, she went toward the lake. If he was looking for her, he'd look on the road.

She got behind the boat trailers and felt safer, but she was still visible, a vertical shape intersecting horizontals. She considered crawling inside the biggest kayak, a tandem. But it would have bulkheads, so maybe she wouldn't fit. Getting in might make noise. She wouldn't be able to see out. And she would feel trapped.

Farther on, the woods. She needed vertical lines to camouflage her legs. She joined the trees like the old friends they were, went in three deep and then remembered her white face and put on the black balaclava.

She waited, feeling the cold nudge its way past her collar, up her sleeves. Her watch told her it was quarter of two. She'd been in Roger's apartment about fifteen minutes, that was all.

If the guy back there moved, the light would come on.

Should she wait for him to leave, or go now? She imagined the line of sight from his position. No, it was too risky to leave. He'd be able to see the first part of the road from where he was. And she felt shaky. She couldn't count on herself to be able to run. Or fight.

She waited. Five minutes to two. She tried not to look at her watch for a while. The light on it was dim but might still affect her night vision. She pondered the question of whether a person might move slowly enough to avoid triggering a motion detector. Possible, she decided. But hard to do. And if you made a mistake—

The light went on behind the building, throwing a huge shadow toward her. Kate gave each side of the building two seconds, switching back and forth. She had to spot him before the light went out.

Back and forth. Nobody.

The light went out.

Damn. Now she had no idea where he was. Maybe she was going to have to spend the night here. She could go deeper into the woods, maybe climb a tree. But she was afraid to move. She could easily step on a branch, give herself away.

He could be moving toward her in the dark.

She'd taken a self-defense course back in college, but what could she remember? She started reviewing moves: pulling back on thumbs to release grips, scraping shins with boots if grabbed from behind, using elbows, knees—

A light came on. An inside light, on the second floor. The guy had broken in after all. No, she'd left the back door unlocked, expecting to leave that way herself.

And the door to the apartment? Had she locked it when she left? She didn't remember. Maybe not. She'd been frightened and in a hurry.

He hadn't broken in. But he'd gone upstairs. Kate swallowed hard. He wasn't a burglar, or he'd go for the store's cash register, on the first floor.

No. He must be Roger's killer. He'd seen her light upstairs.

He was looking for her.

The silhouette of a man filled the front window, his head pointed because of the hood. He looked out, scanning the lot. And then he pulled the curtains closed.

Kate hesitated. Maybe it was a trick. In a second he'd yank the curtains open, see her running for the road.

Right now she knew where he was. But with each second that passed—

She left the cover of trees and moved across the parking area at a fast walk. When she got to the road she looked over her shoulder once—the light was still on upstairs, the curtains closed—and ran until she had to stop, hands on her knees, gasping. She wasn't cold anymore.

She crossed Floodwood Road to her truck and hoped she wasn't waking any of the other campers as she started it up. She drove with just parking lights until she was out of sight of the campground, then hit the headlights and the gas. Putting some miles between herself and Roger's apartment eased her fear that the hooded man would find her.

Kate drove the dark road, avoiding potholes, feeling her heart rate slow to something like normal. She'd probably just set a personal best record for running a mile.

FOURTEEN

Amber didn't look happy. "The handwriting analysis was completed and the prosecutor has sent me photos of the message on the wall," she said. "I'm afraid it's rather compelling." She put her recorder on the table in the little consultation room.

Ellen came up straight in her chair, looking alarmed. "What does it say?"

* * *

Earlier that Friday, Amber had called Kate to ask if she'd be willing to meet with her and Ellen. "I usually talk to my clients alone," the attorney had said. "But Ellen is shaky. She's asked if you could be here, too, for psychological support."

"Of course, yes. I'll come."

"The only condition is that you don't discuss anything you learn here with anyone else. Anyone at all."

Kate thought of how helpful it was to talk with Marjorie. But her friend in Massachusetts didn't need to know all the details.

"I could talk about what gets printed in the *Adirondack Star*, which would be public knowledge, couldn't I?"

"Yes," Amber had said. "But you'd be privy to details from us that are strictly off the record."

"I can handle that."

"Ellen and I are putting a great deal of trust in you," Amber had said. "Don't let us down."

* * *

Amber, a trace of pain under her professional demeanor, glanced at Kate. This was going to be bad news. No wonder she'd agreed to let Ellen have a friend here.

"The message is direct, if ungrammatical. It says 'Ellen W poison me.'"

"Oh, my God." Ellen looked stricken. "I'm—I can't—why would he—say that?" She'd been in the tiny jail cell for five days, and the strain of confinement showed.

"The handwriting analysis should be easy to challenge: the writing of a dying man is not going to be anything like the writing on his last rent check or shopping list," the lawyer said. "And the poison would affect his voluntary muscles first. So I'll argue that the scrawl is not, in fact, a message from Roger. The killer wrote it to divert scrutiny from himself."

The three women sat in silence in the small room.

"What kind of poison?" Kate finally asked.

"Autopsy results show a neurotoxin, a nerve poison, in Roger's blood. It would paralyze the hands and arms and legs first, then the automatic muscles, the heart and lungs."

The heart and diaphragm are *autonomic* muscles, not *automatic,* Kate's biology-major mind objected, but she didn't correct the lawyer.

Ellen looked sick.

"It's strange that the coffee in his cup was fine. No trace of neurotoxin there. He'd drunk most of it. So if it wasn't in the coffee, how was it ingested?"

"This is so confusing," Kate said. "The message is so clear and so wrong."

"I've thought of several plausible scenarios," Amber said. "Whoever killed him wrote on the wall and then pressed Roger's fingers onto the pencil to leave prints. I favor that one, because it's the simplest. It's also possible that the killer forced Roger to write the message, word by word, knowing Roger's state of mind was such that he didn't realize the import of the message as a whole."

"He wouldn't have accused her if he'd known what he was doing. He'd only known Ellen a week, and he liked her." Kate said. "Maybe even loved her."

"I wouldn't call it love," Ellen said. "In retrospect, I think he was nuts."

"Love can mean different things to different people," Amber said. "His state of mind is important—agitated, you would say? That morning?"

Ellen nodded. When Amber pointed to the recorder, Ellen said aloud, "Yes, agitated. I mean, all of a sudden. He seemed okay at first, although I thought it was odd he was up and dressed so early. Then he got all excitable and said those wacko things about our being committed to each other, and I grabbed my bag and left."

"The message is a difficulty. So is the fact that the police found your make-up case in Roger's bathroom and his phone in your purse."

Ellen was clearly startled. "In my purse?"

Amber's voice was quiet. "The police think you took it to prevent him from calling for help. The poison took about ten minutes to be irreversibly fatal."

"That's not enough time to make any difference," Kate said. "An ambulance couldn't get there from South Portage in ten minutes. Let alone get him to a hospital for a diagnosis."

Ellen was crying and shaking her head. "He must have put the phone in my bag."

"Why would he do that?" Kate asked. "Was he protecting the killer? Who would he want to protect that much? A relative? His brother Will? His *mother?"* This was too weird.

"Are you assuming he knew he was going to be murdered?" Amber asked Kate. "He must have put the cell in Ellen's bag before she left, before the murderer confronted him."

"No, that's too crazy. Although it would account for his agitation."

"Someone arrived after you left, Ellen," Amber said, tapping a pen on the table. "I wonder if there are security cameras, either in the store or outside. The police must have checked them. I'll ask." She made a note on her yellow pad.

"There aren't any cameras," Kate said. "An ordinary light on the front porch and a motion-triggered light out back, that's it."

She had Amber's full attention. "How do you know that?"

"I did a little looking around Roger's place last night," Kate said. "I thought maybe I could find out more about him. There wasn't any security, only ordinary door locks. Deadbolts."

Amber's expression changed, and she turned off the recorder. "You broke in?"

Oh, crap. Did Kate want to tell this legal beagle that she'd committed a crime? "No. I had keys."

"Oh," Amber said, her voice still guarded. "Good. So what did you find?"

"One useful thing I got is a list of people applying to work at the store. I'm going to ask around, see if any of them had a motive."

"I'd rather you gave the names to me," Amber said. "I'm local. I'll know more to start with, and my inquiries might be seen as less intrusive than yours."

Kate wasn't sure that last statement was true. Would people rather get asked questions by an unemployed RVer in jeans or an attorney in heels and an expensive suit? But having told Amber about the names, she didn't have much choice. And the lawyer did have local knowledge going for her. Maybe somebody on the list was a known criminal already.

Amber was watching her. "I have staff. Resources. Really, it's better I look into this."

"Okay," Kate said. "I'll text you my photo of the files. But my top suspect is a man who triggered the light behind the store while I was inside."

"Oh, no," Ellen said.

"Can you identify him?" Amber asked.

"No, I didn't see a face, only a guy wearing a hooded jacket and fisherman's boots. Like half the population of South Portage." Neither Ellen nor Amber smiled.

"Oh, Kate, you shouldn't have done that," Ellen said. "That must have been Roger's killer, and if he'd found you snooping around, he might—"

"She's right," Amber said. Her soft voice somehow overrode Ellen's wail. "Did he see you?"

"Not up close," Kate said. She gave a short account of her nocturnal visit to Roger's apartment. "It might have been Dan, but I'm not sure. He didn't look tall enough."

"I don't represent you," Amber said, "but I represent your friend, and complicating her case would not be helpful." She gave Kate a look. "However you got those keys, I would keep it to myself if I were you."

"Okay." Easy to agree to that.

"It would be a great help," Amber said to Ellen, "if you could remember anything more about the vehicle you saw going down Paul's Way." She put the legal pad and recorder into her briefcase. "Put that in your subconscious and see what it comes up with."

"You've asked me that before," Ellen said. "I can't, I just can't—" Her voice cracked.

"All right, Ellen, take it easy." Amber's voice softened. "I'll check in with you on Monday." She stood up. "Thank you for coming, Kate. Here's my card. My email address is where you should send the list of names, and any other—ideas you might have."

Kate took the card, searching Amber's face. Was she encouraging more amateur detective work? A hint of a smile came and went.

At the door, the lawyer turned. "Stay out of trouble." That must be meant for Kate, since Ellen's situation made further trouble impossible.

"I'm going to take a nap," Ellen said. "I'm sleeping way too much. It's how I escape the trouble I'm already in."

Kate gave her friend a hug. "Amber's no slouch," she said. "She's going to get you out of this mess."

* * *

Since Amber had mentioned paralysis, Kate spent another hour on the library computer searching for information on neurotoxins that might cause such a symptom. A syndrome called Paralytic Shellfish Poisoning was caused by saxitoxin, found in blue-green algae and in the bivalve filter feeders that lived on the algae and that were sometimes harvested for human food. Kate's background in biology was useful as she scanned a few scientific articles on shellfish contamination.

The poison came from freshwater mussels and clams, not the saltwater variety. Were they harvested locally in the Adirondacks and served in restaurants? Blue-green algae grew in fresh water, too. Could Roger have been over-exposed because he spent so much time on lakes and ponds? The effect might be cumulative, which would explain why Ellen wasn't affected.

But if the poison had been ingested over years, the symptoms would probably be gradual. An acute, fatal attack argued against algae as the source.

Maybe Roger had eaten scallops or clams at the restaurant Sunday night. She emailed Amber a brief description of saxitoxin and asked her to find out if Ellen remembered what he'd ordered at the Serendipity.

The last article she found gave Kate chills: research into saxitoxin had been ordered by the National Security Agency because it believed terrorists were purifying and stockpiling the poison for use in future attacks on the U.S. The search for an antidote had so far been unsuccessful.

She left the library in a grim mood.

Her next stop was the Sav-A-Lot for groceries. She checked the list on her phone, letting the routine of shopping insulate her from worries about Ellen and about terrorist attacks. Coffee, cereal, soy milk. Tofu. Salad greens, red onions. She'd rolled the cart to her camper and was opening the door when she heard a friendly "Hey" behind her.

"Molly. Hi. Nice to see you."

"How are you holding up? Have you seen Ellen? How's she doing?"

"I just saw her." Ellen's predicament rushed back into Kate's mind in a way that said it had never really been gone. "She's totally stressed out, but at least she's got a lawyer now." Molly didn't have a cart or bags, so he hadn't shopped yet—no frozen food thawing, no lettuce wilting. "Say, you want to come in and have some tea?"

"Thanks, yes. I'd love to see your camper," Molly said. "I see these things on the road all the time but I've never been inside one."

Kate dropped the steps into place. "Maybe you could hand these groceries up to me, and I'll put the kettle on while I stow stuff."

In a few minutes the kettle whistled. Molly had already had the full tour—which was accomplished with them both seated at the dinette while Kate pointed to the highlights: furnace, air conditioner, microwave, stove, hot water heater, over-cab bunk.

"A real bathroom, even, behind that door." She hopped up and opened it.

Molly laughed. "That's the smallest bathroom I've ever seen."

"Okay, so it's also a shower stall. The floor drains to the gray-water tank. It's called a wet bath," Kate said. She poured the tea and put the two cups on the table. "What do you know about Hermit Island?"

Molly didn't blink at the abrupt change of subject. "Oh, wow, that's a great place," she said. "It's s long paddle, but it's awful pretty."

"How often have you been there?"

"One of the portages is something of a trek, so it doesn't get visited that often. I've worked at Boat Camp the longest, and I've only been there once."

"Did you go with some of the other guides?"

"No, it was Roger and me. We took a tandem kayak. Back then I thought he was interested in me, you know, as more than an employee. But he was so up and down." She frowned. "It didn't work out, and eventually I got together with Shag. That put even more distance between me and Roger. I don't know why he doesn't like Shag." She shook her head. "Didn't like Shag. Hard to get used to past tense."

They were quiet. Then Kate asked, "How long have you been with the outfit?"

Molly smiled. "You're pumping me." Her face sobered. "It's okay. I'll tell you everything I know if it can help find who killed Roger. The answer is four years. From the beginning."

"I'd like to go out to Hermit Island," Kate said.

"Cool. I'll go with you, if you'd like."

"That'd be great, Molly. You're a trooper."

Molly looked startled, then sad.

"What?"

"That was Roger's favorite compliment."

FIFTEEN

It was dark and Kate was cold. She'd layered, with long underwear and a fleece under her paddling pants and jacket. She'd be unzipping and venting soon enough. It was amazing how much heat working muscles generated.

Molly was quiet as they unloaded gear and got the boats in the water. She'd driven a Boat Camp pick-up with her kayak in the bed to the Floodwood put-in; Kate had walked from her campsite with her boat on her shoulder. It would take both of them to carry Molly's decked boat, much heavier than Kate's Hornbeck.

It was lovely to be on the water at sunrise. Kate hadn't told Molly that the excursion was based on the map in Roger's home office; she hadn't admitted to stealing the keys and looking over his place, either. Kate felt guilty for not being open with Molly, but she didn't want to risk losing her as an ally. That map was the only thing on Roger's walls: it must be an important clue.

They paddled for hours, Molly in the lead. Kate had a map in a plastic holder tucked under her right thigh, but she only glanced at their route now and then, depending on Molly's knowledge of the waterways. She kept a sharp eye out for other boats. There weren't many. A few canoes drifted in twos and threes near some of the islands she and Molly passed, but the people in them, holding fishing lines, barely looked up.

The first two portages were short. The third one was a real schlep. They carried the boats, went back for the gear. On the fourth carry, the last, Molly fell. "Ow. Shit." She'd been carrying the bow of her maroon kayak, which thunked on the ground. Sitting, she put a hand on the foredeck and rocked a little with pain.

"Are you okay?" Kate put the stern down and ran the few steps to Molly.

"Oh, man, my ankle hurts. Twisted it. That stupid rock moved." She pointed at a rock the size of a dinner plate.

Kate looked at the rock. "You're right. That's the dumbest rock I've ever met."

Molly smiled.

Good, she wasn't too hurt for a joke, then. Kate hoped the twist was minor, not a full-blown sprain.

The guide pulled her sock down and touched the outside of her ankle. "It hurts here."

"Wait a minute, I'll get the first aid kit," Kate said. She found the red packet in her dry-bag and got out an Ace bandage. She'd been an EMT, emergency medical technician, before she got into newspaper work, so she knew how to deal with small injuries.

She didn't take Molly's boat-shoe off, but wrapped the stretchy bandage around the foot and the shoe together and tucked an ice pack under one of the last layers. It wasn't real ice but a chemical pack that got cold when you broke the plastic vial inside. The bandage was the kind that sticks to itself, which was great for outdoor use because you didn't have to fiddle with pins or clips when your hands were cold.

"There," she said. "That'll help keep the swelling down."

"Thanks," Molly said. "The support feels good." She was a guide; she probably knew as much as Kate did about sprains and scrapes and hypothermia.

"How bad is it? Can you stand on it?"

Kate helped Molly to her feet, and the guide made a face. "I think I could walk on it if I had something to lean on. Maybe a paddle?"

"The blades would make that awkward. Maybe I can find a good stick." Kate rummaged under the trees for a minute and came up with one.

They went to the far end of the portage, Molly limping on her stick and Kate carrying her own boat, the lightweight Hornbeck.

"Here's a smart rock to sit on," Kate said. "Nice view."

"Oh, Kate, the rock wasn't stupid, I was. I'm so sorry."

"Don't beat yourself up. Rocks always lie about whether they're going to tilt when you step on them." Starting back for the second boat, she said over her shoulder, "But you've used up your quota. The ankle's the only injury you're allowed today."

Kate dragged Molly's boat along the trail. She didn't like treating kayaks this roughly, but she didn't have any choice. At least Molly's boat was made of fiberglass. Tough stuff. The trails were mostly piney duff with some muddy stretches; rocks were a problem only at the water's edge, at the beginning and end of the portages.

She watched where she put her feet. They could really be in trouble if she twisted an ankle, too.

Kate was a little worried. They'd be slower now, no doubt about it. They had emergency gear with them, but not a lot of food. She hoped they wouldn't be stuck out here overnight.

They talked about turning back, but Molly said they were close to Hermit. "I'd hate to come all this way for nothing," she said.

Fortunately she was paddling well even with the ankle injury. Kate had to push herself to keep up. Molly must be worried about being slower, too, and was compensating.

Hermit Island was heavily wooded. They paddled along its shore, then Molly threaded her boat through a passage that ran between Hermit and another, smaller island. The inlet was narrow, and Kate kept her eyes on the rocks on either side as she glided through—in the narrowest part, there was no place to dip the paddle.

The cove was flat calm: trees on the two islands blocked wind no matter which way it was blowing. Molly's boat was in the shallows of a sandy beach.

"You want to go ashore and have a little walk? I'll wait."

"Good idea," Kate said. "It'll feel good to get out of the boat and stretch my legs without having to carry anything. And you don't want to walk with that sprain." She suggested that Molly pull her leg out of the cockpit and elevate the injured ankle up on the deck. Kate tucked her PFD under Molly's calf. "There, that's even higher."

The trail from the little beach was steep. Moss on the rocks was undisturbed; nobody had been here in months. The island was small: forty steps took Kate to its crest. Stony, with little underbrush, Hermit Island hosted mature spruce trees that rose a hundred feet over her head, their tops swaying gently. A breeze sighed through them, Kate's favorite kind of wild silence.

The main trail went straight, to the other side of the island and the continuation of the canoe route, but there was a trace of another path going right, along the spine of the island. She followed that, dodging an occasional low branch. She'd walk a few minutes, even though she didn't know what she was looking for. Something here had been important to Roger.

The air carried the astringent but pleasant odor of spruce, like orange rind. In sunny breaks, ferns clustered, their arched fronds gone September bronze.

She came to a clearing, with taller ferns and low shrubs taking advantage of the sunlight. Half an acre of weathered, blown-down trunks were evidence of a storm that had taken a bite out of the forest cover.

A red squirrel chittered at her from a branch, the shape of its tail rhyming with that of the bronze ferns.

"What's the matter, haven't you seen a human before?"

The squirrel stopped its racket, as if it were listening. Then something bounced onto the ground in front of her. A chewed spruce cone.

"Too bad, you missed."

Her tiny attacker whisked from its branch and scampered into the next tree, and the next, scratches of sound marking its progress as its claws caught in bark.

"See you later," Kate called after it.

She took a few steps into the clearing, felt the ground go hard where exposure to wind and rain had removed the mat of needles. Then she stopped. The trace of a trail she'd been following had petered out, and she'd simply been keeping to the highest ground. But she wasn't going to climb over all those fallen trunks. This was a dead end.

Whatever had drawn Roger to Hermit Island wasn't obvious. Maybe he liked the wild silence of wind in spruce tops as much as Kate did. She looked in both directions and decided scouting around the open area would take too long, although she might have done so if Molly hadn't been waiting for her.

She was about to turn away when she saw something odd. A pine cone dropped from a tree to her right, but it didn't fall to the ground. It hit something ten feet up and stopped.

Kate worked her way along the edge of the windfall, keeping inside the standing trees where the thick mat of needles lay undisturbed. Ahead of her, the red squirrel chattered.

Then she saw it, half-hidden in a copse of trees. A cabin, small and rustic.

The squirrel had seen a human before. It had seen Roger Benedict.

She went up the two steps, made of logs squared with an axe. A simple latch on the door, no lock.

For the second time in a few days she was in a space that had belonged to Boat Camp's enigmatic owner.

The cabin was dark, with one small window. Kate pushed the door all the way open for light. It showed simple, built-in furniture: a table under the window and a bed along each side.

The walls, though, were cluttered, crowded with dozens of framed photos and plaques.

Her flashlight was in her drybag in the boat, so she had to squint at the plaques. "For service above and beyond. . ." "for meritorious service. . ." The name on all of them was Paul R. Benedict.

Plaques. Framed ribbons. Photos showing groups of men in uniform, saluting, pinning medals on chests. A whole wall.

On the other side of the room, candids. Men in scuba gear, hanging off the sides of inflatable boats. Smiling men standing together, glossy as seals in their wetsuits, on the sterns of ships.

One man in particular, a repeat in picture after picture. Tall. Broad-shouldered. Fit-looking. Well, they all were. You had to be fit to be a special forces operative. But this man was at the center of all the groups.

Paul Benedict.

The cabin was a shrine to Roger's father.

At the cookout, Will had said his brother went through a phase of living in the woods. Roger must have built this place during that period.

The beds were made up with military-style wool blankets. At the foot of one of them, a plastic box. She snapped the lid off.

Ribbons, medals, pins. She closed the box.

Opened it again. None of the medals was tarnished. They'd all been polished and put in clear plastic bags.

Roger had a secret life. Was it Tate who had said he sometimes disappeared for a few days at a time with no explanation? He must have come here, to be with his father in the only way possible. Perhaps even to imagine himself being this man, a leader among one of the toughest combat and reconnaissance units in the world.

And to be with the smiling face of a father who was no longer able to criticize or condemn the son who'd worshipped him.

A wave of dizziness hit her, and she put a hand on the log wall to steady herself. She imagined for a moment what it would be like to have a collection of photos like this of her own father. He'd gone missing when she was eleven, and she had no pictures of him at all. Just before he vanished, she'd asked him if she could have an old photo ID, a construction site pass, that he'd tossed in the trash when the job was over. She'd kept it under her pillow for months before her mother had thrown it away and told her it was unhealthy to dwell in the past.

Kate came back to herself in the cabin, far from her Arizona childhood.

How much time had gone by? Molly would wonder what had happened. She'd better go.

At the door, she turned back. Roger had built this place by himself. Only the window was ready-made, small enough to have been brought here by canoe. Everything else—floor, bed, table—was made of rough, ax-split boards. Gaps in the log walls were stuffed with moss.

A hand-built monument to his father. He must have harvested the logs from the nearby storm damage, a windfall of lumber.

Something hypnotic about the place made her reluctant to go. Or perhaps it was her own history that held her.

Only when she was out in the fresh air did Kate truly extricate herself from the spell. Imagining Molly struggling out of her boat and crawling up shoreline rocks to look for her, Kate backtracked quickly to the little beach.

Molly looked relieved. "Man, I was wondering if you'd been eaten by a bear."

"Nope, sorry to disappoint you. No bears." She smiled at the guide, feeling devious about what she wasn't saying..

SIXTEEN

Kate checked Molly's ankle. Purple-red bruising was coming on, and the skin felt hot. The ice pack wasn't cold any more, so she changed it out. Only one more was left in the first-aid kit.

Molly's pace was slower on the way back.

"You want some aspirin?" Kate asked. "I've got plenty, and it'll help with the swelling."

"No, I'm good. I don't like meds."

An occasional aspirin was the safest medication going, Kate thought, but she let it go. She hoped they could get back before dark. The only night boating she'd done was under a full moon, but those trips were planned ahead of time and weren't as long and difficult as this one.

Worried, she thought about offering to lead, but no—checking behind her to make sure Molly was keeping up would be distracting. Years ago she'd mounted a small bicycle mirror to her paddle to see behind her without turning her boat, but to use it she'd have to stop paddling. Better to have Molly in front.

At least she got to rest at the portages. Kate dragged Molly's boat first, then went back and carried her own, then made a final trip for their drybags. She wished she were stronger and could portage the boats with the gear in them, but pulling Molly's boat empty was strenuous enough, especially on the uphill part of the longest portage. With her own light boat on her shoulder she could carry one of the drybags, but not the other. So each portage meant three round trips.

The two women paddled steadily. Kate's mind was filled with her visit to the cabin. She hadn't noticed if Roger had used nails or screws. She didn't remember seeing the metal heads of those conventional fasteners, so maybe he'd used wooden pegs, pioneer-style. The cabin had a crude beauty that suggested it was all hand-made. It was a work of art.

A work of love.

She moved as fast as she could at the carries, Molly's boat bumping behind her with an occasional scrape as she went over a rock. She breathed a sigh of relief after the last one—now it was all paddle-work, a pleasure even with the time pressure of the oncoming darkness. She lapped her hull with Molly's, knowing the guide's good peripheral vision would pick up that she was there. That would save Molly from having to look behind her.

Molly was leading, but Kate felt like a shepherd with one sheep.

She had a flash of her father, when she was a child. They were out hiking in the Catalinas and met a man with a dog on the trail. Kate had loved the dog, a border collie, and while she was petting it the man said it had "sticky eye."

"I know a good vet," her father said, and the man laughed.

"No, it's not a disease. She flunked out of sheep school because she'd focus on one sheep and the rest of the flock could go over a cliff for all she cared. Kind of a doggie version of OCD, obsessive-compulsive disorder. Like some people can't see the forest for the trees? She couldn't see the flock for one sheep."

Kate smiled at the memory, but her heart was full of longing.

They stopped only once. Molly had put her phone, in its transparent pouch, under the bungee cords forward of the cockpit. When she saw they had cell coverage, she called Shag and asked him to meet her at the Floodwood Road landing. It was her right ankle that was injured, making it difficult for her to drive.

Kate lost herself in the rhythm of paddling, the comforting smell of a wild lake. The boats cut through the water below, through the long shadows of islands above. The day's breeze abated.

Roger must have paddled this route many times, thinking of his father; perhaps he simply banished the painful memories and fostered the earlier, pleasant ones. The cabin's contents suggested that was his strategy.

He'd had twice as many years with his father as she'd had with hers, but his was harsh, judgmental. She was unlucky in one way and far more fortunate in another. She had been loved.

How long had it taken Roger to build his shrine? One season, two? Of course he was fit, capable and driven enough to work in winter, so it wasn't necessarily a matter of seasons.

After he'd finished the cabin, he'd become two people. One was social—ran a business, dealt with employees and customers, got involved in community issues, even dated a few women at times. The other Roger was wounded and withdrawn, grieving for a father who, even before a final, failed deployment, had abandoned his son.

South Portage was a village, and even Saranac Lake wasn't a big town. Someone local had to have killed Roger. Kate felt she knew him better than she had before this trip, but her insights didn't suggest any new leads. Kenny Smallwood had to be looked into. And Dusty, the guide who'd quit Boat Camp. Tate had dismissed Dusty as a suspect, but Kate wasn't convinced a cheerful personality gave anyone a pass. The rejected applicants for guide jobs needed to be checked out. Amber had the names, but maybe Kate could help her out somehow.

She wanted to do something. Her life wouldn't be right until Ellen was cleared of this crazy crime.

The day was fading. Kate worried about Molly. She'd given herself a nasty sprain, and it was almost impossible to paddle without putting at least some pressure on that leg, that ankle—bracing against the foot pegs was how good paddlers recruited their whole bodies into the paddle stroke.

An engine whined in the distance. They really should have lights on their boats if they were going to be out this late. She'd thought to put a flashlight next to her seat before they started back, and she could put on a headlamp and offer her spare to Molly. They hadn't seen much boat traffic all day, only those canoes with lines over the side. But those fishermen would be heading home about now.

The engine was coming their way. Kate glanced back. The power boat had no lights either.

Then she recognized a configuration of rocks she'd mentally flagged as a subject for a future drawing session, and knew they were nearly back to the Floodwood landing. What a relief. Never mind stopping to get out the headlamps—better to get the heck off the water.

Now the engine was much closer.

Molly looked over her shoulder. "What's he doing?" she yelled.

Kate looked back. The boat was coming right at them. It wasn't that big, maybe eighteen feet, with a little windshield and a wheel like a car's. She grabbed the flashlight and pointed it at the windshield, turning it on and off and on.

The boat didn't slow. The beam of her light showed her a figure standing at the wheel.

Steering directly for them.

The engine was deafeningly, frighteningly loud.

Adrenalin surged through her like electricity. Molly had turned toward land, even though they were short of the landing site. She was paddling hard, opening a stretch of dark water between the two kayaks as she headed for water too shallow for an outboard. But there wasn't time.

Maybe the power boater wouldn't actually hit them. Was he just out to scare them? He could be drunk, or playing a joke, but Kate didn't think so.

She put all her anger at the threatening creep into her strokes, catching up to Molly.

"Stop!" she shouted.

Molly kept paddling. Maybe she hadn't heard.

Kate glanced back. The powerboat was so close that she was looking up at it. She had seconds.

Kate ducked under Molly's left paddle blade and slid her own paddle in front of the guide's cockpit, then leaned hard on the shaft. Now the two kayaks were rafted. Held under the pressure of Kate's paddle, they were fixed together like one boat. Double-hulled. Stable.

The power boat's flared bow swept over Kate's head. A wall of spray slammed into her, and the wake swatted the two kayaks sideways, lifting them in a welter of foam, and then dropped them abruptly into the backwash.

The stink of exhaust hit Kate in the face and she coughed.

"Are you okay?" Molly was coughing, too.

Kate had managed to keep the two kayaks together during the worst of the turbulence, but they'd slipped apart at the end. Her open boat was half-filled. While her paddling jacket had deflected the spray, cold water wicked up her long underwear and she was wet to her knees.

Feeling sick from fumes and tension, she watched the boat race away. Without running lights it was only a dark smudge above the dim fan of its wake.

Silence returned, or the almost-silence of watery places. Into it both women heaved big sighs, noticed that they'd done so in unison, and smiled.

"Thanks for thinking of rafting," Molly said. "We'd both have capsized if you hadn't done that." Twilight had turned her maroon boat black, her face and hands pale gray.

"I was betting he wasn't going to hit us. If he wanted to do that, there was no way to stop him," Kate said. "Hey, can I borrow your hand pump? I don't know where mine's gone, and I'm practically awash here."

On the first stroke of the pump Kate squirted Molly in the chest. "Oh! Sorry. The light's gotten so bad I couldn't see where the outlet was." Stupid not to feel for it; she must be rattled.

No surprise there.

"What the heck, Kate, I'm nice and dry inside this jacket. Employee discount means good gear." The guide laughed. "Hey, how about I sell you a boat somebody didn't forget to put a deck on?"

"That's okay, I like this one. Decks are heavy." She turned the pump to the other side and shot water out of her boat, working fast to warm herself up. "I'm glad we're not swimming."

"He saw us just in time," Molly said. "Must be drunk as a skunk."

Kate disagreed, but didn't say so. From now on she'd be careful not to put her friends in danger.

She'd bet her boat she'd just encountered Roger Benedict's killer for the second time.

SEVENTEEN

It was fully dark by the time they got back to the landing. Shag must have called Tate, because both men had come in Tate's Honda and were waiting for them. Shag helped Molly out of her boat and gave her a big hug.

Kate was grateful for their help. She had the easy job of throwing gear into the truck as the men hefted Molly's boat into the bed of the pick-up.

"Thank you guys so much," Kate said. "I was wiped out even before we nearly got run over by some crazy power boater."

"We saw," Shag said. "You were lucky. Guy must have been drunk." He rubbed the top of his head vigorously. "Or thought he was being funny, to scare a couple of girls. What a jerk."

"It was too dark for him to know we're girls," Molly said.

"He did it deliberately," Tate said. "I saw his lights go off when he was still quite a ways out. And then he aimed right for the kayaks." He looked at Kate with concern.

"Hey, Molly, I know you know to keep that leg elevated," Kate said. "Put some real ice on it, okay? Thanks for going on such a great trip with me. It was beautiful out there."

"Sure," Molly said, sounding uncertain. "Great" probably wouldn't be her choice of adjective for the day. "See you later." Shag helped her into the truck and then climbed in himself and gunned the engine. The big truck lurched onto Floodwood and sped into the night.

If Molly hadn't gotten injured, she'd have gone ashore on Hermit and seen Roger's memorial to his father. Kate would have been okay with that. Roger's big secret didn't have to be a secret anymore. But since Molly hadn't gone ashore, probably Mrs. Benedict should be the first to be told where all the photos of her husband had gone.

Then again, maybe it was a good thing Molly didn't know. She would have told Shag, and Shag was still on Kate's short list of suspects. As much as she liked him, he'd resented Roger's treatment of him and he'd been at Boat Camp the morning Roger died. Motive and opportunity.

Tate's voice brought her out of her thoughts, and she realized how cold she was.

"Hey, you're thinking so hard you aren't here any more," he said. He gave her a kiss, a small one, just enough to promise more. "Want to tell me about it?"

"Maybe," she said.

"Be like that."

He shouldered her boat and she picked up her drybag and PFD and they walked to her camper, their flashlights showing the way over the many roots at the edge of Middle Pond.

After extracting a promise that he wouldn't pass her story on to Shag, or anyone else, she told Tate about Roger's cabin. "I'd like to tell Mrs. Benedict first," Kate said. "It only seems right."

"I'm with you there," he said. Then he smiled a delicious smile. "I'm with you kind of everywhere, aren't I?" He touched her arm, then her cheek. "Here, and here, and here, too. . ."

Dinner was late that night.

* * *

Before he left the next morning, Tate said, "Hey. You want to paddle out there and get those photos back for Mrs. Benedict?"

Kate groaned. "Great idea, but I ache all over. Give me a day or two to recover from my paddle and portage marathon."

"Wimp," he said with a grin.

Remembering she'd promised to keep an eye on Ellen's camper, Kate drove to the Fish Creek campground and reclaimed the site adjacent to the Toyota. She got out the drawing she'd done of Ellen resting beside the creek after their lunch with Molly and Shag. That pleasant paddle seemed years ago. Kate lost herself in the work, putting a kayak in the background below a tangle of branches. But when she paused after an hour to make a pot of coffee, her eyes filled as she looked at her friend's peaceful face.

The long trip to Hermit Island the day before had given Kate something to do, kept her from thinking about what a terrible situation Ellen was in. Doing almost always beat thinking. That's why she was working on her art, but maybe she should choose a different piece.

She was flipping through her sketchbook when a knock on the door startled her. Gurgling from the coffeemaker must have kept her from hearing a car drive up.

Remembering the frightening figure behind Roger's apartment and the attempt to capsize her, she pushed the curtain up and had a look at her visitor.

Roger's brother.

She unlocked the door. "Hey, Will, nice to see you."

"Likewise, Kate. Can I have a few minutes of your time?"

She didn't know what to expect from a talk with Will; he couldn't be discounted as a suspect himself. "Sure," she said. "It's so nice outside, let's sit at the picnic table. Coffee? You've got good timing—I made a fresh pot."

"Yes, thanks."

She poured two cups and handed them out to him, then climbed down and joined him on the wooden seat. Her boat, keel-up on the table, left enough room for cups and elbows.

Working inside, she hadn't realized how warm it was. "What a glorious day," she said. "How did you know where to find me?"

"When I was talking to Ellen at the cookout, she mentioned this campground. I figured you'd be here, too."

She sipped her coffee. "So what's up?"

"I've been staying with my mother this weekend. She's doing better than I expected—a friend recommended a therapist, who seems to be helping."

"That's good," Kate said. "She'd been through a lot even before this."

He nodded. "She hasn't been reading the paper because she doesn't want to know anything about—about what happened to Roger."

"I can understand that."

"So she doesn't know what everybody else in town knows, and it was a big surprise to her when I mentioned that Ellen was a journalist." He got up. "Excuse me, I'm way too warm." He took off his dark blue jacket and tossed it over the kayak. "She said Roger hated reporters."

"Really? That's a surprise," Kate said. "He flattered Ellen—flattered us both—about our jobs. Said we were 'word heroes.' His phrase."

"Strange." Will took a hit of coffee. "So that's why I'm here. My mother wanted to know if you're sure Roger didn't know Ellen from some encounter in the past." He looked sheepish. "I'm being a bit of an amateur detective here. I hope you don't mind. I'm asking you because you're more available than Ellen."

"No problem." Kate gave him what she hoped passed for a smile. If he killed his brother, what was he doing here? Hoping to undermine Kate's belief in Ellen's innocence? Had his mother really sent him?

"Of course if I found out anything useful I'd take it straight to the police," Will said. "The real detective, that big guy, um—"

"Jordan."

"That's it, Detective Jordan. He came out to talk to Mum." Will swept his hair off his forehead. Was he sweating?

"I'm sure they didn't know each other before Tuesday night at the Put-In," Kate said. "And Roger seemed to be impressed by us being reporters—I mean, Ellen is, and I was until nine months ago."

Will frowned. "That's odd. Once Mum mentioned it, I remembered that he wasn't a fan of journalists. He got upset about some series in the Syracuse paper on homeless veterans—"

"He brought that up, Tuesday night. Ellen wrote those stories."

Will shook his head. "He told me, back then, that the *Sentinel* was nosing around where it shouldn't go. He thought the vets were being put in a bad light."

"So you're thinking maybe Ellen and Roger got into a fight about her reporting?" She didn't need to tell him that Ellen had said they hadn't.

"That's where I was going with this, but why did he date her if he hated reporters? And hated her specifically, because of the series she wrote?" He sighed and stroked his camera absently. "I can't imagine Ellen killed him. Neither can my mother. She wanted me to ask you about them maybe knowing each other in the past because she wants to know the truth."

"I don't think they did. The situation doesn't make sense," Kate said slowly. "Unless he meant to poison her, in retaliation for the articles she wrote, and something went wrong with his plan."

Will snorted, then caught himself. "I'd say that's absurd, but I guess I should keep an open mind, because the whole situation strikes me as absurd. I can't believe he's gone." He looked at the lake for a long moment, then back at Kate. "He did seek you out, right?"

"Yes, he came over to our table, he was so nice—" Kate's throat got tight as she remembered what a great time they'd all had. "It's a lousy word, 'nice,' but he was so sweet and intelligent and funny. Ellen and I talked on the way back to the campground about how amazing it was to have met him, out here in the woods. No offense."

"What? Oh, none taken. I grew up here, but I'm from Burlington now."

They looked at each other. His family resemblance to Roger was unsettling.

"What was his history with women?" Kate asked. "If you don't mind talking about it." Will wasn't the only one who could play amateur detective.

"Hey, privacy is kind of out the window here, right? I mean, we're talking murder."

"We are."

Will sighed. "He hadn't dated anybody seriously for a few years. There was a period when he was more active—or at least he told me more. Okay, I'll do it chronologically. Ages of Roger. But first I need more coffee. This is good stuff."

Kate got up. "Ouch," she said. "You're lucky I can lurch to the camper. I paddled from dawn to dark yesterday." She brought the pot out and filled both cups. "Let me guess. The first Age of Roger would be growing up tough, aiming to be a Navy special operations guy?"

Will looked startled. "Yeah. How did you know?"

"Some of the guides were talking about it," Kate said. No need to single out Tate as her source. Or name Ellen.

"He trained hard in high school and college, then the Navy turned him down, right?"

"Yeah. Phase one, Man of Iron. Phase two, Navy rejection turns him into a wild guy. Didn't have a job, lived outdoors, God knows where, alone. He had the skills. Dad was away a lot—we think he volunteered for risky missions. My sister and mother fought like cats, then my sister moved away."

"Not an easy time for you, I bet."

"I had my own place by then, I'd gotten a job at the grocery store, but at holidays and birthdays and stuff, when I came back, you're right, it wasn't fun. I started taking pictures because it gave me a way out. Made me an observer, instead of part of that disaster of a family." He touched the Leica again. "Like a duck blind."

"Gotcha."

"Phase Three, which is the most amazing. Dad's declared MIA. The Wild Man comes out of the woods, scrawny and strong. Moves in with Mum. Shaves off his beard. Gets civilized. Decides to open a business, Mum stakes him some dough and he sets up Boat Camp. Bingo. He's Mr. Businessman, hiring people, getting involved in the town. Even some politics, to stop an overenthusiastic mayor from selling the town to the highest bidder.

"That's when he dated two, maybe three girls—sorry, I mean women," he corrected himself as Kate arched an eyebrow. "They stuck with him four, six months. One made it a year, but when they split up she left town.

"Then Phase Four, he put an apartment over the store, moved in, and a few months later stopped dating. Until Ellen."

"That's quite an evolution," Kate said. "The woman he dated who left town—do you remember her name?" Maybe she'd come back, with revenge on her agenda.

"Karen something." Will looked at the sky. "Karen, Karen—Wright? Or Wrightson. Not sure which."

"Thanks." Maybe Amber would know the name. Leaving town after the break-up of a relationship might be a sign of strong emotion. "The last phase was what, a couple years?"

"Right. Oh, I told you at the cookout that all the photos of Dad disappeared, right after Roger moved in with Mum. She was sure he took them, had me go over and look around Boat Camp and then later his apartment when he added it above the store. I looked everywhere. Maybe he threw them into a dumpster. He must have been angry at Dad, although he'd never say so."

"Why angry?" Will might know more than Tate.

"For how he was treated after the Navy rejected him. Dad barely spoke to him."

"That's—extreme," Kate said.

"Dad was an extreme kind of guy," Will said. "You have to be, if you do what he did for a living." He rubbed his face with his hands. "It was a hard time for all of us. My sister and I, we were used to Dad ignoring us, but Roger wasn't. He really suffered. I'm sure he would have been diagnosed with major depression if he'd gotten within ten feet of a doctor. But of course he never did."

"Ellen called him complicated," Kate said. "I guess she was right."

"We all have layers, but his were maybe a bit more—I can't think of a word to describe it. Out of whack with each other."

"Complicated?" Kate asked.

He smiled. "Ellen's word pretty much says it. Probably in the kindest way."

"She's a kind person," Kate said, keeping her voice even.

Kate's boat buzzed loudly and she jumped. Will grabbed his jacket off the upturned hull and fished a cell phone from one of the pockets. With the phone in his hand, the vibrations were quieter, like bursts of a cat's purr instead of a power drill.

"My mother," Will said, looking up from the screen. "She keeps a short leash on her offspring. I don't know how Roger could stand living with her as long as he did." He got up and tucked his phone back in the jacket pocket. "Thanks, Kate. Ellen and Roger didn't know each other before last Tuesday. I don't know where that gets us, but Mum has her answer."

Kate stood and stretched. "Your mother has faced some difficulties nobody should have to face. No wonder she's intense sometimes. Ellen told me about the birthday parties for your father."

"Birthday parties?"

"Didn't your mother invite you and Roger and your sister to parties for your father, even after he was declared MIA?"

"No. Where on earth did you get that idea?"

"Oh, I must have misunderstood something Ellen said."

She hadn't misunderstood. Roger had told Ellen that story. Was he trying to make his mother look bad? Did he have difficulty relating well to women?

His jacket over his arm, Will took a few steps, slowly, as if he were still thinking. "Is there anything else I should know, as I go about pretending to be a detective?"

He was definitely fishing. Out of concern for the truth? Or to make sure Ellen's role as murder suspect was secure? Impossible to tell.

"Can't think of anything," Kate said. "Thank you for believing Ellen's innocent." Amber had explained that the law's categories were *guilty* and *not guilty*, but *innocent* still seemed like the right word.

"I wonder if you'd be willing to talk to my mother," Will said. "She thinks it would help her come to terms with what's happened."

"Oh?" Kate was startled. "I don't know what I could tell her that would help."

"Honestly, I'm not sure either. But I said I'd ask you."

Kate hadn't liked Mrs. Benedict much, but she did feel sorry for her. It couldn't do any harm to talk to the woman. She shrugged. "All right." She said her phone number aloud, twice.

Will repeated it and nodded. "Got it," he said. "Thanks, Kate. I'll let her know."

She followed him around the back of her camper, where he'd parked his car.

A big orange Hummer.

She was glad she was behind him, so he didn't see the momentary shock on her face. On Paul's Way, with the moonlight blocked by trees, Ellen could easily have seen red instead of orange. And the Hummer had plenty of road clearance, the one thing she'd remembered about the vehicle that passed her.

Will opened the vehicle's door and paused. "Please let me know if you hear anything. Unlike my mother I read the paper, the online version. But you're closer to the action." He took a business card out of his shirt pocket and held it out to her.

She didn't respond for a second. She'd been sizing him up. He was about the right height, and build—okay, so were three-quarters of the men in South Portage. But still—he could have been the man at the edge of the woods behind Roger's apartment.

"Kate?"

"Oh. Sorry." She took the business card, gave him a smile. "Hey, that's a nice jacket. Patagonia?"

"Yeah, thanks. It's pretty new."

Biting back the urge to ask him exactly what day he'd gotten it, Kate smiled like the clothes-horse she wasn't. "Could I have a look at it? I need a new jacket myself."

"Sure. Here you go."

"I bet it's comfy," Kate said, holding it up by the shoulders. "Lots of pockets, that's a plus. Too bad it doesn't have a hood. I'd definitely want a hood."

"Oh, it has one," Will said. "It's hidden. Rolls up and stashes away in the collar. See that zipper? That's how you get it out."

"That's great," Kate said. She handed the jacket back to Will.

"Well, thanks for the coffee." He touched his Leica like a talisman. "You'll be staying for a while, I take it?"

"I'm not sure how long," Kate said. "Playing it by ear." She suddenly didn't want to tell him anything.

EIGHTEEN

After Will left, Kate ate a piece of toast and then washed the cups and plate. She found herself staring absently out the window, thinking about Roger's family.

A father who has time for only one of his three kids and eventually throws that one away, too. Then gets himself killed, probably. A sister who flees to the North Woods and cuts off ties with her whole family. A brother who hides behind a camera, calling it his duck blind. A pretty screwed-up crew.

Kate had read that murderers are often close relatives of their victims. Will could easily be resentful of the attention lavished on his brother when they were young. Killing him now? It didn't seem likely. Unless childhood was only the background, and a more recent event had been the trigger for buried angers. She and Tate had talked about former mayor Kenny Smallwood holding a grudge, but one held from childhood could be even more intense.

Will would have had to get up in the wee hours to drive from Burlington in time to pass Ellen that morning on Paul's Way at a few minutes after five. But that wasn't impossible.

At least Kate could cross the sister in Minnesota off her list.

She peered at a bird on Square Pond. A loon, by its silhouette. Flightless now, busy replacing its famous checkerboard plumage, on which chicks had ridden last spring, with the gray-brown feathers that would carry it south in a few weeks to Florida or the Gulf Coast.

South was where Kate wanted to go, too. But first she had to free her friend.

The bird dived without a ripple, the pond surface seamless.

Like Roger, the water had its secrets.

* * *

At the police station in South Portage she asked to talk to Detective Jordan, and after fifteen minutes' wait she was sitting across from him in the room with security cameras.

"You have some information for me regarding the Waters case?"

So it was the Waters case now, not the Benedict case. "I've been trying to find out a little more about Roger Benedict," Kate said. "And I've found out quite a bit."

The pudgy hands were folded on the bare table. No notepad. "Yes?"

"He had a cabin, a rustic place he must have built himself, on one of the islands. Its walls were covered with pictures of his father, and he also had a box of his father's medals."

Jordan shifted in his chair, which creaked. "I don't see your point."

Kate leaned forward. "Roger Benedict seemed to be a normal guy. But there was something wrong with him. He was unbalanced." That sounded too strong. She couldn't think of the right word.

The detective's face showed no reaction.

"The things in that cabin? He stole them all from his mother."

The detective sighed. "Even if what you say is true, I don't see why it matters to this investigation."

"Roger wasn't who he appeared to be. He had a secret life. And if he had a secret life, it's easy to imagine he had friends you don't know about. Some of whom might have had a lot more motivation to do away with him than Ellen Waters had."

"Ms. Corliss, I realize this is a difficult time for you and your friend. But I'm afraid I don't find your information helpful." Jordan stood up. "That Mr. Benedict built a cabin to store pictures of his father may be of interest on a personal level to his friends, but it has no bearing on those of us conducting an investigation into his murder."

Alone, Kate slumped in the chair. She had to admit that what she'd told the detective sounded lame. But her instincts screamed it was important. Elbows on thighs, hands in her hair, she urged her mind to come up with the next step.

If Ellen were free, the two of them would talk this over and figure it out, the way they used to discuss stories they were writing for the *News,* getting a new angle or finding a thread of logic that made sense of a tangle of facts.

Then Kate thought of the next-best thing to talking with Ellen.

* * *

She went outside and bought a newspaper. The small article on the front of the local section, "Murder Investigation Continues," said Ellen had been indicted "based on evidence the District Attorney's office has not yet made public."

Kate sat for a minute and made a mental list of the things she couldn't tell anyone because she'd learned them from her conference with Ellen and Amber. There weren't many items: the fact of Roger's message, what it said, his coffee being untainted, his phone in Ellen's purse and her make-up in his bathroom.

The physical evidence, that was all. Not that those things were evidence of anything, in Kate's opinion. Physical facts. Since they were all of one kind, it would be easy to remember to keep her mouth shut about them.

But she knew quite a lot about Roger she'd found out on her own.

* * *

The *Adirondack Daily Star* was easy to find, both online on her phone and physically, across Broadway from the post office. It was a small white building with the paper's name in large masthead-style lettering.

Opening its green door, Kate scolded herself. She should have called, gotten an appointment with someone.

Then she thought of Ellen, fighting depression in a jail cell. Capable Ellen, sleeping because her life was too awful to stay awake in. Coming here was the least Kate could do. If it turned out she needed an appointment, she'd make one.

At the front desk, she asked to speak to a reporter.

"You have something for us?" The woman behind the desk was older, maybe fifty, with a crest of bronze hair admitting a few silver threads. She'd folded up her copy of the *Star* when Kate pushed through the front door. A silky jacket brought out colors from the woman's hair—umbers and golds.

"Yes, I do," Kate said.

The bronze-haired woman spoke into a desk phone, and another woman, much younger, came into the reception area from the large room behind it. She wore a long blue jacket over a skirt.

The dress code was intimidating, but Kate stepped forward and held out her hand, trying to forget she was wearing jeans and a fleece. "Kate Corliss," she said. "I have some information I think you'll find useful."

"Sure, follow me." The reporter looked like she'd graduated from college last week. She walked quickly. "I'm Laura. What's up?" she said, settling at a desk and motioning Kate to a chair.

Laura's office was tiny, off the large open room in which a herd of desks supported computers, phones, and piles of paper. Only two people were at work even though there was space for ten: the *Star* was a morning paper. A police scanner squawked on a corner shelf.

Filled with nostalgia, Kate turned back to Laura. For a moment she wasn't sure where to start. "I'm a friend of Ellen Waters, the woman accused—"

"Yes." Laura's face sharpened with interest. "I know who she is."

"Ah, good. It looks bad for her, but I'm sure she didn't do it. I've been collecting information."

"Shoot." Laura pulled a lined pad of paper toward her.

Kate gave the information she'd gathered on her own, starting with Benedict family background from Tate and Will. "I'm sure you know a lot of this already," she said, but Laura was writing and didn't look up, so Kate continued.

She described Dan and the unpleasant encounter she and Ellen had had with him, the map she'd found in Roger's apartment, and the cabin on Hermit Island. Then the two alarming incidents—a man lurking behind Boat Camp and a power boater trying to capsize her kayak.

"Wow." Laura put down her pen, then picked it back up. "Did you tell the police about that cabin?"

"I tried to," Kate said. "They didn't want to know."

"You must have talked to Detective Jordan."

"You got it."

"What about the power boat? Did you tell him that?"

Kate shrugged. "No way to identify it." Laura hadn't asked about the man at Boat Camp—she knew telling the police about him would be confessing to breaking and entering, or at least trespassing.

The two women looked at each other. Something was happening between them.

"I was a reporter, until a few months ago, in Massachusetts. Got laid off. I know how important local knowledge is. You can see things I can't."

Laura glanced at her watch.

"Oh, I'm sorry," Kate said. "Do you have to—"

"Want to get lunch? My stomach's growling like an Adirondack bear."

Kate was thrilled. She had a new ally.

* * *

They went to a small café and Laura laid out a few ideas. For one thing, there were cottages on Paul's Way beyond Boat Camp. They were fancy places, second homes of wealthy families. So the SUV wasn't necessarily the murderer's vehicle.

"Damn," Kate said.

"Think of it this way. You must be on the right track, or whoever this hooded guy is, he wouldn't have followed you to Roger's apartment or tried to run you over with a boat."

"That's a good thought," Kate said, and shivered. She realized she'd avoided thinking that she must have been followed the night she found the map in Roger's office. "But maybe it was a coincidence that the guy showed up at Roger's the same night I did."

"You think so?" The look on Laura's face said she didn't. "What, the guy's a burglar who stands around Roger's place waiting for a fellow burglar to unlock the door for him?"

"I guess not," Kate laughed.

"So where did you park, or camp, or whatever, that night?" Laura obviously wasn't into RVs.

"One of those free places on Floodwood Road," Kate said. "Oh, you're thinking whoever followed me, he camped there too? If that's the case, then it wasn't Dan. I sure as heck would have noticed a yellow Corvette." She sat up straighter. "Unless he's using some other vehicle. Something ordinary."

Laura smiled. "Yep. Don't camp there again, because it's remote. Too bad it doesn't have a register we can check for the names of people staying there. You should move to the Fish Creek campground and keep your eyes open. We can find out who else is there. The entrance is staffed during the day, and state park police make rounds at night, so help would be a lot closer there than at Floodwood."

"Good advice. Thanks."

"And the SUV is still important. The timing is highly suspicious. Could have been the brother's. Or what if one of those downstate cottage owners had a grudge against Roger? There can be all kinds of issues between neighbors. Believe me, Roger wasn't happy when he had to allow an easement for those folks to drive through to their fancy homes."

"I'll bet he wasn't," Kate said. "He liked his privacy."

"Maybe Roger came out, running after Ellen to talk to her some more. What if he was in the road and got into an argument with the SUV driver?

She thought of Tate's story about Roger shooting the porcupine. "He had a temper, but I don't think he showed it very often. Still, he was already upset about whatever had gone wrong between him and Ellen. But if he fought with a neighbor wouldn't one of them haul off and punch the other? A physical fight. Not poison."

"Well, maybe the neighbor was a stubborn bastard who'd been carrying a little vial around for a while trying to figure out how to use it on Roger. He could have said he was willing to make some change to the easement, lured Roger back up to the apartment, and doctored his—what? I don't know—coffee, maybe. Or overpowered him and forced him to swallow something. The way I give a pill to my cat."

Kate kept the lid on what she knew from Amber about the harmless coffee. "He was fit, and strong. I'd bet on him to win most fights."

"Or what about this?" Laura said. "However it was done, it was opportunistic: a neighbor saw a chance to get back at Roger and have Ellen take the blame, since she'd just left."

"Yikes. You should write movie scripts. You come up with plots by the handful."

"Thanks," Laura said. "I do better than movies. I write real life." Her face was grim.

* * *

Walking back to her truck, Kate said aloud, "Hope is the thing with feathers." Where did that come from? Probably the lyrics to some rock song, although she couldn't remember its tune.

She drove back toward Fish Creek Pond in a good mood. She not only had an ally, she had an ally with ideas. Laura was going to find out the names of the people who owned properties beyond Boat Camp, and Kate would pass that information on to Amber. Laura had agreed that it was better not to let Ellen's attorney know Kate was talking to a *Star* reporter for now. Later on, when Ellen was cleared, Laura would probably expect Kate to provide full details, the inside story from someone close to the falsely accused. Maybe she would want to talk to Ellen then, too, but that of course was up to Ellen.

For the first time since Detective Jordan said Ellen was suspected of Roger's murder, Kate was optimistic about getting to the bottom of it all.

The GPS showed a different route back to Fish Creek, and Kate followed it for the change of scene. North on Route 86, then a sharp left onto 186. An ice cream store came up on the left, before the intersection. With nobody on the road behind her, she braked hard and turned. The road was high compared to the lot, and the truck's nose dropped sharply as she drove in.

Celebrating the day's progress with a hit of soft-serve was perfect. At lunch with Laura she'd had a salad, so she got a small cone instead of a medium. Sometimes being good encouraged her to be good.

It was a splendid day, and she leaned against the side of the truck, inhaling the papery odor of fall leaves and letting sunshine soften the ice cream between licks. The sun felt good on her jeans and purple fleece, too, like a big heating pad—she was still a little sore from the long paddle with Molly.

Feeling better than she had in a week, Kate pulled back onto the empty road.

A huge bang came from behind her.

Then another bang, even louder. What the heck? She looked in her rear-view mirror.

Behind her, only sky. The camper was gone.

NINETEEN

What on earth? Kate turned and looked out the cab's back window. The camper was squatting in the road behind the truck. The two bangs must have been the rear jack legs hitting the pavement as it slid out of the truck bed, followed by the front legs.

Thank God this hadn't happened with another vehicle behind her.

How could the camper have gotten loose? It was held in place by four big hooks that went through holes in tabs welded to the truck. Adjustable turnbuckles pulled the hooks tight.

No time to figure it out now. She pulled off the road, put on the truck's emergency flashers, and grabbed three bright orange plastic triangles from under the front seat. First time she'd ever used them. She unfolded them as she ran in front of the camper, which was angled across the southbound lane, and spaced them out along the road on the north side of the newly created road hazard.

She didn't see much damage to the camper. The round foot of one of the back legs looked a little bent, that was all. The leg itself appeared straight.

Then she saw the bundle of wires hanging under the camper. Rats.

Normal procedure for unloading a slide-in camper like Kate's calls for unplugging its electrical connection to the truck, then loosening the turnbuckles and unhooking them.

At that point nothing holds the camper in place except gravity. The next step is lengthening the camper's jack legs until they hit the ground and take the weight off the truck, lifting the camper so the truck can be driven out from under it.

In this case, the pigtail of wires had been yanked out by the camper's momentum as it slid onto the road. The plug itself was no doubt still in the outlet in the truck bed, but the ripped-out wires hung from the front of the camper, torn ends glittering.

She called 911, but someone in the store must have already called, because a police car pulled up in minutes.

"So what happened here?" He looked amused. He was probably thinking Stupid Tourist.

"I haven't figured it out yet, but I've driven this rig for years off and on, and then full-time since the beginning of August. Never had a problem before," Kate said.

"You'll need a flatbed," the cop said, and spoke into the mike clipped to his shirt.

Damn. That was going to be expensive. But he was right. Without power to the jacks to extend the legs and raise the camper up high enough for the truck to fit underneath it, the camper was a helpless orphan.

The turnbuckles were hanging loose, and Kate peered at one of them. "Look at this," she said over her shoulder. "This was loosened a lot, recently. The metal threading that goes through the, um, whatever you call the thing in the middle—there's half an inch that's clean and shiny. You can see by the light coat of rust where the thread used to sit."

"I see what you mean," the cop said. "You didn't loosen them?"

"No. Why would I do that? It would be incredibly stupid, not to mention dangerous, to drive around with loose turnbuckles. And it's going to cost me a bunch."

"So what you're saying is somebody tampered with your equipment."

"That's what I'm saying." Kate looked around. "Not while I was in there, getting ice cream. That only took a minute, and I was out here the rest of the time. It would have taken a while to loosen all four turnbuckles."

"Where was the vehicle before that?"

"It was parked in Saranac Lake for a couple-three hours. I bet that's when somebody did this. But why didn't the camper come loose sooner?"

"I'm betting you're a gentle driver. Easy on the gas, easy on the brake, right?"

"Right. Oh, wait, I saw the ice-cream sign and braked hard. Hard for me, anyway. There was nobody behind me, so I could. I braked hard and turned in."

"That's probably what did it. With the turnbuckles loose, the camper only had to shift a little for the hooks to drop out of the brackets." He gestured at the edge of the pavement. "This road sits higher than the parking lot, and besides that it has a high crown to help it drain. So when you came out of there, the front end of your truck was lifted, and—boom." He nodded, satisfied he'd figured it out.

"Actually, more like boom BOOM," Kate said.

He smiled. "Whereabouts in Saranac Lake did you park?"

"In front of the post office."

"Hmm. That's a pretty busy place. I'll check to see if there are any security cameras on the building." He thought a moment. "People passing by might have thought the perp was working on his own camper, making it safer. They'd have to watch for a bit to see he was actually doing the opposite."

"I hope he's a film star on security camera footage," Kate said. "Or the digital equivalent."

"Smart thinking, putting out those reflective triangles and getting your truck off the road." The officer nodded again. "Good luck with getting it put back together. The flatbed driver will recommend a couple of garages that can help you out."

"Thanks," Kate said.

"I'll be in the cruiser, writing this up, until he gets here."

"Okay." Kate considered telling him about the power-boater and her belief that somebody was targeting her because she was looking into Roger's murder. And that Dan was at the top of her list of suspects. But she didn't remember Dan's last name, she didn't have a shred of info that could identify the boat, and she certainly didn't want to say she'd been followed when she'd broken into Roger's apartment.

No, she'd have to be careful. Keep her eyes open, see if she could get a look at her stalker's face, or anything about him that would lead to an ID.

Forty-five minutes later, a flatbed pulled into the parking lot. Kate could see an employee at the glass door of the ice cream store looking out at the excitement. She should go in and thank whoever had called 911.

The cruiser had moved north of the marooned camper, blue lights flashing.

The flatbed driver was tall and lanky, wearing a wrinkled blue shirt with "Ron" embroidered in white—or what used to be white—on the pocket.

"So why'd you park your camper in the road?" He had shrewd blue eyes and a sharp face, with acne scars under stubble.

"Well, the turnbuckles—"

Ron laughed and waved a hand. "Relax, I'm pulling your leg. Let's check this out." He strode to camper and looked it over, then fingered the wires hanging underneath the front corner. "You know, this is a no-parking zone. You could get a ticket."

Kate was ready for him this time. "Please, officer sir, please don't give me a ticket. I really needed an ice cream cone. I really had to stop."

He laughed. "I think I've got just the thing." He went to his truck and pulled something heavy out of an outside compartment. He thumped the big box on the ground next to the camper.

"That looks like a battery to go," Kate said, when she saw the coppery jaws of alligator clips, one tucked into each end of the box.

"You might be right about that." Ron spread out the ends of the wires in the bundle hanging from her camper and chose two. To these he attached his portable battery with much smaller versions of the big alligator clips Kate had noticed. "Where's the remote for the jacks? I think we can put this puppy up in the air for you."

"Fantastic." With the "puppy" up high, Kate could back the truck under it and drive the camper to a garage herself. She unlocked the door and got the remote, pushed the button and watched the camper tilt a little as the front left leg extended.

"Hey, great," she called to Ron, and moved the right leg up.

It took a few minutes to get the camper high enough. Kate moved around, raising each corner a bit at a time, with the front always a little higher than the back.

Ron watched her, arms folded. Then he waved. "That looks good," he said.

Kate was glad the cruiser was still there. Only a few cars had come along, but they'd slowed down, crawling south past the camper in the northbound lane. Now she had to move the truck onto the southbound side of the road to back it under the camper.

Getting a truck to line up perfectly with a slide-in camper is tricky. Kate hadn't done it all that many times because she'd lived in a city and stored the camper on the truck. She was very aware of Ron and the cop in the cruiser watching her as she edged the truck back, glancing between the two side mirrors. The clearance between the camper legs and the side of the truck was about half an inch. She did not want to screw this up.

Ron was watching from behind her, standing near the front of the camper. He gave her a grin and a thumbs-down sign in the driver's-side mirror.

She pulled out and tried again. It was like trying to thread a needle. A huge needle, and a thread that was only slightly less wide. She wished her truck was new enough to have a back-up camera, one with red lines to show the truck's projected position.

Second try. Ron's thumb went down, and his grin was bigger. If she blew it again, she'd have to ask him to do it. She couldn't keep him and the cop here all day.

The third time she got it. Ron gave her the closed-fist sign to stop. She wiped her forehead and jumped out.

Ron was already using the remote, which she'd left on the back step of the camper. Her little house was humming first at this corner, then the next, as its legs shortened and it settled onto the truck bed. The Ford sank on its suspension as it took the weight.

"Thanks," Kate said. "You did that a lot faster than I would've." He must have dealt with a few truck campers.

He helped her more, shortening the turnbuckles, getting the hooks lined up in the holes, and cranking down tight. He didn't ask how the accident had happened, but he could see how loose the turnbuckles were. When they were done, he said "You could get some padlocks for these."

"That," Kate said, "is an excellent idea. Thanks. You've been a huge help."

"No biggie," Ron said. He picked up the battery-to-go.

Kate drove her rig to the right side of the road and parked on the shoulder, then ran back across the road to the flatbed. She waved at the cruiser as it left, its blue lights doused.

Ron was in the cab with the window open, writing on a clipboard.

He handed her a couple of business cards. "There's one of mine," he said, "which I hope you don't need. And there's one for an RV place I recommend. They work with truck campers all the time, and getting a replacement plug on those wires of yours will be a cinch."

She pulled a twenty out of her pocket and handed it up to him, but he waved it away.

"Take it, Ron," she said. "Hey, you did yourself out of a job."

"Nope, I get paid for the call, whether I bring in a big fish, a little fish, or no fish at all." He put his hand up again the second time Kate offered the bill, so she put it back in her jeans pocket.

"Thanks," Kate said. "So now I have a question."

"Shoot."

"Why'd you bring this whole darn truck with you when all you needed was the battery-to-go?"

His laughter mixed with the sound of the flatbed's big engine as he started it up.

Ron's attitude and expertise gave the day a happy ending. Kate drove back to Fish Creek thinking of ways to tell the story as if it were funny. She'd ask Marjorie and Ellen, What's the difference between a loose cannon and a loose camper?

She backed the truck into her campsite and plugged into shore power. A rock on top of the gray pedestal held down a piece of paper. A note from the campground host?

The cartoon was crude: a stick figure in a boat beside a ball with a wick at the top, a child's idea of a bomb. Underneath, the initial D, the same way the note in her coffee pot had been signed.

A chill ran through Kate. Not such a happy ending to the day after all.

TWENTY

Laura had suggested checking out the campground to find out if Dan was staying at Fish Creek, so the next morning Kate got herself out of bed early, put on long underwear under her kayaking pants and jacket, and paddled around Square Pond. Tate hadn't stayed on board the night before, and that had turned out to be fine. He was wonderful company, but he was new in her life and she wasn't used to sharing the camper's small space.

She remembered an older friend at the newspaper in Massachusetts saying to her husband, "I married you for life but not for lunch." Having some alone time was important, especially for an artist. She hadn't forgotten how long it had taken her to fight back to a habit of work after ignoring her talent for years.

It sure wasn't something she wanted to do again.

The sky was overcast but the day was off to a warm start. The campground looked busier than she'd expected. Was it the weekend? She was losing track. No, it was a Tuesday.

A family in a fifth wheel was up early, a girl around ten helping with breakfast, holding open a carton of eggs beside her mother, who cracked one on the edge of the frying pan on the grill. The smell of bacon came to Kate and she had a momentary urge for that hot, salty treat, even though she hadn't eaten meat in a couple of years. The girl's brother, around six, stood at the water's edge waving a yellow plastic shovel. Kate waved back with her paddle and his laugh bounced across the water.

Two old folks sat at the picnic table at another site, the woman still in her bathrobe and slippers. They were reading a newspaper the man must have gone out to get. They looked like an ad: a class C Winnebago in the background, coffee cups on the wooden table. Fortunately no bacon—Kate wasn't sure she could resist a second time.

Across the pond from her site, three men in their twenties sat on top of a table, facing the water, feet up on the seat. Their truck and camper were old and beat-up.

Kate paddled close to the shore. "Hi," she said.

"Morning," said the one in the middle. He appeared to be the oldest and wore a green sweatshirt with a leaning pine tree on it, a couple of sizes too big. "Early for a paddle."

"That's the way I like it," Kate said. She was telling only half a complicated truth: she did enjoy morning, the freshness in the air and in her brain. But after years as a reporter covering meetings at night—zoning boards, city council meetings—she had night-owl tendencies too.

A fourth man came out of the camper with a coffee pot in hand and a bouquet of mugs in the other. Kate's kind of guy. He passed out the cups and poured, then looked at Kate.

"Want some?" He was wearing a green sweatshirt, too. Beside the leaning pine tree, block letters said PAUL SMITH'S COLLEGE.

"Thanks, no, I'm fine," she said. "Say, have you seen any single guys camped around the lake?"

"Oh-ho," the coffee bearer said. "She's looking for single guys, guys."

"Hey, wait a minute," Kate said, laughing. "No offense, but you guys are probably ten years younger than I am. I'm looking for—a friend of a friend."

"Yeah, yeah, sure." Mr. Coffee Hound slid onto the corner of the table and bumped hips with the next man. They all scooched down to make room. "You need a better cover story."

You're right about that, she thought.

"But to answer your question, nope, haven't seen any single guys. Seen a lot of families, couples. And of course a group of alluring young studs." He grinned at her.

She laughed. "Hey, thanks, stud," she said, and took a stroke.

"Good luck, cougar girl," one of them yelled after her.

Gosh, they were young, weren't they? One-track minds.

Well, that was okay. They didn't need to know she was hunting a murderer.

She turtled the boat on the picnic table and locked its cable. Some campsites were set back from the water, so she took a walk on the road around Square Pond to check them out.

What was she was looking for? A big red SUV like the one that passed Ellen on Paul's Way as she fled from Roger would be nice. Or a single guy of medium build wearing a raincoat with a hood.

Good luck with that, girl, she told herself. Like he always wears a rain jacket, always with the hood up?

The posts at only a few sites had tags showing they were reserved. One was occupied by a big RV, a class A the size of a Greyhound bus, and two by trailers. At the site farthest from the pond, a VW camper-van was just pulling out. Nobody was hanging around outside now; it had started to rain. The vehicles parked near the trailers were pick-up trucks. Nobody here had an SUV, let alone one the right color.

Too bad Ellen hadn't gotten much of a look at the vehicle that night. But the light of a half moon on a road through dense woods hadn't been enough. And of course her state of mind wasn't the best for careful observation.

* * *

Kate checked that the turnbuckles were tight, then drove to the RV service company in Saranac Lake that Ron had recommended. She'd made an appointment, and while she waited for the repair she called Molly. The guide's ankle was much better, the swelling down substantially.

"I bet the bruise is turning all kinds of interesting colors," Kate said.

"That it is." She could hear the smile in Molly's voice. "But not being able to drive is giving me cabin fever."

After the call, Kate looked at the RV supplies on the store's shelves. The turnbuckle locks were nice-looking but expensive. Then she sat on a bench out front rather than staying in the customers' lounge with its looming TV. A bright, blue day like this one was the best place to be.

She waited less than an hour.

What a pleasure to get her house back, good as new. To a full-time RVer, a vehicle is not just a vehicle. It's home.

Her next stop was a hardware store to get some short, eye-end cables to slip around each turnbuckle hook and connect in the middle with a small padlock. That way the turnbuckles couldn't be loosened. She needed cables exactly the right length, and the hardware store was great—they let her take a couple of sizes out to try. The first two were too long, but she got it right and bought eight of them, plus four padlocks.

Fifty bucks. Ouch. She could have gotten less expensive padlocks but she didn't want to deal with four sets of keys. The locks she got had three-digit combinations, which she re-set so they were all the same.

At least Dan, or whoever had sabotaged her camper, wouldn't be able to do it again.

Or wouldn't be able to do it the same way

TWENTY-ONE

Kate sent an email to Amber, telling her about the second homes beyond Boat Camp on Paul's Way and about Roger's antipathy to the easement. Maybe the attorney already knew, being local, but it couldn't hurt to draw her attention to another group of possible suspects. Kate should have sent the information sooner, but the accident with her camper had distracted her.

Mrs. Benedict had called, and Kate had agreed to a visit. She had no idea how she could be of help, but it wasn't a bad idea to get to know the woman a bit before revealing Roger's secret cabin and returning the photos of her lost husband.

* * *

A long driveway curved into a wooded lot; the Benedict place came into view slowly. A one-story ranch, painted pale yellow with white trim, it was unremarkable except for its proximity to Lake Flower. A patio angled from the house to a small boathouse and dock, beyond which the water flashed in the sun, throwing out bright invitations to play.

At the door, Roger's mother was as tall as a waterfall, and as cool. Her face was strained and her eyes puffy, but she'd clearly pulled herself together for her visitor. She struck Kate as more dignified than the busybody she'd seemed to be at the cookout.

Her asthma must have given her a good day: after murmuring a greeting, she moved easily into the living room.

Two sofas were arranged in a V so that each had a view of the lake, with a small coffee table in the vertex between them. Mrs. Benedict waved Kate to one of the sofas and sat across from her.

"Thank you for coming." Her voice was loud; she must be hard of hearing. "I wanted to learn more about your friend Ellen. It still doesn't seem real, what's happened." She looked at the lake for a moment, twisting her wedding band. "But I need to accept it. And to do that, I need to know everything I can possibly know." She managed a small smile. "Tell me about your friend."

"First of all, I'm so very sorry about Roger," Kate said. "I met him, paddled with him, and thought he was an unusually intelligent and thoughtful man."

"Thank you." The head bowed momentarily.

"I've known Ellen for more than four years, worked with her for two, and I am completely sure than she is not someone who would end another person's life."

"Well, she's your friend, and you support her. I don't know where the truth is, but I would like to know as much as I can. How did you come to know her?"

"We were both reporters for—"

"I don't understand it." Mrs. Benedict said. "Roger detested reporters."

Irritating to be asked for information and be interrupted after a only few words. But Kate had to cut Roger's mother a good deal of slack: she had to be in gut-wrenching emotional pain, even if she was trying not to show it.

"Was it possible he didn't know that about her?" Mrs. Benedict asked.

"He knew. He stopped by our table before dinner at a restaurant downtown. We talked about her work."

The older woman shook her head. "I understood where he was coming from. I don't like reading newspapers, either. They make everything sound so—sordid. But I must come to terms with how my life has changed. We—I thought seeing you would help."

We? She might be referring to the psychologist Will had mentioned, or perhaps to Will himself. To "come to terms" with something was the sort of thing therapists helped people do, but the expression was one Kate had always found mystifying: it sounded as if a person could sit down and negotiate with difficult events.

"Please go on."

Kate went over the history of her friendship with Ellen, starting when they were both reporters for the *Danvers Daily News* in Massachusetts. How they'd spent time with each other on weekends, biking and cross-country skiing. Ellen's sense of humor and thoughtfulness. Her skill with a camera. Kate felt as if she were at a vicarious job interview, presenting Ellen's experience and achievements.

"We worked and played together," she said. "Shared ideas for stories. Ellen dated one of the photographers, picked up tips from him and got pretty good with the camera. The editors loved sending her to cover a story because they didn't have to send a photographer with her."

Mrs. Benedict nodded. "She sounds like a resourceful person."

"She is. She's a good friend, and I'm sure she did no harm to Roger. I'm trying to figure out who did."

"I hope you can discover the truth," Mrs. Benedict said. "The police seem sure Ellen is guilty, but I suppose they could be wrong. And that would be terrible." She looked at Kate with troubled eyes. "You seem like the kind of person who'd have trouble sleeping when you know a friend is in trouble."

Mrs. Benedict probably knew what it was like to have trouble sleeping. "I'm sure she's innocent," Kate said. "I'll do my best to clear her."

"Thank you for coming. I feel somewhat—clearer. It was good to meet you."

* * *

Kate went out into the crisp fall air, feeling more sympathetic to Roger's mother. She'd seemed inquisitive and a bit difficult at the cookout, but more dignified and self-possessed in this conversation. Amazing what different impressions the same person could make in public and in private. Perhaps she was as uncomfortable in crowds as Kate was, but expressed it differently, pestering Ellen with all those awkward questions.

Of course the woman's circumstances had changed completely since then. In a sense she really was a different woman.

Returning the lost pictures was the least Kate could do.

She called Tate and told him she was ready to paddle to Hermit Island, but warned him that someone had been making her life difficult and was perhaps following her. He'd been concerned about the power boater try to swamp her, and now she told him about her camper's turnbuckles being loosened.

"Why's somebody after you?" Tate asked. "Does he know you're trying to clear Ellen?"

"If it's Ellen's former boyfriend Dan hassling me, part of the reason might be that he jumped to the conclusion I'm a lesbian. He may even think I stole Ellen away from him." When Tate didn't say anything, she added, "I'm not even bi. Ellen and I are simply good friends."

"Okay. And if it isn't Dan?"

"Whether it's Dan or someone else, he has to be Roger's killer. If Ellen goes free the police will be looking at other suspects, and they might find him."

"We'll be okay on our trip," Tate said. "Some of the lakes are off-limits to engines, and of course nobody can portage a power boat. So once we get beyond the first carry we won't have to worry about a capsize attempt. We'll go in a tandem canoe, a nice long one," he said. "That'll be faster than you and Molly were in the kayaks. And we'll have more room for cargo."

"Hermit's beyond cell phone coverage, isn't it?"

"Yeah." He paused. "Thanks for letting me know about the danger this guy is to you and to anybody who's with you. We'll have to keep our eyes open."

"I grew up in Tucson, where there are plenty of guns, but I stopped carrying when I moved east. This is the first time I've wished I had one."

"I don't have a firearms license," Tate said. "But I'm thinking spear-fishing gun. Shag has one I could borrow."

"Should we wait on this? Until Roger's killer gets caught?" The thought of being out of cell phone range was giving her cold feet. But even within cell phone range, a call for help if they were attacked wouldn't bring help very fast. The area was wilderness, after all.

When Tate didn't answer right away, Kate had a feeling that he wasn't optimistic about the cops changing their minds about Ellen.

"Stop worrying. We're good. Pick you up at six?" He laughed. "That sounds like such a first-date line."

Kate laughed, too, her mood lifting a bit. Tate was reliably upbeat.

"Hey, let me fix that," he said. "I'll pick you up at six in the morning. No first-date guy says that."

The night-owl in Kate rearranged its feathers and set the alarm on her phone for five.

TWENTY-TWO

She met Tate at the Floodwood put-in. He gave her a kiss that lasted until she put her hands on his shoulders and pushed him gently away.

"I'm worried, Tate. Let's get this done first."

He'd driven a Boat Camp pick-up with a sixteen-foot aluminum canoe on its rack, along with three paddles for her. While she was deciding among them, he took two big plastic bins with lids out of the truck cab.

"Waterproof," he said. "Or so Walmart would have me believe." He laughed. "The cashier actually called them bullet-proof."

The memory of the power boat attack rushed through Kate's nerves. "Did Shag give you his spear-fishing gun?"

"No." Tate laughed. "He told me I was an idiot. It's designed to work in water, so in air it'd have one hell of a recoil. He said it would take my head off, or a shoulder. Or something else."

"So we're, um—" The word "helpless" came to mind, but she didn't want to say it.

"Sitting ducks?" He took the two rejected paddles from her and tossed them into the cab. "No way. We're low-flying, jet-assed ducks. We'll have to be faster than whoever's after you. After us."

Nice of him to include himself, but she didn't think the two of them could outrace a power boat. She was glad he'd said they'd be safe after the first portage. She trusted his knowledge of the rivers and lakes.

They got the big canoe off the truck and down to the water's edge, went back for drybags and PFDs.

"We'll have to keep a sharp eye out for villains."

Villains? Either he was making light of the danger in order to reassure her, or he didn't realize how great the danger was.

When she got a chance, she'd return the keys to the boxes under the counter at Boat Camp. She still hadn't confessed her theft to Tate, or her visit to the apartment over the store, so he didn't know about the man who had frightened her that night. She'd told Tate that Roger had mentioned Hermit Island in conversation. Kate rarely lied, and she was surprised she'd done so this time. She hadn't known Tate very long, and if she told him the truth he might be angry with her for swiping the keys, or for going to the apartment without him. She felt guilty, though, hiding the truth.

They launched into the darkness, Kate at the bow. They paddled well together, she setting the pace while he used his strokes for steering as well as speed. The canoe was noticeably faster than the kayaks had been on her first trip to Hermit with Molly.

The light of another perfect September day expanded around them, and each maple leaf flared like a match as the sun hit it. It was surprisingly warm by the time they glided through the narrow inlet, paddles high, into the cove behind Hermit's Island.

Kate re-traced the way to the cabin, she and Tate each carrying one of the plastic boxes. He let out a whistle when he saw the place. "It's amazing," he said. "To think he did this by himself. I wonder how long it took him."

"I don't know, but I bet he built it in his Wild Man phase." She told Tate about Will's description of the four phases of Roger's life.

"Ah, Wild Man was before I knew him," Tate said. "But I can imagine."

The cabin impressed Kate all over again. She had to admire Roger's skill and persistence. He was a man with an obsession. No, wait, a compulsion—not an idea but an action, building this place, this museum, and then filling it with his father, or as much of his father as he could get his hands on.

Then what? Where does a fulfilled compulsion leave someone?

They piled the photos into the bins, wrapping the largest in wool blankets from the beds to protect the glass. There were so many framed items that Kate wondered about the weight of the boxes.

She picked a bin up at one end. "Yikes. I think this is enough. We can always come back for more."

"We've got most of it. There are some clothes here I'll take a picture of, a wetsuit and a dress uniform. Mrs. Benedict can decide if she wants us to come back for them."

They skidded the rubbery boxes through the trees and lugged them down to the beach. It was heavy going, and Kate was sweating by the time she set down her end of the second bin.

They floated the canoe a few feet from shore and Kate held a gunwale while Tate hefted the bins between the thwarts.

"The wind will be on our stern most of the way back," he said. "These tubs stick up high enough to give us some sail action."

"Windage at work," Kate said.

She didn't set as fast a pace on the return trip. The canoe was heavier, lower in the water. Tate was right, though: they made good time even at the slower stroke rate because of the brisk wind coming from astern. Wavelets jumped and foamed and sparkled.

They stopped for lunch: gorp—good old raisins and peanuts—and oranges.

"I'm glad we're out of there. That place is pretty remote," she said. "I was afraid the guy following me would try something. I know we're not back yet, but so far, so good."

"Yeah, I was thinking the same thing. And we're more than halfway."

"Yes, back in civilization. We've got cell coverage," Kate said, holding up her phone.

"Hey, you know what? We could paddle right up to the dock at Mrs. Benedict's house. Then paddle back to the truck with the canoe empty. More efficient."

"Sounds like a plan."

"She's going to be thrilled," Tate said, tapping the number into his phone.

Kate untied the trash bag from the thwart and dumped their orange peels into it, listening to Tate's half of the conversation with Mrs. Benedict. He said he had "something to give her," but didn't say what it was.

"You left her wondering what the heck is going on."

"Hey, I want to surprise her with this loot."

"Come to think of it, seeing the photos might be a bit of a shock," Kate said. "I'm glad you didn't tell her."

Mrs. Benedict must have been watching for them; she stood at the sliding patio doors as Kate jumped from the canoe and cleated it off at both ends. With the bins on board, it was too heavy to pull up onto the dock. Tate kneeled in the canoe and hefted each of the tubs in turn to his shoulder; Kate grabbed them and slid them along the boards. Then two trips across the patio and into the living room.

"Watching you two lug those things up here made me tired," Mrs. Benedict said, her tone less reserved than when

Kate had talked to her in her living room. Was it because Tate was there? She must have known him for a few years now, and who could resist being friendly to Tate?

Roger's mother wore a big green cardigan sweater with matching sash over what looked like a nightgown; her feet were in suede slippers. "What on earth have you got in those boxes?" Her breathing was apparently no problem; she was smiling, anticipating a pleasant gift. It might be bittersweet and upsetting to be flooded with dozens of images of her late husband. And to find out that her son was a thief and a liar.

Kate said, "Why don't you sit down, Mrs. Benedict? I'll slide this bin right over here next to the sofa." Tate gave her an appreciative look.

"You think I need to sit down? Is this some kind of bad news?" Now Mrs. Benedict looked more nervous than excited.

"I think you'll be very happy to have the things in these bins," Kate said. "They may come as a bit of a shock, that's all." Tate joined her, standing close. She felt his warmth.

"Ooookay." The older woman sat, leaned forward, and tried to pull one of the lids off, but couldn't. Tate knelt and popped it loose.

"There's a trick to it," he said, setting the lid aside.

Mrs. Benedict glanced at him. "You're saying that so I won't feel like a clumsy fool." She picked up the top photo and gasped. Studied it for a long moment, then looked up, eyes spilling over. "Where on earth did you—" She smiled through her tears, and her hand went out for another photo. "All my pretty ones."

Kate sat down on the sofa next to her, pulled Tate down beside her. "We'll tell you everything, when you're ready," she said. "Take your time."

They waited. Mrs. Benedict reached for the next picture, a shot of a young Paul in the water with his scuba mask lifted above his eyes. "At his first training camp," she said. "So many years ago." His arms were up on the side of a rubber raft, his expression serious, eyes narrowed.

Perhaps because she wasn't seeing well through her tears, Mrs. Benedict set the photo too close to the table's edge and it fell, the frame separating at the corners when it hit the floor.

Kate gathered the wooden pieces and put them on the table. "Good thing the glass didn't break," she said. "It could have damaged the print. But it's fine." She passed the photo to Mrs. Benedict and picked up the cardboard backing. There was a piece of paper on top of it that must have been between the backing and the picture.

"What's this?" She unfolded it.

The handwriting was blocky and forceful. *You've done well. The son of a hero, soon to become a hero yourself. It will take all you have. Congratulations.* The date was almost a decade earlier.

She passed the note to Mrs. Benedict. "I'm sorry, I read it before I could think not to."

The yellowed paper crackled in the older woman's hands. "That was the year Roger graduated from high school," she said. "He was so bright. So driven." She pulled a tissue from the cuff of her sweater and wiped her eyes. "What a couple of pirates you are. The good kind. You've brought me treasure chests, and I'm extremely grateful."

"Hey, thanks," Tate said. "I like being a pirate."

She sat back. "Tell me where they came from, my dears."

"We found a cabin we think Roger built out on Hermit Island," Kate said. "These pictures were hung on all the walls. There are medals, too, in the other box."

"I knew he took them." She shook her head. "I asked him. I said to tell me the truth, it was okay no matter what. But he stuck to his lie."

A tremendous bang from behind the house made all three of them jump.

"What the hell? That was a gunshot," Tate said. He ran for the door.

"Tate, are you crazy?" Kate shouted. "Don't go out there!" But she was right behind him.

"I'm calling 911," Mrs. Benedict quavered.

Kate stopped just outside. Tate was on the patio. At least he was being cautious, looking along each side of the house and then disappearing behind the boathouse. Kate held her breath until he reappeared and went onto the dock—to the end, fully exposed to fire if anybody with a gun was still around. If he was on foot. If he had a vehicle—

Kate dashed around the end of the house and ran for all she was worth down the driveway to the street.

Yes. A shape taking the curve. She got only a glimpse. It was big, boxy. Could have been the infamous SUV she'd been looking for, but there were too many trees in her line of sight to have any idea of make, model or even color.

She met Tate in the driveway. They had a good hug, then Kate said, "She'll be worried," meaning Mrs. Benedict, and they walked back toward the house together.

He was shaking his head. "They shot the canoe."

"What?" It sounded like a joke.

"Holed it. Pretty big slug," Tate said. "Boat's full of water."

"You didn't see anybody?"

"No."

"I got the barest glimpse of a big vehicle taking the curve down there. Wish I'd been faster, mentally and—"

"Hey," Tate said. "At least we know he's gone."

They heard a vehicle behind them. Police car. The window slid down and the driver said, "You reported a shot? Where did it come from?" He was the same cop who'd called the flatbed for Kate's camper.

"Back of the house," Tate said. "Shooter holed a canoe at the dock."

The cruiser sped up to the front door and the cop jumped out, drew his gun and edged to the corner of the house, peered, then went quickly down the side.

"Doesn't hurt to make double sure the shooter's gone, I guess," Tate said.

"You shouldn't have run out there so fast."

They found Mrs. Benedict pulling more pictures out of the box, laying them on the coffee table. It was covered with Pauls.

The officer came up the back steps and took their statements, which were brief. He'd seen the holed canoe.

He looked at Kate. "You," he said, "are trouble."

"No, trouble follows me around. Big difference."

"You two know each other?" Tate asked.

"This is the officer who helped me when my camper tried to learn how to fly," Kate said.

"I'm Sam." He turned to Tate. "If you have any influence with this young woman, tell her flying lessons are available at the regional airport, half an hour from here." Then he turned to Roger's mother. "Have you seriously annoyed anyone recently, Mrs. Benedict?"

"I don't think so."

"You haven't gotten into fistfights with the neighbors? Hosted wild parties? Your dog isn't barking at three in the morning?"

"I don't have a dog," she said. "Parties and fights? I plead the Fifth."

Sam smiled. "Let me know if you think of anyone, anything." He turned back to Kate. "We didn't get anything useful from the post office security cameras. You'd better watch yourself. Don't go out alone at night."

"I'll take care of that," Tate said to Kate. "You're staying with me, or I'm staying with you. You decide."

* * *

Sam, Tate and Kate looked down at the swamped canoe, the painters at bow and stern taut with the weight of water.

"Well, I guess we're not paddling that back to the put-in," Tate said.

"I can drive you to your car," Sam offered.

"That's quite a hole," Kate said. "Pretty big caliber ammo. How hard is it to patch aluminum?"

"We do it at the shop all the time. There's stuff you can get in a tube that's called a weld even though it's really a two-part plastic."

"Just epoxy, then."

"Right," Tate said. "They label it for marine use and bang—it costs three times as much."

"Well, let's get this critter up on the dock," Sam said.

He uncleated the stern and tossed the painter into the water. The boat sank slowly until that end touched bottom. He and Tate hauled the bow up and held it while Kate unfastened the painter, then they levered the canoe through ninety degrees so it was at right angles to the dock, the bow resting on the edge.

They flipped the boat keel-up to dump the water out, then dragged it onto the dock, gunwales scraping noisily. Once it was all the way out, they turned it again: a metal boat afloat on wood instead of water.

"Bingo," Tate said as the big silver tube clanged onto the boards. "Good thing it's aluminum. Harder to do that with the weight of a classic wood-and-canvas number."

Mrs. Benedict applauded from the house. "Bravo," she called. Kate hadn't realized she'd been watching.

"We'll come back for the canoe," Tate called up to her. To Sam he said, "Thanks for your help."

"Yes, thanks a lot," Kate said. She and Tate could have handled it, but she liked how Sam took his job to be more than filling out an incident report. He clearly cared about his town and the people in it, and was kind and funny, too. She wished all cops were more like him.

"Sure thing," he said. His pants were wet from the knees down, splashed when he and Tate flipped the canoe the first time. "Where's your vehicle?" His shoes squelched as he walked to the cruiser.

Riding to the Floodwood put-in, Kate couldn't help but think of Ellen and her trip in a patrol car last week. Wire mesh between the back seat and the front made a passenger feel already jailed. Worse, the back doors didn't open from the inside, as Kate discovered when they got to the Boat Camp truck.

Tate and she drove back to Mrs. Benedict's house, put the canoe on the truck rack, and then he took her home. Dinner was cheese and apples. She could hardly keep her eyes open to eat. She crawled into bed and a minute later she felt him join her. She was so tired she fell asleep before they'd had a chance to make love.

They made up for it the next morning.

TWENTY-THREE

"Yes," Kate said. "He built a rustic cabin and filled it with memorabilia of his father's career in the Navy." So much had happened since the last time she'd been here; Kate wanted to catch Ellen up not only out of friendship but to do some brainstorming the way they used to do over newspaper stories. Was Dan the murderer, or just a nasty nuisance? If it wasn't him, who was it?

Some things Kate withheld, of course. Her romance with Tate wasn't something she wanted to bring up, since it would only highlight her freedom and Ellen's lack of it; and her relationship with Laura was under wraps, for now, because Kate didn't think Amber would approve.

Two trips to Hermit Island, the attempt to capsize the kayaks, her camper sliding off the truck, the gunshot that sank the canoe at Mrs. Benedict's dock, the houses on Paul's Way beyond Boat Camp—oh, plenty of news. Kate talked fast because the visit was limited to fifteen minutes.

But Ellen was in a philosophical frame of mind rather than a brainstorming one. "A secret shrine to his father, deep in the wilderness," she said. "A sanctuary for Roger's wounded spirit. How strange. He seemed like he really had it together."

"Roger had a good act," Kate said. "He charmed the socks off both of us."

"More than socks, in my case," Ellen said. "But you're right, he seemed so—normal. Dan, on the other hand, flubbed his act months ago. I finally realized he was a sad, sad man, but I didn't peg him for a criminal. And now, murderer or not, he's harassing you because I'm out of his reach." Her smile was wobbly, but it was a smile. "That's the only good thing about being in jail. For me. Not so good for you."

"Jail stinks. As soon as you get sprung, we'll go for a paddle."

"Kate, I would so love to do that. But by that time the ponds might be frozen."

* * *

Someone else needed updating. From her camper in the parking lot at the police station, Kate called Amber.

"I'm eating lunch," the lawyer said. "And I'm tied up in court this afternoon. Want to come to the Put-In Pub and tell me about it?"

The Put-In. Not Kate's favorite place.

She slid into the booth and discovered a cup of coffee waiting for her. "Thanks," she said. Then she filled Amber in on the same events she'd told Ellen about. "I'm sure Ellen's described our encounter with Dan, and how he admitted he'd been spying on us. No, 'admitted' isn't the right word. He seemed proud of it. He's a good candidate for these crimes—so far only property crimes against campers and canoes—but maybe for Roger's murder as well."

"Ah, but he's been clever," Amber said. She'd almost finished a bowl of what smelled like butternut squash soup.

Kate hoped her rumbling stomach wasn't audible across the table. Ramen noodles in the camper were in her near future. "Are you saying there's nothing I can do? Aside from scaring the heck out of me a couple of times, he could have killed somebody with that slide-out camper stunt."

Amber wouldn't get the joke: the kind of camper Kate had was called a slide-in, not a slide-out.

"I'm sorry to say this, but you have nothing to tie Dan to those attacks. You said you couldn't see the boat numbers because it was nearly dark, and unless the officer found some relevant pictures from the post office's security cameras you don't have any evidence about who loosened those straps on the camper, either."

"Turnbuckles." It popped out, and she smiled an apology.

"Whatever. Not my field."

"That's why I haven't gone to the police. Detective Jordan would have said exactly that. And I want him to focus on finding Roger's killer, not solving my plague of problems. But the same person might be behind both."

"That's true," Amber said. "Thank you, by the way, for sending me the names of applicants for Boat Camp jobs and the information about the houses farther out on Paul's Way. I've got my people working on those leads."

"Can I do anything?" Kate asked. "Besides dodging bullets, I mean."

Amber's laugh was short. "Seriously, wasn't that a little scary?"

"Absolutely," Kate said. "Just because I don't talk about how frightened I am doesn't mean I'm some kind of fearless Superhero chick." She finished her coffee. "But it's so obvious Dan's the killer. Just the fact that he's in South Portage instead of tending to his oh-so-important businesses in Syracuse—isn't that strange?"

"Yes, it is strange. I'll relay your recent adventures to the police, and they may want to question him. But I wouldn't get your hopes up. He can easily say he's here on vacation, like all the other out-of-towners. 'Oh, my ex-girlfriend is still in town? I didn't even know that.' See?"

"Yes." Kate had hoped for some new strategy from Amber.

"Don't despair, Kate. From that incident at the gas station, we know Dan has an ugly side, and he might involve himself in a fight and get picked up by the police as a result. It's great that he's in a distinctive car—he'll be easy to spot. Sometimes when shifty people are faced with trained questioners, they make mistakes. We don't know what might come to light when Dan—if Dan gets questioned."

"I just don't get it. Dan's motive is so much stronger than Ellen's. Hers is nonexistent."

"I agree. But they have that message that appears to have been written by Roger, so their minds are made up. I'm afraid we're dealing with a small town cop shop, and the decisions that get made aren't always the best." She took a credit card out of a maroon leather wallet and returned it to the matching purse.

"Could the police look for Dan's fingerprints in Roger's apartment?"

"That's a great idea, Kate, but I don't think it's going to happen. There's only one thing you can do to change their minds."

Ah, paydirt. "What? I'll do it."

"Physical proof. Evidence. Something physical that links Dan to Roger and Roger's apartment early Monday morning."

"The police already did that kind of a search, right? For fingerprints and hair and, and—footprints? Stuff like that? That takes expertise and equipment I don't have."

"Yes, they found Ellen's fingerprints all over the doorknobs, light switches, dishes—including Roger's cup. A hair on his pillow. She was there, and before he died he pointed his finger at her. End of story, or so they think."

Kate didn't know what to say. It was hopeless.

"Don't give up. Call me or the police if Dan does anything else, especially if you catch him red-handed and get a good enough look to identify him. A cell phone picture would be excellent. He could be our killer. I'd love to see him in the interrogation room with Detective Jordan."

"Me, too," Kate said. "Believe me, I've been watching for that obnoxious yellow car of his."

"Let's hope he makes a mistake, and soon. Let's hope he's dumb as a duck," Amber said, standing and picking up the check. "I'll let you know if any of your leads pans out."

Dumb as a duck? Before Kate had finished laughing, the lawyer was gone.

Kate got in her truck and heated water for noodles, chopping up green onions and thin-slicing some red cabbage to add to the pot.

Dan's unwillingness to accept Ellen's rejection had been festering for weeks. If he killed Roger, he must have been following Ellen. But where was his car? Was he on foot? Did he lurk outside the Boat Camp building all night, and see Ellen leave early the next morning?

And then what? He'd somehow gotten Roger to ingest the poison. Dan must have scrawled the accusation on the wall. Roger didn't write it, Kate was sure of that.

But if you didn't know Roger or Ellen personally, then the conclusion the police had drawn could seem valid. Kate thought of Chinese finger-traps, the woven straw cylinders you put your index fingers into, one at each end. The harder you pull to get your fingers out, the tighter the trap holds them.

So simple. So impossible.

* * *

The best way to think was to work.

When Kate had scouted the Fish Creek campground a few days earlier looking for the SUV, she'd noticed a huge beech tree. She went to it now with her large sketchbook and pencils. Before settling in to draw, she stroked the smooth, light gray bark and looked up into the mass of leaves, their tans and golds. She took a dozen reference photos from different angles with her phone, and walked backwards to find the right working distance from her subject.

A mixed flock of small birds flew to the tree and flitted among the leaves, twittering. Probably warblers, but Kate couldn't see them well enough to identify a single one. Fall warblers, their bright breeding plumage replaced with duller feathers, are often hard to identify, and she'd come to believe they all used one foot to hold leaves in front of their tiny bodies, like fig leaves writ large. They didn't want to be seen.

She sat with her back against a smaller tree and took in the beech. Sunlight came through its canopy, and the backlit leaves near the top were a different, more vibrant color. She made a joke to herself about "gold leaf" and said aloud, "You must be a saint."

The tree didn't answer.

Then she thought of money growing on trees, and wished she hadn't. Staying at the Fish Creek campground was adding up. It was a relatively inexpensive place, but Kate's budget was thin. Still, she couldn't leave until Ellen's case got resolved.

She had to think of some way to prove Dan was the killer.

Kate roughed out the big beech in her sketchbook. As she began work on the finer details, she got lost in the color of the leaves, her first impression of gold replaced by a mix of yellow and burgundy. She had to work with stronger colors soon, a different medium than pastels. She'd get herself a set of acrylic paints as soon as Ellen was out of jail.

If that ever happened.

When her cell made its bird-call sound, she almost ignored it. But then she remembered what was going on in her life, and snatched up the phone without looking at the caller's name.

"Hadn't heard from my most exciting friend in a while. Any developments?" Marjorie asked. "Is this a good time to talk?"

It wasn't, but Kate's concentration was already gone. With two small children at home, Marjorie sometimes had trouble finding a time when she wasn't besieged by them and the housework they generated, so Kate went with the conversation.

"Developments? Gosh, yes." Feeling guilty she hadn't updated Marjorie in a while, Kate described Roger's secret cabin, her near-capsizing, and the sabotage of her camper. "I'm coming up with some likely suspects, and whoever's doing these things most likely killed Roger."

"Who are your suspects?"

"The boyfriend Ellen just broke up with, who's come out here from Syracuse to harass her." She filled Marjorie in on the incident at the gas station. "Also Roger's brother, one of his old girlfriends, and a political rival. Plus people who applied for jobs at his business and weren't hired."

"At least you've got it down to a couple of dozen."

Kate caught the sarcasm. "Okay, you're right, there's a lot of work to do. Ellen's attorney is looking into some of the leads, but I worry she isn't working fast enough."

"An arrest tomorrow wouldn't be too soon, considering all the threats to you."

"Arrests aren't happening," Kate said. "There's the small problem of proof."

"Small problem? Good thing you don't want a career in law enforcement." Marjorie must have missed Kate's irony.

"I sure don't. Dealing with scary people for a living doesn't appeal."

"Be careful, Kate. Ellen's ex-boyfriend sounds volatile."

"I think he's the one. But I've got to connect him, or some other suspect, to Roger's place right after Ellen left."

"He sounds like such bad news. Come to think of it, Roger wasn't a paragon of mental health, either. A hidden memorial, where he surrounded himself with smiling photos of the father who rejected him? He was troubled."

Kate listened to Marjorie's stories about her children, half-distracted and admitting as much afterwards. "I feel the way I do when I'm looking for something I've lost—the car keys, a book, the scissors. I look where the thing is supposed to be, and then I look everywhere else. Then I look where it was supposed to be again, and there it is. How did I miss it the first time?"

"It sounds like you know something but haven't connected the dots," Marjorie said. "Good luck with it. But while you're figuring it out, please remember your own safety."

After ending the call, Kate worked for a while on her drawing even though the original inspiration had evaporated. If she'd learned anything from her mentor in Maine, she'd learned to work when she felt like it and to work even harder when she didn't feel like it.

Only when the afternoon dimmed did she pack up her pencils and sketchbook, preoccupied.

Dinner was beans and rice, with wilted spinach on top. Kate was two-thirds of the way through *H is for Hawk*, and this part of the book exhausted her. Our emotions are where we live, but sometimes they're overwhelming.

Still, the book was excellent distraction from the difficulties of her own life. And Ellen's.

* * *

With Kate's first swallow of coffee the next morning, an idea jumped into her mind and shouted. She called Tate. "Hey, pirate. Want to go with me to Mrs. Benedict's to look for hidden treasure?"

Sometimes making art was the best way to let her mind work out a problem. And sometimes talking to a friend was the best way. Kate was grateful to Marjorie for calling the previous afternoon. And to herself for taking the call even though it had interrupted her communion with the beech tree.

She waited for Tate outside, watching Square Pond invent color in the morning sun.

He picked her up, and she explained as they drove to Mrs. Benedict's. "That note we found was hidden behind an early print of Paul. We ought to look behind the rest of the photos, don't you think? Maybe there are other hidden messages."

"Not a bad idea, fellow pirate."

"And over coffee this morning I thought of something else. Remember I told you Roger paid for dinner that night Ellen and I went to the Put-In Pub, back when we first got here? He gave the waitress a hundred-dollar bill?"

"Yeah," Tate said. "Kind of a memorable story."

"He kept that bill someplace safe."

"In his underwear?"

"No. In his wallet."

"Original." Tate's eyebrows were bunched. He was still working on it.

"Behind his father's picture in his wallet."

It took a second. Then Tate gave her an excited look. "Oh-ho. I see where you're going with that. He used photos of Paul as a front, literally."

"He was obsessed with his father. Look at what he named the road to the store—Paul's Way. Roger took his father to be a supreme role model. Those photos might be a gold mine." Kate laughed. "Or a minefield."

"Tally-ho. Or whatever pirates say."

* * *

Mrs. Benedict answered the door. She was wearing the same sweater-over-nightgown outfit, and she looked tired. But her voice was upbeat. "Hello, my lovely pirates. You said you want to look at your booty again? I haven't even finished looking at them all, there were so many. But I put them all back in the bin for you."

Kate sat on the floor in the living room, removing frames and looking between the cardboard backing and the photos. Tate sat on one of the sofas and did the same. Most of the photos were held in place with soft metal tabs. Working quietly, the couple replaced the photos carefully in their frames and put the ones they'd checked on the coffee table.

It took an hour. Kate's hope faded as she picked up the last photo.

Glass, photo, backing. Nothing else.

"I guess I was wrong."

She and Tate looked at each other.

Mrs. Benedict, seeing what they were up to, had made herself scarce. Now the older woman reappeared and took in their disappointed faces. "Oh, dear," she said.

* * *

"It was a really smart idea, Kate," Tate said as he drove her back to Fish Creek.

"Not smart enough."

"And now you want to go someplace and draw rocks and bushes?"

She gave him a sharp look. "How did you know?"

"It's what you do when you need to think. It's what you do when you need to stop thinking. It's what you do when you're sad. It's what you do when you're feeling on top of the world. How did I know?"

Kate laughed. "I guess you've got me there."

"I wish I hadn't set up a date to work on this guy's truck," Tate said. "But he's helped me with my Honda, and we've got the use of a service bay he rented. So I can't back out now." He gave her a look. "You could come, you know."

"And watch you two play with lifts and torque wrenches? Not gonna happen."

"Can't you stay at the campground? Draw from the picnic table at your site? At least there'd be people around, if Dan tries to bother you."

It was too soon to return to her drawing of the beech tree; sometimes she needed to give her work a rest to see it with fresh eyes. "It's such a beautiful day. How about you name a pond I could paddle on that's busy, or near a busy place? He's not going to attack me in public."

Tate thought a bit. "Osgood Pond is nice. And it's right next to Route 30, which has a good amount of traffic. I've seen some houses on the north shore. Sound safe enough?"

TWENTY-FOUR

She launched her little boat into Osgood and paddled along the shore, scouting. Told herself to relax and enjoy the lake, the sweet air.

Or the almost-sweet air. The breeze that made the water sparkle also brought road noise and the odor of exhaust. She paddled a little farther.

A wooded peninsula extended into the pond, with a tiny outlying island off its tip. Kate punned to herself: the point was an exclamation point. Opposite the topological punctuation, half a dozen cabins with docks clustered along the shoreline—a reassuring sight. Between the traffic on Rte. 30 and the lakeside residents, the pond was public enough to keep Dan from trying anything. She could concentrate on her work.

The water was shallow and the sandy bottom glowed in sunlight. Minnows scattered from the boat's shadow as if she'd thrown a handful of black rice. The shoreline was rocky, topped with blueberry bushes spreading their red September foliage.

Kate laid her paddle across the gunwales. She'd brought a lapboard and drawing paper, but before she started drawing she used her cell phone in its waterproof pouch to frame reference shots. In places the rocks looked like a glacial jumble, granite chunks of differing textures lodged against each other, some sparkling, some creamy and marbled; elsewhere the rocks were sedimentary, with layers of ochre and tan and gray tilted at various angles. She included the blueberry bushes in some of her photos, but the sedimentary striations increasingly drew her interest. She held her phone horizontally and drifted, finding plenty of promising compositions.

Color excited her even though today she'd brought pencils and was working in black and white. She reminded herself of the message from the saintly beech tree: she should start working in acrylics. The next step in her development as an artist.

But for now, composition was reward enough. She drifted, looking at the cell. Filling the screen with rocks, excluding the bushes above and the water below, gave her images that reminded her of Arizona, her childhood home. Rocks talking about time were everywhere in her native state, not just at famous sites like the Grand Canyon or the Petrified Forest. In the West the earth bared its structure, making her place in the landscape clear.

Caught in the tangled green layer of the Northern Forest, the wooded Adirondack wilderness stretching for hundred of miles in all directions, she felt, for a moment, homesick.

And moved on. Her work was her freedom. The pond opened and the day opened and her mind found the quiet she needed to work. She loved working outdoors. She was with wind and water, rock and sky, and at the same time very much in her head. She was an eye and a hand working together, and the person called Kate was somewhere else.

Looking at shapes, making shapes. She was a mind balancing the two, a mind absorbed in translation.

An occasional birdcall fluted above her. Wind shushed through pines. It pushed small waves against the hull, making those small watery comments that always filled Kate with joy. A boat engine grumbled to life somewhere near the road. Maybe a fisherman would be joining her in this quiet spot.

Well, fishermen tended to be quiet people, too.

She turned her attention to leaves. The shadows they made on the rock pleased her. Some of the leaves caught the sun, and when she made drawings from these photos she'd leave the paper untouched in those shining places. The lower leaves were dark, candidates for pencils with the softest leads.

The boat engine got louder, and a pang of alarm shot through her. She hadn't been paying attention. To her life. She looked around. She'd drifted behind the point, into a part of the pond screened from the road and far from the cluster of cabins.

A boat was rounding the tiny island. It wasn't a very big boat, and it wasn't moving very fast. Relax, she told herself. Not every motorboat was driven by a murderous psycho.

Still, she kept an eye on it as she picked up her paddle. Lost in imagery, she'd drifted close to shore. She took a stroke, the shaft warm from the sun.

The right blade exploded and the paddle flew from her hands.

Kate threw herself to the left, capsizing, then scrambled to her feet and scampered through the shallows, her hands and knees stinging where they'd hit the gravelly bottom. She yanked herself up the bank, grabbing at roots.

Something smacked into the mud beside her, spattering her hand. A big round, not a .22. This guy meant business.

Cover. Where?

She ran for the trees, veering from a straight line twice. Not enough to slow her down much, enough to throw off the shooter's aim.

She hoped.

He must have a silencer: the report had been muffled. She risked a quick look back. A man was dropping into the water over the side of the power boat.

A path ran north, but she didn't take it. A path was an obvious route, and open. Good for pursuers, bad for targets. She ran along the shore. She hadn't realized how extensive the pond was, how far she'd drifted from Route 30. She could forget about escaping back to her camper, at least for now. Had she seen any buildings? She hadn't been paying attention to anything on land.

She should have been more careful. Remembered Sam, the cop, who told her not to be alone.

The land was narrowing. She was on another point, and the trees were thinning. Damn.

Was that a shack ahead?

She was at the edge of a cove, on the other side of the strip of land where she'd come ashore. A wooden footbridge stretched across the cove, as long as a football field, leading to a boathouse.

The bridge was worse than the path. Full exposure, the whole length. Not a twig's worth of cover.

But she didn't have anywhere else to run. He must be ashore by now. He'd either go down the path, assuming she'd take that fastest route, or he'd follow her footprints and be right behind her.

Probably the latter. She'd been too panicked to think of keeping to rocks or hard ground to avoid leaving a trail.

She ran for the bridge. At the other end of it, the boathouse was a beacon of hope. It marked some well-to-do landowner's property. With luck, it wasn't an empty summer home.

Between her and the boathouse, a sun-drenched wooden corridor of extreme danger.

Even though she ran on the balls of her feet to reduce the noise of her footsteps, they sounded like thunderclaps in the quiet cove. The whole bridge shuddered.

Panting, she paused and turned. No sign of the man. But he would be coming. Soon.

Counting to thirty, she ran at top speed, noise be damned. Then she slid under the handrail and into the water as gently as she could.

The pond was shallow; the water wasn't shockingly cold. Her PFD kept her afloat, and she looked up, panting from the sprint. The boards were tight, the splinters of light in her dark ceiling few. Standing on the bridge, he wouldn't be able to look down and see her.

But from land, she was entirely visible. Posts and crossbeams supported the walkway. A person among posts, her silhouette was unmistakable.

She reached up and grabbed a crossbeam with both arms, held it hard, swung her hips up and snagged it with one heel, then the other. Crossed her ankles above the beam.

Now she was hidden, tucked up under the footbridge. But how long could she hold this position?

She focused on her breathing, not on the muscles of her arms and legs. She would have to stay here. She would listen.

The beam's corners pressed sharply into her ankles. Her shoulders ached a little already.

Breathe.

First possibility: he'd follow the footprints she'd carelessly left. He'd get to that point of land with the shack, discover the long walkway. Seeing nobody on it, he'd think he'd missed her, that she'd taken the path. It probably led to the house that must be inland from the boathouse. He'd go look there.

Second possibility: he'd seen the path and assumed she'd taken it. He'd run down it, looking. The landowner would see a man with a gun and call 911.

In her dreams.

The first scenario was more likely. The problem was that she wouldn't know if her pursuer had come, looked, and left.

Breathe.

Her arms were numb. She peered at the next crossbeam. Was there room enough on top of the beams for her to get above the one she hung from? If she could lie along the top of it, then her muscles would get a break. She'd have to worry about hypothermia, but she could last longer if she wasn't using all her energy holding on.

She'd wait until it was dark enough that she wouldn't be such a target, then see if her boat was still in Osgood Pond. If not, she'd have to walk back to Route 30. Watching her back.

No, there wasn't enough room for her to lie on top of the beam. Three or four inches. Forget it.

Her arms were shaking. Breathe.

The shoreline was wooded. She'd be able to stay under cover most of the way to her truck. But would he be waiting for her there?

Breathe.

She couldn't hold on.

She was going to have to convince her numb ankles to unlock, convince her arms to hold out for a few more seconds, long enough to lower herself gently into the water.

A series of vibrations ran through her. Footsteps. Someone was walking on the bridge.

She couldn't let go.

Wait. If he was on the bridge he wouldn't be able to see her. Now was indeed the time to let go. She could tread water and let the blood flow back into her arms and legs.

As long as she did everything quietly.

She thought longingly of her cell phone, which had gone into the water with her art supplies and lunch.

The footsteps were louder. She unhooked her ankles and let her legs drop into the water. Her cold muscles weren't able to do it slowly, and the splash sounded huge to her.

But he wouldn't be able to hear it over the noise of his own footsteps on the wooden planks.

Would he see the ripples?

Something was wrong. The steps were coming from the boathouse end of the bridge, not the shack end. He must have followed the path to the house, then found the bridge there, at the other end from where she'd started.

The footsteps were closer. They were mixed with a rumbling noise.

What was going on up there?

Voices.

". . . tell you it was the perfect spot? It's my favorite place on the planet, Mama. You are going to feel better in a hurry, I just know it."

A woman's voice, cheerful, untroubled.

"Stop here, dear. I want to look," an older woman said. Her voice had a quaver. "What a lovely breeze."

The two were right over her head.

"Here's your blanket, Mama. Don't catch a chill, now."

Obviously these two had not met a man with a gun. Kate didn't want to alarm them, but she had to get out of the water. She was starting to shiver.

"The lodge was built in the 1800s," the first voice said. "And some old president stayed in it, maybe a hundred years ago. We're living in history here."

"I *am* history," the older voice said. "I'm old as the hills. As the lakes." A small laugh, a cough.

Should she warn them?

No, Roger's murderer was not going to risk being seen by more than one person. He'd only reveal himself to Kate.

Lucky Kate.

Keeping within the dark path of water under the footbridge, she swam on her side toward the end the women had come from. Much quieter than the crawl, the side stroke meant she could keep one ear above water. If another set of footsteps hit the boards over her head, she wanted to know.

She got to the end and looked out at the wooded land where it curved to meet the bridge. He could be behind any one of those trees.

Or he could have given up. Maybe he was sitting in a diner somewhere, drinking coffee and eating a croissant.

It wasn't the wisest way to make a decision, but the thought of steaming coffee and a chocolate croissant hit Kate the way catnip must hit a cat. She pulled herself up on the lake side of the bridge and clambered over a row of concrete planters, banging a knee on one of them. Crouching, she scanned the woods along the cove.

Nobody there.

She glanced down the walkway. A figure leaned over a wheelchair, adjusting a blanket around the seated person.

So far so good. Time to get indoors. She was shaking with cold.

When Kate turned around, she almost fell backwards in fear. A man had come out of the boathouse with a gun in his hand.

TWENTY-FIVE

It wasn't a gun, it was a dark brown bottle. A beer. He stared at her with his mouth open. In his late sixties with a bit of a paunch, he wore yellow pants and a pale green sweater with an alligator logo. "Are you all right?"

* * *

A few fragments of memory: someone in blue leaning over her, toweling her hair dry and pulling off her wet pants and shirt, helping her into a thick bathrobe. Bright fireplace shouting with flames, cup of cocoa held to her lips, soft blanket around her shoulders.

Then a familiar voice said, "What? *You* again?"

Kate looked up. "Hello, Sam," she said weakly.

"Where is that no-account boyfriend of yours? I thought I told him to stick close to you." He sat beside her on the loveseat and pulled out a notepad. "Fire away," he said.

"Would you mind rephrasing that?"

* * *

Then Tate was there, and she stood up in her blanket and wrapped her arms around him. She licked him where his chest hair showed above the top button of his shirt and inhaled the warm smell of his skin and said something inarticulate with a lot of m's in it.

"I guess I'll be going," Sam said morosely.

Kate half turned. "Oh, I'm sorry, do you have more questions for—" When she saw the teasing expression on his face, her apology changed to a laugh. "Yes, don't you have some paperwork to do back at the station?"

"As a matter of fact, I do," he said, looking instantly gloomy. "For real. Did you have to remind me?"

She rested in front of the fire with Tate, the blanket across their legs. Sam had reassured her that he and two fellow officers had checked the grounds and buildings, finding nobody lurking, armed or otherwise. He'd also told her the South Portage police didn't consider a man taking potshots at people a minor matter. At all.

Sam liked to joke around but he took his job seriously. She was able to breathe easy. At least for now.

A tall woman in blue, who introduced herself as Joanne, brought Kate's clothes, neatly folded. It felt glorious to get dressed, pants and shirt still warm from the dryer.

A few minutes later, when Joanne returned, Kate said she felt well enough to leave. "You were an angel of warmth," Kate said, "in more ways than one. Thank you."

"Our specialty is reviving our guests," Joanne said. "Although usually it's a more psychological process." Her slacks were cobalt blue, and the matching sweater was cashmere or some other fuzzy, expensive yarn. No white uniform, but she'd handled the blood pressure cuff with the casual skill of a trained nurse.

"Thank you for getting her warmed up for me," Tate said with a smile.

"Most people stay a bit longer here at Great Camp. And most of our visitors don't swim under the Tea House bridge." She must have listened to Kate's conversation with

Sam, or talked to him afterward. "We do have beaches, you know. Won't you both come back when you're able to enjoy our facility in a more orthodox manner? "

"She's definitely not orthodox," Tate said, tilting his head toward Kate. "The way things have been going recently, I think she must be easily bored."

As they walked to his Honda, Kate said, "That shack was a tea house? Dang. First tea house of my life and I missed it."

"Maybe you didn't look closely enough," Tate said. He drove toward Route 30, along the edge of Osgood Pond. The road was narrow, the pavement sandy. "You were busy at the time, remember?" He pulled up next to her truck. "Shall I follow you back to Fish Creek?"

"I was hoping you'd ask," she said. "There are parts of me that aren't completely warm yet."

* * *

The next morning Kate yawned and stretched. "I am so looking forward to a quiet day."

"I didn't know you had quiet days," Tate said.

"I used to."

"You can have one later. First we have to recover your sweet little Hornbeck and your cell phone."

They went to Boat Camp in Tate's Honda to pick up a canoe to search Osgood Pond.

"Sure, take the truck. Take another canoe," Shag said. "But try not to let anybody shoot it, please?"

Although he was joking, Kate was glad no other vehicles were parked in the small lot next to the pond. She and Tate launched the canoe and started toward the point.

Of course, Dan could drive up at any moment. Or whoever the guy was who'd shot at her.

"Relax, Kate," Tate said from the stern. "He's not going to try again in the same place."

She realized she'd been looking over her shoulder. "How do you know that?"

"It's a rule," he said. "Must be in the labor union contract. You know, the AMU? American Murderer's Union?"

Kate shook her head. For once, Tate's sense of humor didn't click with hers.

They scouted the pond for the Hornbeck and found it swamped, lodged against the bank near where Kate had scrambled ashore the day before. Its foam seat and the wood trim around the gunwales kept it from sinking entirely. With a yelp of glee she scooped up her cell phone in its waterproof pouch. The bags with her art supplies and lunch were full of water, but the pencils would be usable after they dried out, and the tangerine and unopened Clif bar were fine.

She pulled the boat half up on the mud and flipped it to drain. Tate passed her the paddle he'd borrowed from Boat Camp, and she edged along the bank.

"What are you doing?" Tate called. He was crouched low in the canoe, moving forward to trim it for solo use.

"Looking for my paddle."

"I thought you said a blade shattered. It's not a paddle anymore, it's junk."

"That's the point. I hate to leave litter." But she couldn't spot the remaining blade and shaft, and she didn't like being on the lake, even with Tate. Too exposed. They paddled back to the Route 30 lot and put the boats in the truck, but it wasn't until they were on the road that Kate felt her tense muscles loosen.

Halfway back to Fish Creek Kate's phone chirped. She held it away from her ear because Mrs. Benedict's voice was loud with excitement. "I have a present for you," she said. "Would you mind coming over?"

She looked at Tate and he nodded. "Okay if I bring Tate?"

"Both my lovely pirates? Even better."

Mrs. Benedict didn't look as robust as her voice had sounded. Her door was open and she was sitting in the living room. She waved a small plastic bag at them almost before they'd gotten inside. "I have the bullet . . . that put the hole in the canoe."

"Really? How did you find it?" Kate asked.

"I called . . . old friend of Paul's. Retired." Her breathing was audible. "He and a buddy came over. With wetsuits. Took ten minutes." She smiled, but her face was strained.

"Hot dog," Tate said.

"Not deep. No air tanks. Wetsuits . . . masks."

"Mrs. Benedict, are you feeling all right? You sound short of breath," Kate said.

"Asthma's bad today," she said, but she clearly wanted to use what little breath she had to talk about the discovery. "Beneath the dock. Rocky place. Paul's friend said . . . bullet lying there looking. . . like a diamond ring. In a jeweler's case."

"That is so great," Kate said. "What an awesome idea, to call a friend of Paul's."

"They were careful. Didn't touch it. Neither did I. They just . . . scooped it. Into this bag." She paused to catch her breath. "Does a bullet . . . take fingerprints? Would the water . . . wash them off?"

"I don't know," Kate said. "But it was smart of you not to touch it."

"I'd like you . . . to take it. To the police."

Kate hesitated. "The fewer people who handle it, the better. Why don't you have an officer pick this up directly from you?"

"Ah. Of course." She looked annoyed with herself, then sad. "Wanted to . . . to see you. Do you mind? That I called you? So wonderful. Young people . . . coming in the door again."

Sympathy for this woman who was facing so much loss surged through Kate. She sat beside her. "No, we don't mind at all."

She'd gotten to know Mrs. Benedict in layers—the inquisitive woman at the cookout, the dignified mother struggling with grief who'd questioned Kate about Ellen, and the vulnerable, lonely person she'd just revealed herself to be. Her asthma could well be triggered partly by emotions, and then its physiological effects, like lowered oxygen levels in the blood, could have psychological consequences. A vicious circle.

Kate put her hand on the older woman's. "This is a hard time for you." She waited, listening to the older woman's breathing. "I'm worried about your asthma."

"Yes. Bad day. Feeling dizzy." She took an inhaler from a pocket and shook it, then gave herself a hit and held her breath, her eyes closed.

Kate looked at Tate, wondering if it was unusual for the symptoms to be this bad. Had he been around Roger's mother enough to be familiar with her condition?

He seemed to understand the question on her face, and held his hands out, palms up. He didn't know.

Mrs. Benedict opened her eyes. "I'll lie down . . . for a bit," she said. "Bedroom."

Kate helped Roger's mother get up and stayed close, a hand under her elbow.

"Should we call your doctor?" Tate moved to the older woman's other side.

"Saw her yesterday. Said I might have vertigo. New medication . . . for anxiety. Said I'd . . .adjust."

The bedroom was dim and cool, the air tinged with the scent of lavender.

"Thank you . . . my dears." Mrs. Benedict sat on the bed. "Be all right. Few minutes." She twisted at a finger to remove the rings. "Hate to take off . . . my wedding band, but . . . swelling." She set the rings down on the bedside table with a little clink and turned on a small lamp.

The rings gleamed below a picture of Paul Benedict, sitting on a folding chair on the patio, sunglasses dangling from one hand. He was wearing only dark blue swim trunks and his dogtags, which reflected the light.

A photo from some bright day well in the past.

Mrs. Benedict saw Kate staring. "Oh, yes. Handsome, isn't he? Oh!" She picked it up and handed it to Kate. "Forgot this one."

Kate bent back the tabs, then held the frame over the bed and tapped the glass. Backing, picture, and glass fell noiselessly onto the comforter. Her hand shook as she moved the glass and looked under the picture. Last chance.

Ah, an extra piece of paper. She unfolded it and read the handwritten word "Son" at the top, then handed it to Mrs. Benedict. "This looks private. You'd better read it first, then decide if you want to show it to us."

She looked at Tate and they went back to the living room and watched the whitecaps flickering on Lake Flower. Such a lovely landscape before them—the glistening water, then a rocky shore below a vastness of forest, the wild colors of maples accenting somber evergreens.

So much beauty before them. In the next room, so much pain.

"Dears."

Kate moved quickly to the bedside, Tate behind her.

Mrs. Benedict looked dreadful. She held the note out toward Kate.

Kate unfolded it, and she and Tate read it together.

Son. I'm not coming back this time. I have my way. You remember? I showed you. And I gave you what you need. Use it. Do not fail again. Paul.

Kate read it twice, her mind racing.

She and Tate looked at each other, stunned.

Mrs. Benedict's face was wet. "He must have—" A sob stopped her.

"It's a suicide note," Tate said quietly.

"Paul planned. To disappear. On his last mission," Mrs. Benedict said. She lay back on the bed.

"A suicide note and a suicide command," Kate said. "To his own son." She read it again. Hard to believe a man could tell his son to end his life. But what else could it mean?

"I lost them both. It felt like two . . . two terrible events," Mrs. Benedict said. "But it was one. Linked."

"This has been a terrible shock," Tate said. "I'd feel much better if you checked in with your doc."

Mrs. Benedict didn't seem to hear him. "Some sickness in Paul . . . I never saw. I thought he was—what did I call it? Gung-ho. Overly . . . enthusiastic." Her voice was low, hoarse. "It was him. He killed . . . himself. He killed our son." She closed her eyes.

Kate tried again. "Wouldn't it make sense to touch base with your doctor's office and make sure there aren't any issues with your meds?"

Her eyes opened. After a moment she sighed. "All right, dear. All right." She picked up the bedside phone.

Kate called Will from the living room. "Your mother's had some more bad news. I thought you might want to be with her."

"Bad news? What could be worse than losing Roger?" Will asked.

"I didn't say worse," Kate said carefully. "I said more. But I don't think I should say. I'd rather you hear it from her." She already was as deep into Benedict family trauma as she wanted to go.

No, she was deeper.

"Well, as a matter of fact, I'm headed there now. I've been worried about her, how she's sounded on the phone, so I cleared my calendar and I'll stay with her through next weekend. I should be at the house in half an hour."

"Great," Kate said. "I'll stay with her until you get here."

He sounded friendlier. "Thanks for that. And for the heads-up."

Tate went into the bedroom, came back out with the note. "Mrs. Benedict talked to a nurse, and now she looks like she's sleeping. This phrase, 'what you need'—that was—?"

"It must have been poison," Kate said.

"Roger took it himself."

"Yes."

"Good God."

They sat on a couch together. "So your friend Dan is in the clear," Tate said.

"For the murder."

"Right. All the other fun and games are probably on his head."

"Are elite military units issued some kind of poison to use in case they're captured?" Kate asked.

"I don't know," Tate said. "I've never had much interest in the military. Not my bag."

"It sounds humane, in a crazy way," Kate said. This was unfamiliar territory for her; she was thinking out loud. "If I were captured and facing torture and certain death, I suppose I'd like to have the choice of ending things quickly."

"Roger's father brainwashed him into some kind of samurai mind-set."

"So Roger dated Ellen to set her up," Kate said slowly. "Ellen had to be at his apartment, to leave a hair or two on his pillow and her fingerprints on the cups and light switches."

"It's wild," Tate said. "I bet he planned it for a long time."

"He'd been waiting for years for the right victim to come along," Kate said. "Like a spider in a web. He must have been thrilled to get Ellen—not only a journalist, but the one who'd written a series of articles he'd had strong feelings about."

Kate felt as if she'd been thrown in the ocean. She was cold all over. All over, inside and out. She pressed herself against Tate's warmth, and he put an arm around her.

After a while he said, "Roger was a careful, planning sort of guy. Into spreadsheets for all kinds of angles on his business."

"Too bad all that care and intelligence went for such a hideous goal," Kate said. "But his father was where all this started. He damaged his son, deeply."

Mrs. Benedict had married a very sick man, and apparently never suspected.

TWENTY-SIX

The next morning Kate went to her familiar spot at the South Portage library, got on the Internet and searched on "special forces suicide pill." Saxitoxin came up, the shellfish poison she'd suspected Roger had eaten accidentally at dinner. For military use the stuff was of course refined and concentrated. The LD, or lethal dose, of engineered saxitoxin was one-eighth the size of a grain of sand.

Then she went outside to call Amber, who was, as usual, the voice of pragmatism.

"That's the strongest theory you've come up with yet."

"Theory? It's not a theory, it's—"

"Kate. Listen. You've done so much. Go one step more. What was the poison in? How did Roger carry it around? Or how did Paul? How does one carry around a tiny piece of death? You can't keep it with your pocket change."

"In the sugar bowl? Ellen said he put sugar in his—no, wait, you said his coffee was fine."

"Look, Kate, I've got to go. See what you can do. It'll make all the difference to the police if you can provide the complete scenario. Call me when you've got something."

Mrs. Benedict sounded half-asleep when Kate called her.

"Sure, honey, you come over. I didn't put the photo back in its frame. The door's unlocked. Will just went out for some groceries."

Kate drove to a drugstore in Saranac Lake and bought a magnifying glass before going to Mrs. Benedict's house.

She didn't read the note again. She looked carefully through the magnifier at the photo of Paul on the patio. She wanted a closer look at those dog tags.

Yes. There was something else on the chain around his neck besides the flat tags. Something smaller than a pencil eraser.

A tiny container, like a miniature beer keg.

You could kill someone with a gun, or a knife, or a piece of rope. Amazing that you could do the same job with an object way smaller than a grain of sand. Saxitoxin: she'd bet that's what it was in that container.

She looked at some of the other photos in the pile she'd put back in their frames. Whenever there was enough of his neck showing, the chain was there, under his shirt. Even when he was wearing civilian clothes.

"He wore his dog tags all the time."

Kate jumped. Mrs. Benedict had ghosted into the room. She was wearing the same nightgown she'd had on the day before and she looked devastated.

She dropped heavily onto the sofa.

"Mrs. Benedict, should you be up? Shouldn't you rest?" Her breathing, at least, was better, probably due to the effects of the inhaler on the coffee table.

"Rest? I don't know what that means anymore." She leaned back, looked at the ceiling. Her voice was subdued. "Paul's dog tags. I'd say, couldn't you take them off at night, in bed? But he wouldn't. He even showered with them on."

She must have figured it out, too.

"I asked him what that other thing was, the little round thing on the chain. He said it was a radio tracking device, that he was required to wear it. And I believed him. I said, 'So the Navy knows you're right here, in bed with me.' He laughed and said yes. And I kidded him. Asked him if he was sure there wasn't a camera in there too."

"I'm very sad for you," Kate said. "What a shock this must be."

"Honey, get me the big white bag. In the hall closet." She waved her hand weakly toward the front door. "It's what they gave me. After Roger . . . after I saw him. I had to go say it was him, I had to see him, all—"

"Stop," Kate said. "You don't have to think about that now." She found the bag, brought it back to the sofa. It said PERSONAL PROPERTY in big black letters.

"I didn't look in there. Didn't want to. But now—"

"Yes." Kate looked in the bag. Watch, coins, wallet, small jackknife. And what looked like dog tags. She lifted the chain that held them.

"Paul got those tags for Roger when he got his first job, as a lifeguard, and a social security number. That's what's stamped on there. Roger was so proud to wear them. Like he was in the Navy already."

"That's unusual."

"More than unusual. I look back on it and wonder why I didn't understand—" She paused, caught her breath. "What was going on, it wasn't right. To find out now, so much later, these things about Paul. About the two of them."

Kate held the chain high so the tiny container was at eye level. It looked like the one in Paul's pictures, except that the top and bottom weren't as tightly connected. With the magnifying glass she could see metal threads that wouldn't be visible if the two halves were screwed tightly together. "Look," she said.

But Mrs. Benedict was asleep.

Kate went out on the patio, closed the door quietly and called Amber. Looked out over turquoise water, maples flaring above it like torches. She got voicemail, left a message that she'd done what the attorney had asked.

The lake was peaceful. Kate breathed deeply, doing her best to inhale that peace. She needed to counter the images that had come to her: a man near death, fumbling with a tiny capsule he desperately wanted to reassemble. Not getting the two parts to line up, maybe cross-threading them, starting over, his vision fading, his fingers going numb.

Why hadn't he taken the chain off his neck and destroyed it? Thrown it into the woods or the lake?

Because he didn't have enough time. His strength would have been ebbing, and he put what he had left into the note that condemned Ellen to a jail cell.

And because anyone who knew him would expect him to be wearing those dogtags, alive or dead. He probably did as his father had done, wearing them to bed, wearing them in the shower.

Perhaps he'd expected to plant the bottom half of the capsule in Ellen's purse, along with his phone. She may have disrupted his plan by leaving as quickly as she did.

As she turned to go inside, Laura called from the *Saranac Lake Star*. "Just thought I'd check in, Kate, and see how things are going."

"Are you psychic? Five minutes ago there was a huge break in the case."

"Hooray," Laura said. "Shoot."

Kate hadn't noticed before how often people said that. "I can't tell you yet. The family should get the news first." Mrs. Benedict knew, but Will didn't.

Laura, of course, wanted to know everything right away. "You want to clear Ellen's name as soon as possible, don't you?"

"Mrs. Benedict has been avoiding newspapers since Roger died, but Will reads the paper. I don't want him to get the news in print, or on your website."

"Let's make a deal," Laura said. "You tell me everything you know, I get it all written up, then I promise to wait until you give me the green light that the Benedicts have been told." She paused. "Of course, you'll have to trust me."

Kate went on instinct. "I trust you, Laura." She took a deep breath. "This is going to take a while."

"Okay, I'm bursting with curiosity," Laura said. "Who killed Roger?"

"Roger."

"Yes. Who killed him?"

"Roger."

"Kate—" A pause. *"Suicide?"* Another pause. "Are you sure?"

"Very. Listen." As Kate told Laura the details, she could hear the sound of the reporter's keyboard. Roger Benedict's strange story was going straight into the *Star's* computer.

"You're amazing, Kate," Laura said afterwards. "This story is great, and the case was one tough nut to crack. If you're looking for a newspaper job, here or anywhere else, I'll put in a good word for you. Write you a letter. Remember that, okay?"

Kate checked on Mrs. Benedict, who was snoring gently on the sofa.

Will's orange Hummer came down the driveway, and Kate opened the door for him, her finger to her lips. He had a paper bag of groceries in each arm.

He saw his mother asleep on the couch. "Thank you," he whispered to Kate. "But I think I'll wake her and get her into bed. Her neck's at such an awkward angle, it can't be good."

"I think the police will want to have these items back," Kate said, putting the dogtag chain, the wallet and other items on the coffee table back into the white bag. "Your mother can tell you what we've figured out."

Mrs. Benedict's eyes opened and she smiled weakly. "Will, dear," she said. Then the smile vanished. "I have something important to tell you about your brother."

TWENTY-SEVEN

Kate drove her truck down the driveway, turned onto the road, and parked on the shoulder, too excited to postpone calling Marjorie.

"You were so right about the Benedicts being a messed-up family. But it's even worse than you thought." She told her friend about the dog tags and the container with its tiny payload of death.

"Poor Mrs. Benedict," Marjorie said. "What total hell, to cope with all that. Her son is dead, then she discovers he killed himself and tried to frame somebody else. And her husband instigated the whole train wreck."

"Horrible, isn't it?"

"Roger did a good job of setting Ellen up."

"Yes. His plan nearly worked," Kate said.

"I wonder about Roger's state of mind," Marjorie said. "His pride must have been struggling with what he saw as his duty to his father."

"That must have been why it took him so long. Five years. He probably thought of Paul's command every day. What a way to live."

"Enough time to come up with an ingenious way to avoid the stigma of suicide."

"So self-worth versus his allegiance to his father," Kate said. "Do you think that when he found out what Ellen did for a living, and that she'd written the homeless veterans articles, that it tipped the balance?"

"Yes, that makes sense. He probably thought there'd never be a better opportunity."

"Never be a more appealing victim to frame, you mean?" In her side-view mirror she saw a police car turn into the Benedict driveway.

"Exactly."

Kate drove back to her usual site at Fish Creek and plugged in. Roger's murder was solved and Ellen would be free soon, but whoever had been harassing Kate was still on the loose. And he was dangerous. Kate couldn't forget bullets thwacking into the bank beside her as she scrambled out of Osgood Pond.

But she still didn't have any evidence that Dan had fired those shots.

He'd been so relaxed when he confronted Ellen at the gas station back before Roger died. That calmness was frightening. He'd been sure he was right, even though his ideas were way off base. Kate and Ellen a lesbian couple? No way. He didn't recognize friendship. Relationships, for him, were about power and sex. He didn't know what love was.

Lost in thought, Dan's figure standing large in her imagination, Kate jumped when her phone chirped.

Amber's voice was as professional as ever. Excitement percolated through it, though, when she heard Kate's news.

"Excellent work! When I asked you to find physical evidence I honestly didn't think you had much of a chance. I didn't think there was any evidence, other than what the police had already found at Roger's apartment, all of which implicated Ellen. This is extraordinary."

"It was such a fluke. If Mrs. Benedict hadn't felt unwell and gone to her bedroom, I might not have seen that last photo."

"A fluke—and your sharp eyes," Amber said.

"So when will Ellen be released?"

"Probably tomorrow. There's paperwork, of course,. But first we have to meet with Jordan and present the facts."

Had she heard right? "We?"

"Kate, you're the one who collected the evidence. You found the cabin on Hermit Island, you discovered the notes behind the pictures, you even worked out the detail about where the poison was stored. I think it would be useful for you to be there."

"Jordan already knows about the cabin—I told him. He blew it off." Kate remembered how small she'd felt after that meeting.

"That was before you had the complete scenario, with evidence to back it up. Now we've got the whole package. I think he'll listen."

"Okay, I'll go." Maybe it wasn't a bad idea. It would be satisfying to see the detective admit he'd been wrong about Ellen. "When?"

"I'm sure we'll be able to see him tomorrow. I'll give him a call and let you know."

"Let's ask him to put some effort into finding Dan. He's a dangerous man, and who knows how he'll react when he hears the news that Ellen has been released? He might even be a danger to her."

A pause. "That's a valid point," the attorney said. "Jordan's not the most responsive type, but I'll see what I can do."

"I wish I could prove Dan unhooked my camper. That was far more dangerous than shooting an empty canoe. If there'd been a car behind me when that thing went off the truck, people could have been killed."

"That's true," Amber said. "And he shot at you. The canoe was relatively minor property damage. A routine repair, I imagine? Canoes must get holes in them all the time."

Get holes in them? "You make them sound like sweaters," Kate said. "But yes, they get holed. Usually when paddlers are having too much fun, and kiss a rock."

"I'll work on Jordan. If the police are willing and able to locate Dan, they could question him about the AWOL camper and the shots at Osgood Pond."

Kate ended the call and filled her coffee machine, wishing Amber had been more positive that Dan would be apprehended and questioned. *If* the police were willing, she'd said, and she'd called Jordan unresponsive.

And wasn't that what Kate had been thinking about Dan before Amber had called? How calm and unresponsive he was? Sure, Jordan's coolness might be a professional style—detectives can't act warm and fuzzy. And maybe he'd seen enough crime scenes to harden him. But his immediate assumption of Ellen's guilt, and the way he'd tried to pit Kate against Ellen—those things made Kate feel bullied.

Was what she saw of Jordan only a role he played for his job, or was it his true personality? Where better to conceal a lack of feeling than in police work?

She told herself to stop thinking. She told herself to go to bed.

* * *

The meeting with Jordan wasn't as gratifying as Kate had hoped. Amber did most of the talking, and the big detective accepted her summary of Kate's discoveries with his usual poker face. Roger's dogtags were on his desk in a clear plastic bag, and he ran his fingers back and forth over them as he listened.

He'd have read the report from the officer who'd collected the dogtags, of course, and Mrs. Benedict's statement, so he couldn't have been surprised by what

Amber said. Still, Kate had expected some kind of reaction, perhaps even an apology for what Ellen had been through.

"My client, Ellen Waters, is not guilty of murder. Roger Benedict obeyed his father's fatal directive and killed himself," Amber said. "We have the directive in writing—the note Kate found behind Paul Benedict's photo. To conceal his suicide, Roger framed Ellen by dropping his phone into her purse and pointing a posthumous finger at her with the message he scrawled on the wall."

Jordan shifted in his chair. He wasn't making eye contact with the attorney.

"We have the container in which Roger carried the lethal substance. Your forensic chemists will no doubt be able to find traces of that substance in the container." She leaned forward. "Do I have your assurance that my client will be released in short order?"

Jordan looked up from the dogtags and nodded once. "I'll talk to the prosecutor," he said. "We'll take care of it."

"I know he was convinced by the accusation Roger wrote on the wall," Amber said, "and by his phone being in Ellen's purse. Of course, it was easier to cast blame on the nearest out-of-towner than to proceed more cautiously."

Jordan's head snapped up and he stared at Amber as if deciding whether she'd just insulted him. But his voice was tired. "I said we'll take care of it."

"One more thing," the lawyer said.

Kate had planned to put in her two cents' worth when Amber described the urgency of finding Dan, but she did such a convincing job that Kate didn't have anything to add.

"Okay," Jordan said, and stood.

Did that mean "okay, this meeting's over" or "okay, we'll find Dan"? But Amber gave Jordan a big smile and got up too.

Outside the station, Kate said, "I'm not sure I was much help."

"Don't worry about it," Amber said. "I wanted you to be there. After all you've been though, I thought you deserved to see Jordan eat crow."

The slang expression startled Kate; the lawyer's language was usually so formal. "Eat crow? He did? No, wait—he just sat there like a sack of flour."

Amber grinned, and Kate felt energy flowing out of the small woman. It was almost palpable, like a strong sunlight. "Consider this an educational experience, Kate. When powerful people are forced to eat crow, many of them have learned to do it discreetly."

"No bones on the plate?"

The lawyer laughed and gave Kate a quick hug. "Not even a feather." She hopped into a neon-blue sports car and zipped out of the lot.

Kate pulled out her phone on the way to the camper. Now that Mrs. Benedict had had plenty of time to explain the unusual circumstances of Roger's death to her younger son, and the police had all the evidence showing Roger had killed himself, Kate was happy to let the *Star* publish the story. As she tapped Laura's number she sent a silent apology to Roger's spirit, should it exist, imagining all the people who would unfold their newspapers or open their tablets the next day and discover his harrowing secret.

"This is your green-light call," Kate said. "You can tell the editor you've got a big scoop."

"You're an ace," the reporter said. "Remember what I said about giving you a reference."

Kate didn't feel like an ace. Not with Dan on the loose.

Was there anything she could do about that?

* * *

"This is your favorite vic," Kate said the next morning, using the shorthand for "victim" she'd heard on some TV show. "Kate Corliss."

"I hope you're not calling to report another crime," Sam said. "Haven't you caused enough trouble?"

It had been easy to get in touch with him, since the South Portage police department was small. Asking to speak to Officer Sam had done the trick, and he'd called back half an hour later. Kate doubted the approach would work in larger towns.

"No new crimes yet. I thought I'd give you a chance to catch up on my backlog. Any progress?"

"You didn't give us much to work with," Sam said. "Seriously, no numbers from the boat with the shooter or the one that tried to capsize you near the Floodwood landing. No physical description of the guy who drove those boats or messed with your camper. The only good news is that we got some .38 slugs out of the mud at the edge of Osgood. They match the ones Mrs. Benedict's Navy friends collected. I wish we could find this guy and ask him a few questions."

"I'm glad to hear that," Kate said. "And I have an idea."

* * *

Kate was hardly in the door at the police station before she got a huge hug. Ellen was laughing and crying at the same time.

"Oh, Kate, you can't imagine what it's like to be held in that tiny, ugly place. It was beyond awful. I can't believe I'm out of there."

"So let's get you back to your home away from home."

"Hang on a sec. They're going to give me my cell phone and stuff."

A big cop came into the entryway, holding a white plastic bag. Kate recognized him: he'd knocked on Ellen's camper door two weeks earlier. The bag was marked PERSONAL PROPERTY and looked just like the bag Mrs. Benedict had gotten from the morgue, which gave Kate the creeps.

"Have a look inside and make sure everything's there," the officer said. "Except the baggie of marijuana, of course."

Ellen peered into the bag, shaking it. "This is everything," she said. "You've got my keys, Kate, right?"

"Right."

"You're good to go," the cop said. "A misunderstanding. Roger fooled everyone." But Ellen was out the door, Kate on her heels.

Almost to the truck, Ellen stopped and threw her head back, inhaled deeply. "I'm free. It's so beautiful," she said. "Air. Sun. Trees. I was afraid I'd never see them again."

"Yes, the air is sweet. But did you hear what he said? This was all a misunderstanding?"

"Misunderstanding?" Ellen squawked. "Two weeks in jail was a misunderstanding? I'd hate to see an actual argument."

"An argument is twenty years to life," Kate said as they climbed into her truck.

"Those were the worst weeks of my life," Ellen said.

Kate was silent. She'd had a worse time not too long ago, in Maine. At least this time the person who'd died hadn't been someone she dearly loved.

She shook off the memory. "Let's go out for dinner, to celebrate."

"Great. Anywhere but the Put-In Cafe."

"Deal," Kate said. "And I have a proposal for you. Something for you to consider after you've had a good meal and a glass of wine."

"What am I supposed to do with my major-league curiosity until then?"

Kate backed the truck out of the parking space. "Ditch it. Curiosity killed the cat."

"Kate, I could see every square inch of that cell. I even looked under that miserable excuse for a bed. There wasn't any cat to get killed."

Wonderful to hear her friend being silly after weeks of bad news and the bleakness of a jail cell. Ellen would be fine; she was already bouncing back.

TWENTY-EIGHT

Ellen had made the front page of the *Star* the next morning. A photo of her leaving the police station with Kate got full play on the front page, below a banner headline: BENEDICT DEATH RULED SUICIDE, SYRACUSE WOMAN CLEARED.

"When I fill up column-inches in a newspaper I usually get a byline," the Syracuse Woman complained. She and Kate were sitting in a gazebo on the South Portage Commons, a strip of land at the edge of a pond just outside town. The park was narrow enough at this point that the gazebo was close to the road, and passing motorists could easily see the two women. Ellen wore an eye-catching pink fleece.

The breeze off Raquette Pond was chilly, but the park seemed busy anyway: shouts from a nearby volleyball game reached them, and bicyclists whirred by on the paved path. When Ellen had parked her camper in the small lot, she chose the space closest to the road, next to a white van with a bike rack on the back.

"You look great in the photo," Kate said, folding up the paper. The wind made reading the long article by her pal Laura impossible, so she'd have to catch it later. "Grinning like a dentist's ad. I don't think you looked that way when I picked you up the first time."

"No, but I got a second chance. After I washed my hair and spruced myself up. That photographer was a sweetie. Did you hear him tell me I looked like a movie star?"

"No," Kate said. "If I had, I would have told him that was my line." She moved closer to Ellen. "Let's get this show on the road."

The two women embraced. Ellen's laugh was right in Kate's ear. "It really is a show, isn't it?"

"Let's hope Dan falls for our amateur acting." Ellen's arms protected Kate from the wind, but they also restricted her field of view. "Want to rub cheeks?"

After Sam had agreed to Kate's plan to use herself and Ellen as bait to trap Dan, the two women invented a fake kiss that would look convincing from a short distance away. They did that for a while, and then went back to hugging.

"My back is tired of twisting. Time for a break?" Ellen asked.

They separated. "Yeah, let's be realistic," Kate said. She stood and went to the railing over the pond. "Even if we were lovers, we wouldn't clinch continuously." She turned to face the gazebo, her elbows on the top rail.

"I like it that you're watching my back," Ellen said. "Any Corvettes in sight?"

Kate scanned the road in both directions. "Nope." She flipped the collar of her flannel shirt up. "Wish I'd worn my leather jacket."

"I'm freezing," Ellen said, crossing her arms. "Too used to wearing a jail cell, I guess. It's a tight fit. Smaller than this gazebo. No breezes, ever. And no views."

The sun was out, at least. The volleyball players—only two on each side of the net—were taking a break, one of them looking toward the gazebo.

Ellen glanced at her watch. "I think if he were going to show, he'd have made his move by now. Maybe I'm not the attraction we hoped. Do I look fat in this fleece?"

Two bicyclists cranked by, heads down. One was a heavy guy, and his seatpost wasn't high enough. He was going to wreck his knees if he spent much time with it that low. His bike was out of adjustment, too, chain rubbing on the derailleur with a rapid clicking that would have driven Kate nuts.

The volleyball rose over the net again, with thumps and slaps marking the game's progress. The four players were good: the ball arced back and forth, the men shouting encouragement and taunts.

A mud-spattered Jeep pulled into the parking lot, and a tall man in a camo jacket got out.

"Lights, camera, action," Kate said.

Ellen looked up sharply and turned toward the lot. "That's him." She stood and raised both arms in the agreed-upon signal.

The volleyball thudded to the ground, players drifting off the court. The cyclists turned around and headed back toward the gazebo.

Noticing the four players coming his way, Dan walked faster. One of them called out, "Police! Stop. We want to talk to you."

Dan sprinted for the gazebo, his jacket flapping open. Was that a holster under his arm? He was fast, dodging a tackle by one cop and twisting away from another's grip on his shoulder.

"Kate—" Ellen's voice quavered as she clutched Kate's arm. Dan was ten yards away, reaching under his jacket as he ran, his face lit with some kind of dark joy.

The smaller bicyclist shot in front of Dan and slammed on the brakes. In a tangle of limbs and wheels, both men went down. Dust rose as they struggled, but the fight was short. The volleyball players arrived, and in seconds Dan was handcuffed and hauled to his feet. Two of the plainclothes officers patted him down.

Ellen dropped to the gazebo bench, looking dazed.

The small cop sat up, one hand pressed to his side. His shirt was bloody, but he grinned at Kate. "Captain of the wrestling team, SUNY Plattsburgh."

"You go, Sam!" Kate said. "But you're hurt." She started toward him, but a fellow officer got there first, kneeling to check the wound.

"Just a scratch," Sam said, getting up and unclipping his bicycle helmet.

"Scratch or not, you're going to the ER to get it looked at," the other cop said. "When was your last tetanus shot?" He scooped a nasty-looking knife out of the dust. "Switchblade. We'll probably find some more weapons in his vehicle."

"Got one already." A player in a Nike sweatshirt held up a heavy hand gun.

Once it was clear Sam's wound was minor, the officers' mood changed from efficient to upbeat. A couple of the volleyball players high-fived. "Damn," Nike said. "We have to go back to work now?"

"Yeah," another said. He looked at Dan. "Why'd you show up so soon, dude? We were having fun. My partner and I were winning."

"The hell you were," said a guy in a faded New York Jets shirt.

Dan stared over their heads, his jaw clenched.

"What happens now?" Kate asked.

"First we see if he has a license for that gun," Sam said. "Also whether it's stolen, or been used in other crimes. Then we check the gun against the bullets we have from Mrs. Benedict's and Osgood Pond." Sam smiled. "Then we—chat with him."

"Chat?" Ellen joined them.

"You know, Detective Jordan's not exactly pleased with this guy. Stories all over town about some nut case firing shots in residential neighborhoods and near fancy resorts.

So I think Jordan would like a long, personal conversation. If the bullets match, we've got him on the Osgood Pond incident and the canoe shooting. We can put out his photo and ask around at boat rental places. Maybe we can connect him to the near-capsizing, too."

"He was following me in that damn Jeep," Kate said. "And I was looking for a Corvette. No wonder I missed him."

The heavy cyclist picked up Sam's bike and rolled it toward the rack on the back of the white van in the parking lot just as a police car pulled in. Two uniformed cops put Dan in the back of the cruiser.

"Perhaps our newest jailbird can be persuaded—" Sam cocked his head and looked at the sky, as if he were imagining Dan being questioned in the room in the police station Kate knew only too well.

"Persuaded?" Ellen said.

"Persuaded to admit to loosening turnbuckles on Kate's camper, for instance. And any other sins he might like to confess."

Kate and Ellen looked at each other. "That sounds kind of sinister," Kate said.

"By the book," Sam said. "Strictly by the book."

Kate was glad she didn't need to be persuaded of anything by Sam. Or by Detective Jordan.

TWENTY-NINE

Molly called Kate with the invitation: a going-away party for her and Ellen.

"The party was Tate's idea," Molly said. "And I'd better warn you it won't be swordfish and Guinness this time. More like hot dogs and Bud. Boat Camp's budget got put on a diet. By Mrs. Benedict—I mean Sharon, she wants us to call her Sharon. She's our new boss, but she's asked Will to run the place."

"Bud's fine with me," Kate said.

"And we're not inviting a cast of thousands, like last time. Just the Boat Camp staff, and you and Ellen."

"That's fine, too." Wasn't that the truth. "Hey, do you think Roger's last cookout was meant to be a farewell party? He must have already decided what he was going to do the next day."

Molly didn't answer, and Kate wished she hadn't made the comment. Better to look forward. "Boat Camp will be a different place from now on. Calmer."

The pause lengthened. Kate was relieved when Molly said, "It'll be a good change for all of us." Her voice was subdued. "We were all afraid Mrs.—I mean Sharon—would close the place down. She has zero business experience, but Will's done okay with that photography studio of his in Vermont."

"They'll be fine. I've gotten to know her a bit. She's a decent person."

"God, can you imagine—husband and son? She'll be in mourning for the rest of her life."

"I hope not," Kate said. "She deserves better."

"She does. Well, see you Friday."

* * *

"I can't believe I'm going to be back at work next week," Ellen said. "It seems like a year since I left for my little trip to the Adirondacks." She shook her head. "The editors were so understanding. They're giving me an extra week of vacation to use later on."

Kate poured red wine into their plastic cups. "That's great. They figured out you need a vacation from the vacation you just had."

The store was closed for the day. The guides had come early to set up grills and put out some chairs and one table. Irving was at his post at the gas grill—no surprise, cooking was still a refuge for the shy guy. Molly and Shag unloaded a couple of coolers. Jennifer set out a stack of paper plates and opened boxes of plastic forks and spoons.

Kate and Ellen had tried to help when they first arrived but were chased away by Molly. "No way. Guests of honor. Scram. Go away and drink wine."

"An offer I can't refuse," Kate said. "Where's Tate? His Honda's here."

"He's in the store. Be out soon. Now shoo."

The two friends sat by the boat trailers. Ellen put her arm over the bow of a turtled kayak. "You know, I love the shapes of boats. The hulls. Their shapes are so—clean."

"I know what you mean," Kate said. "I love these smooth, sexy, hydrodynamic shapes, too. I love how the water moves all kinds of ways, all around them, and their shape stays itself, does its work by holding firm."

"Kind of like a person," Ellen said. "Life is a mess, the water going all this way and that, and you, the boat, you have to stay steady and fixed and true."

"Wow," Kate said. "All that on half a glass of wine."

Tate came out of the store, looked around. Kate waved.

"Ah, there you are."

"I hoped it was me you were looking for."

"You bet." He sat on the ground beside her.

"You rate a chair, you know."

"Nah, this way I get to look up your shorts."

Ellen said, "You guys want me to leave?"

"Don't listen to him. I'm not even wearing shorts."

An orange Hummer came down the road. Good, Will and his mother.

Tate got to his feet. "This is Roger's mother," he said to Ellen. "And his brother. You maybe remember them from the cookout? But so much has gone down since then. C'mon."

The three of them met Will at the table. "Let me put this bowl down," he said. "Potato salad."

"Yum," Kate said. All of a sudden she was hungry. It was a bright day but cool, and the wine was making her a little dizzy. She helped herself to a couple of pretzels.

His hands free, Will helped his mother down from the high-clearance Hummer. She was moving well, looking much better than the last time Kate had seen her.

"So much has happened since the last time we talked,'" Mrs. Benedict said to Ellen. "I'm sorry my son—I'm sorry for what you had to go through. Being in jail is no picnic."

"No, but this is," Tate said. He and Kate were the only ones who laughed.

"Let's let the past be past," Ellen said. "I'm very happy to see you again. I'm free. You and Kate saved the day."

"Kate is a genius. I'd totally overlooked that picture by my bed."

Was it the wine or the praise that made Kate's face heat up? "Don't forget Amber," she said. "She had a lot to do with justice getting done. But I agree with Ellen—let's think about the future. You're now the proud proprietor of Boat Camp?"

"I am," Mrs. Benedict said. "But I want to change the name. How do you like 'Adirondack Paddlers?'"

"I like it," Kate and Ellen said together.

"I do, too," Will said. Instead of potato salad he was now carrying a can of Bud in each hand. He held them both out. "Your choice," he said to his mother with a wink.

She pretended to have difficulty deciding, moving her hand toward one beer and then the other. "Of course you like Adirondack Paddlers. You thought of it. Your first act as manager." She took a drink and looked at the can. "You know, Paul used to say Bud was like Ford Motor Company and black coffee."

Will nodded. Kate, Ellen and Tate looked at each other.

"How so?" Kate prompted.

"If you're in some small town in the middle of nowhere and there's only one car dealership, what's it going to be? Ford. If you're in that same small town and there's not much choice in the liquor store, they're going to have what? Bud. And if you're in a small boat in really the middle of nowhere, the nautical version, there'll be coffee, even if it comes out of a Thermos. But there may not be sugar and it's downright unlikely anybody's going to come up with cream."

"Simplify, simplify, simplify," Will said. "His motto."

"Don't forget redundancy," his mother said.

"Who wants burgers?" Irving called from the grill, and the group migrated toward him. Kate grabbed a plate and helped herself to both kinds of potato salad and a couple of devilled eggs.

"Ah, so you're a vegetarian?" a familiar voice said. Someone had come up behind her as she served herself.

Kate turned. "Amber." Their eyes met. "Yes. This potato salad is great. It's got little bits of celery and red onion in it. Crispy. Must have been made this morning."

"I can take credit for that," Jennifer said. "I somehow remembered you were a plant-eater. A herbivore."

"I am, too," Amber said, taking a plate.

Kate introduced her to everybody. "This is the woman who rescued Ellen."

"Not exactly," Amber said, and smiled at Kate. But she didn't contradict the statement, or change the subject. There was a lesson to be learned from this small woman about how to operate in the world.

* * *

Kate gave Tate a minute or two after he went into the store, then followed. She went quickly behind the counter and slipped the keys she'd stolen back into the boxes under the counter. When he came out of the bathroom at the back, he smiled at her, but a little sadly.

"Hey, sweetie," she said. "I feel like you've been avoiding me."

"Why would I do that? You know I like hanging out with you." He slid up next to her, put his hand around her waist. "In case you hadn't noticed."

"Yeah, but you're holding out on me. What's up?"

"God, am I that obvious? Well, okay, here's the thing: Will offered me a job as assistant manager at Boat—at Adirondack Paddlers. In line to be manager as soon as he can train me. He says six months."

"Tate, that's wonderful. And it makes perfect sense. Will can't run both his photo studio and this place."

"It's an opportunity to learn a lot. I don't know a, a ledger from a ledge. My asset from a hole in the ground."

They laughed quietly, their breaths mingling.

"So you've been avoiding giving me some good news?"

He looked down. "I'd built up this idea that I could travel with you. Not in your camper." He laughed at the look on her face. "No, I was thinking the job here was over, and I'd get a camper myself and go with you. Not all the time, I'd peel off and check out something along the way you weren't interested in, and then meet back up. A kind of loose arrangement."

"You never said anything about it."

"I was thinking. Trying to see how I could afford a camper, looking at them on-line, used. There are so many kinds. I didn't want to hit you with a half-formed idea, I wanted to be sure I could do it first. And then this job came along. And I, I'd—"

"—be a fool to turn it down," Kate said.

"Yeah. Like that." He didn't look very happy. "I went to college for a couple of semesters, hated it. I couldn't be a manager of anything else, anywhere else."

He pressed against her, wrapped her up in his long arms. God, she was going to miss him. Or—what if—

He nuzzled her ear, licked it. Then said very softly, "I don't suppose you'd be willing to, um, stick around?"

"Oh, Tate. I don't know what to do. You're a lovely man, but I've known you less than two weeks."

"Gotta start somewhere." He stepped back a little. Reached out and wiped a tear from her cheek. "You think about it."

"Okay." She nodded, ducked her head, heard the door shut behind him.

* * *

One thing Kate hadn't anticipated when she'd decided to go on the road for a year was how many times she'd be saying goodbye. Like a kaleidoscope, her life shifted dramatically every few weeks, its patterns and colors rearranged.

Mrs. Benedict hugged Kate and Ellen and cried, and said they were welcome back any time. "Come and stay with me, Kate, whenever you like. You changed my life."

"I don't know about that. I had a part in a very difficult transition you had to make."

"You know, dear, what happened was going to happen. You got to the truth of it. I could have gone the rest of my life full of ill will and anger toward an innocent person." She smiled at Ellen.

Will stood behind his mother and put his hands lightly on her shoulders. "Thank you, Kate," he said. "I know I was on your shortlist of suspects for a while. Glad I'm in the clear. You and me both, Ellen." He gave a hearty laugh.

Will, his mother, the guides—everyone was in a good mood. Difficult as it was to understand Roger's choice, the truth was out. An innocent woman was free and the grim prospect of a murder trial had been avoided.

Jennifer came up behind Will and nudged him, handing him something.

"Here it is, Ma." He stepped in front of his mother, his back to Kate and Ellen, and the two of them fumbled a bit, then Will moved away. Mrs. Benedict held, awkwardly, a new Werner paddle, disassembled, the two blades spooned together. Red, lustrous in the sun, they looked like the fins of some aquatic creature yearning to play at the seam between water and air.

The two halves of the shaft were tied together with a big red bow.

"Why is there a ribbon on that paddle?" Before she finished the question, Kate knew. "Thank you so much, Mrs. Bene—Sharon," she said, accepting the gift with a smile. "I'll use it well." The red paddle was carbon-fiber, feather-light in her hands.

"I know you will, dear. Tate told me your good paddle was in smithereens at the bottom of Osgood Pond and your spare was a cheap plastic number. We all know you earned the best Adirondack Paddlers has to offer."

Kate marveled at Mrs. Benedict's resilience. She was going to be all right. What had happened wasn't easy to deal with, and she probably had a long way to go. But knowing the truth would encourage healing.

"Tell Kate about Sarah," Will said. He was standing behind his mother again.

"Such great news. I heard from her, my daughter in Minnesota," Mrs. Benedict said. "For the first time in—what, Will, six years? She somehow heard about all this, about Roger, and about Paul, too, she didn't even know about him being officially MIA. Maybe she saw it on the Internet, or some Facebook friend told her. Anyway—"

Kate's eyes met Will's, and something in his expression told her exactly how Sarah had found out about what was going on in Saranac Lake. Good for him.

"—she's coming to visit. Next month. I'm thrilled," Mrs. Benedict said. "Out of my mind with excitement. I'm worried I won't even recognize her, made her promise to send me a picture."

"I'm going to get you set up with email so she can send you pictures every day," Will said.

Doubt flickered across Mrs. Benedict's face. "Now, Will, I'm no techie. Can't she put them in the, what do you call it, snail mail?" She laughed. "I just learned that phrase. I think it's so cute. I used to love getting those bright yellow envelopes full of snapshots—"

"Mum. The Great Yellow God is long gone. That chrome yellow was the Kodak color, and the company crashed in what, the 1980s?" He rolled his eyes, but his tone was affectionate.

"I'm fine the way I am. I like to get my snail mail, my snail newspaper. I'm so happy to be able to read the paper again, now that nobody on the front page is related to me."

"Thank you for supporting print media," Ellen said. "We love our hard-copy subscribers."

Will shook his mother's shoulders gently. "I'm going to drag you kicking and screaming into the twenty-first century."

"Better than the alternative, I suppose."

"Another thing," Will said. "You're going to get a hearing aid."

"What?" his mother asked, and everyone laughed.

Mrs. Benedict took Kate's hand, gave it a squeeze, and said, "Remember. Come visit."

"Thank you," Kate said. God, she hated goodbyes.

THIRTY

"I don't know what to do," Kate said on the phone that night. "I feel like I'm being torn in half."

"Sounds like a win-win to me," Marjorie said. "Either you hang out with this really sweet man, or your do what you planned to do, wander the country in your RV doing your art in beautiful places."

"I guess you could see it that way. But you could also call it lose-lose. I have to give up a sweet man or I have to give up my freedom."

"Kate, you're not in the best situation to decide."

"What do you mean?"

"I mean you've come through a hair-raising situation. A good friend was in jail, charged with murder, and you were the only person doing anything to help her get out of a dreadful situation. And a month or two ago you were in Maine, struggling to find your way as an artist, and you lost a very lovely man who mentored you and cared for you. What you had with him wasn't a romance, but he gave you the emotional support of an older man, something you've needed since you lost your father."

Kate's throat had tightened into a knot. She couldn't speak.

There was a long pause as Marjorie waited. "It's okay," she said.

Kate knew her friend understood her silence. She tried to make her throat relax, but it was impossible. It had been so long since she lost her father that she sometimes thought the pain was gone, but of course it wasn't. The way Marjorie had connected his loss with a much more recent one had shaken it loose like a flock of startled birds rising into the sky of Kate's mind.

"You need to give yourself some alone time before you make any big decisions," Marjorie said, her voice gentle. "Walks, drawing sessions, paddling now that you know you won't be shot at. Give yourself some peace."

Eventually the ache in her throat ebbed, and Kate managed to speak again. "Oh, that pain I get in my throat when I want to cry and can't." she said. "It's awful."

"Yes. I know. So listen, Kate, there's no rush about this. Tate really likes you, you're attracted to him in all the right ways. Take your time. He'll be there a month from now, six months. You need to give yourself a chance to recover from what's been—a trial. Pardon the pun."

"Marjorie, that was bad. I think you're going to have to talk to a judge about that one." Kate's smile eased her throat even more.

"Be kind to yourself. You've been through a lot. More than I think you realize."

"Thanks. You've helped me a lot. And we haven't talked about you in the past couple of weeks. How are you, really?"

"My life is dull and boring, the way I like it."

"Go on, Marjorie, you have two kids. I'm sure dull and boring is not how it's going for you."

She laughed. "Yes, I was kidding, but there's an element of truth there. What I mean is that I know what I'm going to do each day when I get up. No big surprises. And I like it that way. It's fun to watch my boy learn how things work—he's so curious, I have to really watch him. And my little girl is sleeping through the night, finally, so I'm loving that."

"That beats getting up every three hours the way you had to for a while." Kate had never had the urge for children, but many of her friends had. Those she'd know in college, in their thirties now, were having to get on with that project or admit it wasn't going to be part of their lives.

"I love my life," Marjorie said. "It's the only way to live. Love yours, Kate. Love it hard."

* * *

She'd driven to Boat Camp dizzy with a strange mix of sadness and joy.

Tate must have seen her truck pull in, because he came onto the porch and waited. His face was more serious than she'd ever seen it; he must be feeling some powerful emotions himself.

She joined him on the porch. "You amazing person," she said.

His hand reached for hers and held it lightly.

"I loved the time we spent together, Tate. But I need to be by myself for a while, to get over what happened here. To calm myself. Become who I am again."

"I understand." His voice was husky. "For now, the road leads south?"

"Yes."

"Roads that go south go north too," he said. The smile wasn't his real one; it was crooked, and brief. He closed his gray eyes and opened them. "Don't forget me."

"Tate. How could you think that's even possible?'

They left it there, with a question. He turned and went inside, the door closing gently.

* * *

The next morning Kate and Ellen readied their campers for the road. Kate gave her friend the drawing she'd finished: Ellen lying on her back beside a creek, next to a kayak half out of the water.

"I love this," Ellen said. She put it down on the picnic table and gave Kate a hug, then picked it up again and studied it. "You started it on our first paddle, before everything happened."

"Yes."

"It'll remind me of how peaceful life was then."

"Hey, life will be that way again," Kate said. "You'll be back in Syracuse soon. You can go to the airport in a few days and pick up your parents."

"I'm so glad for those few days. I need to settle in, let myself recover from everything that's happened. Things won't ever be the same, though—I can't take peace for granted any more." She put a hand on Kate's shoulder. "I only wish I could spend more time with you. You saved my life."

"Oh, go on. I did what anybody—"

"No, I don't know another person who would have done what you did. Snoop around Roger's apartment, paddle all the way to Hermit Island twice, find that note hidden in the picture—" She dropped her hand, ran it over her face.

"Hey, the hard part was dodging your delightful ex-boyfriend," Kate said. "I thought he was the murderer, trying to keep me from clearing you of his crime."

"You weren't totally off base. Dan wanted to keep me in jail, all right. He wanted me to suffer because I'd dumped him."

"And he wanted to frighten the wits out of your friend, because that would upset you. And he was jealous, although I don't know if he really thought I was your lesbian lover. Maybe he just liked having a woman to harass, so he could feel powerful."

"Good thing he was stubborn, along with all his other sterling qualities," Ellen said. "He couldn't stop until he thought he'd won. Like it was all some kind of game."

"Smart of him to rent that Jeep when I was looking for the yellow Corvette."

"Not so smart to have a gun without a permit. He said he aimed wide at Osgood Pond, just wanted to scare you, but I don't know if I believe him."

"It wasn't wide by much," Kate said. "And what if he'd aimed wide and missed?"

"Maybe he's in the same cell I was in. I hope they never let him out."

"Amber told you he'll be in prison for a while, right?"

"Yeah, thank goodness. Assaulting a police officer is a heavy charge, with no gun permit and resisting arrest on top of it. So I won't have to look over my shoulder all the time, back in Syracuse." She touched Kate's shoulder lightly. "Where are you going this fine fall day?"

"I don't know," Kate said. "I was looking at the map last night, but I had two glasses of wine at the party. Took me three hours to drink them, so I didn't think they'd affect me, but I was so sleepy I decided to wait until today to choose my route." She laughed. "That was the long version. You want the short one?"

"Sure," Ellen said. Her movie-star smile was tinged with the sadness of parting.

"South."

Ellen smiled. "That's all you need to know, isn't it? You're migrating. Like a bird. You're free as one."

They had another good hug and Kate went back inside her camper so she wouldn't have to watch Ellen drive away. It had been an intense couple of weeks. Thank goodness everything turned out as well as it had.

She got the atlas out and turned to the New York page. Pages. Four for upstate, one for the City. Well, she wasn't going down there. As she ran her finger along possible routes, she thought of Roger doing the same on his map of the St. Regis Canoe Area. The worn path he left had led her to the truth about his death.

Marjorie had come up with a word for Roger's suicide: over-determined. Somehow this comforted Kate. There were many reasons Roger had decided to end his life. His father's influence was major, of course, but Roger's own temperament was a factor, too, and his mother's apparent ignorance of the dark side of her husband's perfectionism. Other aspects of his personality and family life, unknown to Kate, would also have been at play. Roger had been planning his death for years, and looking for someone to use as a cover.

A secret suicide? Not easy to pull off.

He'd been such a good actor. Looking back, Kate doubted his meeting her and Ellen at the Put-In Pub was a coincidence. A truck camper, even a stowed pop-up, would be easy to spot in the restaurant parking lot, and he'd have recognized Ellen's rig since she'd driven it to Boat Camp earlier that day.

Kate closed the atlas. Route 30 to Route 28 would take her south through the Adirondack Park, sure to be a pretty drive. When she got near Utica she'd have another look at the map, choose another road. Right now she agreed with Marjorie: after all the excitement of the past few months, in Maine and here in the Adirondacks, boring was good. No surprises.

Or a few surprises, good ones. Morning light through the leaves. A fat gray squirrel scolding her as she climbed into the cab. The freshest air on the planet coming through the truck window. A yellow leaf falling, scalloping its way down, taking its time, navigating the air in sideways swoops.

Like the leaf, she would take her time, enjoy the ride. She would find her way.

Thank you for reading!

If you enjoyed this book, please consider leaving a review on Amazon, Goodreads, or wherever you spend time online. Even a few words can make a major difference to an author.

Look for other novels in the Art of Murder series: *Drawing Fire*, Book 1, and *The Double Magpie Murders,* Book 3, are available on Amazon. *Frozen Fire,* Book 4, is coming soon!

Find news of further releases at www.PamFoxAuthor.com.

Comments? Email the author at PamFoxAuthor@gmail.com or follow her on Twitter at @PamFoxAuthor.

Made in United States
North Haven, CT
18 October 2024

59088614R00157